The Thing About Men: Stories

Gregory J. Wolos

Červená Barva Press
Somerville, Massachusetts

Červená Barva Press
P.O. Box 440357
W. Somerville, MA 02144-3222

www.cervenabarvapress.com

Bookstore: www.thelostbookshelf.com

Cover Art: "Silhouette of Man During Nighttime"
Courtesy of Wikimedia Commons

Cover Design: William J. Kelle

ISBN: 978-1-950063-58-1

Library of Congress Control Number: 2023931075

ACKNOWLEDGMENTS

"An Evening with Willie Freeze," *Baltimore Review*, winter, 2012; winner, *New South Fiction Award*, 2011 (as "Who's Akela?"); Pushcart Prize nominee

"Still Life," *Superstition Review*, issue 14, fall, 2014; winner *Rubery Book Award*, 2014; Pushcart Prize nominee

"Boy Strangling Goose," *Glimmer Train*, issue 103, fall, 2018; 2nd Place, *Glimmer Train Family Matters Contest*

"Cat Calls," *Solstice*, summer, 2016; winner, *Solstice Short Fiction Award*, 2016

"Mister S, the Mysterious," *Los Angeles Review*, spring, 2012

"Dead White Male Body," *FRiGG*, summer, 2011

"Glorious Vessel," *Shooter Literary Review*, summer, 2018

"Balance," *descant*, winter, 2018, winner, 2018 *Frank O'Connor Short Fiction Award*

"Knuckles," *Florida Review*, spring, 2017

"Beast Music," *FRiGG*, fall, 2016

"Dirt," (as "Out of the Basil Pot"), *Dark Lane Anthology*, Volume 6, winter, 2018

"Diorama," *Baltimore Review*, summer, 2015

"Convenience," *Thrice Fiction*, spring, 2019

"Cupids," *Storyglossia*, April, 2011

"Wisent: a Love Story," *Superstition Review*, issue 9, 2012

"Karaoke for the Deaf," *Jersey Devil Press*, October, 2014

"The Wild Pandas of Chincoteague," *Post Road*, winter 2014; *Glimmer Train* finalist

TABLE OF CONTENTS

For Mendel, Ilina, Bear, and Indigo

The Thing About Men: Stories

An Evening with Willie Freeze

The Cubmaster introduces our guest speaker as George White Eagle. I don't recognize the name, but his face is familiar—it's a twist of rawhide, eyes hooded to a slit under bruise-purple lids. You'd think they were shut completely, except a gleam sneaks out now and then that reminds me of the husky dog we had when I was a kid. Wolfy slept with his eyes half open, and the dead look in them made me shiver, like he was watching us from some evil world. George White Eagle's black hair is tugged back into an inch of ponytail. New blue jeans cinch his waist, and his flannel shirt, rolled up at the sleeves, bags at the chest because he hunches.

"Mr. White Eagle is going to tell us some Indian lore and play his flute for us," the Cubmaster says. His face is ham red, as if his yellow neckerchief is too tight. "So let's quiet down, kids, okay?"

The scouts are sugared up on soda pop and cupcakes, unconcerned about whatever is happening on stage. They shout and bang folding chairs and play keep away with stolen caps or sneakers. The Cubmaster raises his hand and calls, "Akela." A ten count passes, and he repeats: "Akela!" The kids sag to the tiled floor in front of the cafeteria stage as if their bones have dissolved. Benny and I have been sitting for five minutes—sugar is not part of my nephew's diet. He rocks slowly, careful to stay on a black tile. He's fixed his attention on a heel mark on the white tile in front of him. The other kids keep their distance. Benny attends this school too, but he's in special classes. He doesn't meet eyes.

With all the kids and dads on the floor, the Cubmaster leads a recitation of their oath. Only Benny and I and Mr. White Eagle abstain.

The cub scout follows Akela.
The cub scout helps the pack go.
The pack helps the cub scout grow.
The cub scout gives good will.

After the oath, the chattering starts again. The adults don't help—two dads near me discuss creosote buildup in chimneys while one of their boys, his cheeks smudgy with chocolate, chokes his freckled pal.

My sister Tara thinks scouting is a good idea for her son. Her boss at the Walmart made it all the way to Eagle. As I see it, Benny will never be management material. Tara calls his autism "mild Asperger's." He's not a head banger yet—Tara doesn't need to hide his red curls under a helmet—but doctors warn that it's a possibility down the road.

Often at pack meetings a father will sidle over during refreshments, usually dragging his son, who'll be smirking around at his friends. As Benny presses against me, swaying to his own rhythm, the dad will say, "How's the boy—how ya doin', son?" Benny won't answer. Maybe he rocks harder. Maybe he makes a keening sound. To fill the awkward moment, I ask my default question: "So who's this Akela, anyway?" The dad will smile without answering. "We'll see you later," he'll nod, and shift away, while his son zips off like a released fish.

Tonight, I touch my nephew's shoulder, and he flinches. I think I hear him humming, and I slide my hand from his shoulder to his back, but I don't feel the purr I expect— only the ridge of his spine and the ladder of his ribs. The sound comes from the stage: Mr. White Eagle is chanting. The hubbub in the room subsides until everyone except my sister's son is staring at Mr. White Eagle.

"Respect," he whispers. His purple lids are squeezed shut, as if we're something he doesn't want to see. "My people use a special, holy word: *Blah-dee-blah.*" The syllables melt together. "It is a tradition that passes from fathers to sons. Say it with me: *Blah-dee-blah.*" We try. We watch each other's lips. "*Blah-dee-blah,*" Mr. White Eagle repeats, and we catch on. "*Blah-dee-blah.*" Our chorus echoes through us, as if we're in church. Benny's mouth is shut, and he's still staring at the heel mark.

"It is with respect we treat our elders, our parents, our guests, each other," Mr. White Eagle says. The Cubmaster bows. These are the values we hope to instill in our boys. Several dads nod, too. I'm still trying to figure out where I know George White Eagle from.

Respect hasn't been part of the formula with a lot of our Pack's guests: the young veteran of the Iraq war lost the kids to giggle fits when he couldn't keep from swearing and quit his speech in the middle; the professional football player who'd never made it off the Oakland Raiders taxi squad only took questions. He said "yes" or "no" to a few, then stationed himself at a table where he signed autographs for two dollars each. After twenty minutes he stood and asked, "Who do I see about my fifty dollars?"

But Mr. White Eagle commands the kids' attention. He blows three long, sad notes into his wooden flute. We hear wide open plains and forests full of wildlife. "These are mourning songs," Mr. White Eagle tells us. "Songs of loss. Songs of death. Loss is part of the great circle of life, boys. Life begins with creation. Sex is creation. The mating of creatures. Of your mother and father. We have respect for sex—*Blah-de-Blah*." Our "*Blah-de-Blah*" is automatic, but "sex" has some fathers frowning. The Cubmaster's got a glazed look; his ears and neck are crimson.

"I'm going to tell you a story about respect." Mr. White Eagle speaks in a slow, measured beat, with his head still and his eyes closed like a blind man's. "It's an important story. It's about my people, the Creek. And America." I expect something about the world on the back of a big turtle, about brave warriors.

"Not too long ago, I was driving on a long stretch of Interstate 10," he begins, "just into Arizona from New Mexico, on my way to visit some people in Ohio. My car was borrowed from a friend in Bakersfield. The highway stretched far and wide in front of me, with great mountains in the distance. I was smoking— a cigarette—something you shouldn't do, boys. But when my people smoke, we're mourning our losses." Several adult heads bob, most likely the smokers. "It was a bright afternoon. No one else was on the road. Then, in my rearview mirror I saw a car, a state trooper, closing in quickly, and I said a prayer of welcoming. The trooper's lights started flashing, and I said another prayer to speed him safely to whatever emergency called him. When he pulled up beside me, he looked at me. I nodded at him through my open window, and when I smiled, my cigarette fell out of my mouth. I couldn't see his eyes behind his mirrored glasses, but I saw his lips curl with hatred. He pointed to the side of the road, and I pulled over."

Mr. White Eagle has been speaking in a prayerful monotone. From time to time there's a glint from between his shut lids, as if there are jewels hidden behind them. He continues his story: he's asked for his license and for the registration of the vehicle his Bakersfield friend apparently failed to renew; he's ordered to wait with his hands on the hood of the car while the trooper searches it; finally, he's handed citations for littering (the fallen cigarette) and the lapsed registration, and the trooper races off, lights still flashing.

"Do you see?" Mr. White Eagle asks the boys and their dads. "Shame—it sucks the warmth from the sun and the sparkle from the lakes; it steals the sweet scent from the pines. Do you see? It's this—" and he presents his profile: his hatchet nose, his high cheekbones and crag of a brow, the stump of the pony tail he waggles between his thumb and forefinger. There's a hush. Then Mr. White Eagle turns toward us and opens his eyes fully wide for the first time, and we gasp. His eyes have no whites—they're silvery irises set in absolute black—eyes that belonged only in nightmares. And I remember where I'd seen Mr. White Eagle before.

He's nearly whispering now. "What that officer showed was the ugliest thing in the world: prejudice. Against me. Against my people, for nothing more than a ponytail, and for skin a few shades too dark." He doesn't mention his eyes. He doesn't have to. "No respect. *Blah-dee-blah.*"

I'd seen him about a year ago, at the first and only AA meeting I'd ever attended. That's when Tara and my now ex-girlfriend, Janie, got together and "intervened," as they called it. For Tara the few joints a week I smoked, the six pack or so that helped quench my dry mouth and round off my buzz, made me a doubtful risk around her son. "You've got to be a better role model for him," she said, knowing how much I depended on his company.

Janie's reason for wanting me sober was more complicated; it was another aspect of the situation that forced me to move out of the rented bungalow we shared, the one on the river bank where there used to be an amusement park almost a hundred years ago. I've seen old photographs of a midway and a carrousel, and a ferris wheel at night all lit up and reflected in the black river. I can match up the shoreline to my fishing spots. I liked to tell Janie when we were in bed that the wind rustling the leaves outside our window was the ghosts of happy people laughing. I moved out because Janie was pregnant—not by me, though I wish that would have been possible. Janie had the best one-time job I'd ever heard of—she was a surrogate. The fertilized egg of a rich woman had been implanted in her womb; she didn't know who she was bearing the baby for, only that she was to be paid a small fortune when the kid was born—exactly how much it wasn't my business to know yet, she said. She also received a monthly sum to eat properly, and a nurse visited once a week to check on the progress of her pregnancy.

Janie is beautiful and ambitious—she has a college degree, and when she was picked to be a surrogate, you'd have thought she won the lottery and bags of gold would soon be dropped off at our door. "You can't stay here," she told me. "They think I'm single. I signed something. You'll have to get an apartment, and I'll visit you there. And if I am going to visit, you'll have to change your habits. There'll be no smoking or drinking around this baby. He's going to be my down-payment on life."

I should have noticed that she said "my down-payment" and not "our down-payment." But I promised both Janie and Tara I'd go to an AA meeting, and I quit smoking and drinking. When Janie started swelling, I talked to the baby in her belly, which she let slip was a boy. Janie would sneak over to my tidy little apartment every weekend at first, but she visited less and less frequently the more and more pregnant she got. She stopped letting me touch her. It wasn't that she wasn't horny any more—she said she was "superstitious" about my fingers and tongue so close to "the portal," which would be the rich child she was carrying's access to the world. Sometimes I thought Janie was afraid I would contaminate the unborn kid with my ignorance—as if she had just enough class for him, but I'd never be in the same league.

When her nine months were nearly up—it was just after the night of that one and only AA meeting where I saw Mr. White Eagle— I suggested that we could deliver the kid ourselves, then take off with him and start our own family somewhere far away—a tropical island or a village in the Brazilian rain forest. I thought it was a funny idea to have to kidnap something inside of you. I never saw her again after that night. I don't know where or on which day she had the baby, and when I returned to the bungalow on the site of the old amusement park, there wasn't a scrap to indicate she'd ever lived there, let alone a note.

But while I waited in the dim fluorescence of the Methodist church's meeting room for that AA meeting to begin, I'd thought I was opening a new chapter on Janie's and my life, not closing the final one. Maybe two dozen folks, mostly men, sat in three rows of folding chairs. Despite the ban on tobacco, the room reeked from clothing steeped in smoke. The people in charge were welcoming, but there wasn't much chit-chat. Everyone was too intent on publically nursing a private woe. I thought I'd be required to share my story, and I decided I'd tell the assembly about the testicular cancer that left me single-balled and sterile. I'd reveal that I'd never be able to father a child of my own, and that the heart-wrenching disappointment had driven me to anesthetize my sorrows in drugs and drink. The truth is, I'd never had cancer, just a sperm count approaching zero—I'd been tested periodically because I'd grown up in a tract house my folks bought that was built on a nuclear waste dumping ground. That situation involved some mismanaged lawsuits, and if anyone in my family reaped a penny from it, I never knew. But a cancer story would draw more sympathy than a lawsuit, I concluded. I imagined the eyes of these hardened substance abusers filling with tears at my tale of woe.

Tara and I don't talk about it, but she grew up over the same nuclear waste I did, and maybe her irradiated eggs caused Benny's problems. Her husband left after the weight of Benny's turning out to be the kind of kid he is cracked marital ice that was already thin. Tara and Tim didn't have it in themselves to deal with the situation as a team, which is why I'm scooched up next to my nephew at this scout meeting while Mr. White Eagle has resumed sounding melancholy notes on his flute. When I look at him I can't believe I didn't recognize him immediately from the Methodist church basement.

He sat in the first row, and when he popped up to tell about his tribulations, he made no effort to dim the effect of his frightful eyes: they were like dimes floating in black ink.

"I have been a conman and a terrible human being," he began. His tale was set "in another city" where he had custody of a little girl, a toddler "not really my daughter." To make his very long story short, somehow he managed to scam the congregation of a church into believing that this child entrusted to his care was dying of "something like leukemia." He'd thrown himself on the mercy of the big-hearted congregants. "The good people organized a fundraiser," he told us, and he'd netted a "blessed" profit in the thousands from the gullible church folk before skipping town.

"I have paid my debt for that and other offences," he said, by which he meant he did prison time, "and as a confirmation of that payment I inked my eyes." I shivered. I hadn't known it was possible to tattoo your eyeballs. "These eyes are my public admission of the midnight thoughts that always lurk inside. They warn everyone I meet, 'Trust me if you dare.' Being seen as I am is part of my daily battle."

Anonymous no longer, here he is, "George White Eagle," toodling his flute and yammering about *Blah-dee-blah* to a pack of Cub Scouts for the sake, I assume, of fifty dollars. How, I wonder, had the scout leaders found him? How had Mr. White Eagle advertised himself?

I'm fidgety, and at a loss as to what to do with my knowledge. Is there a statute of limitations on anonymity? What if Mr. White Eagle's got a bigger scam in mind than just that fifty?" "You okay?" I ask Benny, mostly to calm myself down, and my nephew doesn't respond, but the father next to me shushes me and gives me a look like I've just violated *Blah-dee-blah*. I raise an eyebrow at the shusher and cock my head toward Mr. White Eagle, but the dad misses the signal. His plump son's mouth hangs open as if the nonsense Mr. White Eagle is feeding him is better than a cream-filled donut.

What I should do is get up and take my information about Mr. White Eagle to the Cubmaster. He stands at the back of the room, smiling at the stage; but if I leave Benny, I'm afraid he'll start howling, like he did when I left him on a movie line with a nice old lady so I could get the wallet I'd left in the car.

Mr. White Eagle has stopped playing and addresses us again. His silver and black eyes gleam. There's a beat in the pit of my stomach like a tom-tom.

"*Blah-dee-blah*," Mr. White Eagle intones.

"*Blah-dee-blah*," almost everyone replies. Benny makes his own sound.

"Boys," our guest says, "you make my heart glow. Your ways, the ways of scouting, are the ways of my people.

And there are two things we must value as much as *Blah-dee-blah*: Truth and Vigilance."

Heads nod, though I'm sure few of the boys know what "vigilance" means. This is the real deal, dads are telling themselves, this is why we signed our boys up for scouting. Not to tie knots. Not to carve race cars out of blocks of pine. Not to earn badges for taking out the trash. But to grab hold of those old virtues, Truth and Vigilance. Virtue, I think, and that's when I decide that it's up to me to unmask Mr. White Eagle. I'm panting, and the hand I rest on Benny's knee is damp.

"And so," our guest continues, "I offer you myself as a lesson in Truth and Vigilance." He bows deeply. I brace myself—there's the kind of hush that Benny often fills with a wail. But his breathing is regular, and for a moment I understand the relief of fitting in. Who would it hurt to let the whole thing slide? But then Mr. White Eagle smiles—for the first time this evening—and the way his face twists beneath those eyes hits me like a blow to my manhood. I'm being disrespected—no *Blah-dee-blah*.

I remember the first father-son Cub Scout project Benny and I undertook. Tara had dropped Benny off on a Saturday morning at the bungalow I'd re-occupied after Janie's desertion. He sat at my kitchen table with a milk mustache while I whittled away at a Pinewood Derby car with a steak knife, the closest thing I owned to a tool. The magic marker for Benny to color the raw wood had dried up, so I gave him a Bic pen, and he slashed stripes along one side of the car, again and again and again, hundreds of them, then said, "TV," and I said, "Okay." We brought the car to Derby night, where other scouts displayed glossy, aerodynamic racers they seemed to be handling for the first time. Their dads swapped details about weight distribution and wheel bases, decals and metallic paint. Compared to the others, our car looked like it had been gnawed into shape by squirrels. I caught one father looking at it and muttering to another with a shake of his head, "You'd have thought . . ." The other dad shook his head too, staring at our scarred chunk of wood. The first dad repeated, knowing I was in earshot, "You'd have just thought." I turned to my nephew, who clutched our car to his chest like it was a gold ingot. "Who the heck is Akela, Benny?" I demanded. "Why can't anybody tell me that?"

So I have no choice. Mr. White Eagle must be exposed. But I'm still waiting for a sign that the moment is right when he beats me to his own unmasking.

"Truth," he says. "The truth is, I am not who you think. There is more to George White Eagle than meets the eye. I was baptized George DiBello, but I have gone by many other names. I have been William Smith. In prison they called me Willie Freeze." His words seem to echo from a pit that's opened beneath us. The blood has drained from the Cubmaster's face. "Truth: I was not born a Creek Indian. I am of Italian and Greek descent." He grins, and his eyes flash. "And now you think I have deceived you. That's good—you're being vigilant. There are those who will tell you lies, boys—you will meet such people as you journey through life."

Confusion reigns—dads look to the Cubmaster and to each other for some kind of reassurance, but there's none to be had, and as the boys feel their fathers' grips loosen, their eyes round with fear. It's frightening and exhilarating at the same time. It's a feeling I wish I could get credit for creating.

"But even now I have fooled you," Mr. Whoever says. He waggles a finger. "Truth and Vigilance— I became a Creek in prison. My cellmate was Creek, and after an intimate ceremony, we became blood brothers. He assured me I have full tribal rights. Then I had my eyes inked—I gave up their whites. And now, the blackness is a symbol. As I look out at you, my darkness is behind me. So, learn this lesson, just as I learned the lessons of my adopted people, the Creek—don't trust what you see. Don't cast judgments until you know the whole Truth. That trooper who pulled me over? He was wrong about who he thought I was—but he was also right, do you see? But in the biggest way of all, *Blah-dee-blah*, he was wrong."

Silence. There's too much to digest to understand it all. But the Cub Scout oath prevails: "*The cub scout shows good will.*" A unified opinion settles like a golden cloud on Mr. Dibello-Smith-White Eagle's audience: *The subject was Truth. No one has been deceived. Good people chose this speaker. We will all sleep well tonight.*

"Thank you, boys, fathers, Cubmaster." Our guest is reluctant to leave the stage. I'm waiting for one more "*Blah-dee-blah*" when I feel Benny seething next to me. He's rocking on his haunches, forward and back. His lips part.

"Boo," Benny says, the sound a burst bubble that only I hear, because everyone else, all the dads and their kids, have begun to clap—louder and louder, applause that grows bolder as it justifies itself. Benny tilts his head back, and his jaws seem to unhinge. "Boo!" he bleats. "Boo, Boo, Boo!"

"Shh, quiet!" the dad behind me growls, and "Hey" and "Quiet" and "Shh" erupt around us. "Get him out!" another dad nearby hisses, because Benny won't shut up— "Boo-boo-boo-boo-boo—" he rattles like a machine gun. Outrage swells, and in a second I'm on my feet, and I pull Benny up, too. He's looking at the floor, and he stumbles stiffly after me as I lead him out the emergency exit that takes us into the parking lot and the night. "Boo-boo-boo-boo-boo," he's muttering. I haven't once told him to knock it off. Behind us I hear the Cubmaster's enthusiastic voice, muffled, then more applause. Did he just thank the speaker—had he apologized for my nephew and me? I take Benny into the darkness, onto the playing field stretching beyond the parking lot, walking him almost all the way to the trees at the far end. It's a cool evening, and it feels good to move. After a while Benny stops booing.

"Look at the stars," I say, catching my breath. I drape my arm over his slight shoulders. He doesn't say a word, but he lifts his eyes. "There's the Big Dipper," I say, "and the

Milky Way." I haven't really found them, but I know they're up there somewhere. Benny's staring up— at the stars or the spaces between them. I plan to stay out on the field until the parking lot empties. Then I feel Benny freeze—he senses before I do that we've been followed across the field.

"The Seven Sisters," a voice whispers. It belongs to the man I first saw at AA. He points at the heavens as he circles around us until he blocks our way. "The Creek tell a story about them." His back is to the trees. There's an odor from him like incense. He lowers his gaze and I can feel its blackness spreading over us, thicker than the night. "You booed me," he says, addressing me, not Benny. "Do I know you?"

The truth is, maybe I did boo him. Maybe Benny got the idea from me. I don't say anything for a few seconds. Up close he's not very tall, almost a head shorter than I am. His grin is tight, hiding his teeth. "We're just tired," I say. "It was a long night."

"There's something wrong with your boy," he says matter-of-factly. *There's something wrong with your eyes*, I want to say, but hold my tongue.

"He's my sister's kid." The moment I say it, I feel bad. "I can't have my own," I add, but it's too late. I have never before in my life hit another human being, but I'm feeling the instinct for it. My arm tingles and my hand closes into a fist. The man holds his flute like a club, as if it's heavier than anyone would think, and I assess how much it might hurt to block a swing with my forearm. Then I ask him, "Who's Akela? You should be able to tell me that."

"Akela? It's another name for the Great Spirit. Shawnee, I think."

"Wrong," I say. "It's Hindi. It's *Indian*-Indian, not Native American. From Kipling's *Jungle Book*. Akela is the lone wolf—the lone wolf who leads the pack." A lot of truths can be found on the Internet.

"I'm a hypnotherapist. And a homeopathic doctor," he says. "Maybe there's something I can do for the boy. For you, too." I twitch as he reaches into his jeans pocket, but he pulls out a card. I relax my hand to accept it. "Give me a call. We can work something out. No charge for session one." He looks at Benny, whose gaze has fallen from the starry sky to the turf. "*Blah-dee-Blah*," the Creek adoptee says. He salutes us with his instrument and turns toward the trees. I see now that there's a path through them to a lit street not more than fifty yards beyond, and he's striding toward it. "Boo," he throws back over his shoulder, followed by a laugh that turns into a smoker's wheeze.

By now my sister will be wondering where we are. I might have to tell her we're done with scouting, and I'm trying to think of how to break the news. Maybe I don't have to say anything; maybe on Tuesday nights Benny and I could just do something else, like bowling or a movie. What we won't do yet is visit Dr. DiBello—that's the name on his card. The parking lot looks empty now, but I no longer care. The school's big classroom windows are bright yellow, and we can see the late-shift custodians moving around. I palm Benny's back and guide him forward.

"Akela" I say.

"Boo," my nephew says, his eyes on the night-blue turf he kicks at with each step.

Still Life

I'm late, and I'll be much later; the dead dog I see through the slats of the louvered door is to blame. I haven't the art class instructor's telephone number. What will her students use for a model when I don't show? Who or what will occupy my stool? I will be replaced by an object. Still life. A piece of fruit. Perhaps a ripe tomato. A coffee mug. An interesting piece of found trash? All my folds and wrinkles, my hairy and hairless patches would have been on display. My retired penis would have awaited the skill of the boldest among them. But on the other side of this door Sirarthur is dead. His name was a compromise: Susan wanted something spiritual; I favored Sherlock Holmes. If she hadn't predeceased him by a year, our dog's stiff bulk would have brought my wife to tears.

When Susan passed, I was posing. My cell phone, set on vibrate, was in my pants pocket, left with my shirt, socks and underwear behind a screen erected for my convenience. I had emerged, as for every class, in my yellow terrycloth robe, which pooled on the floor as I assumed the session's position. We thought Susan had months, even years, that this hospitalization was just one more in a cycle of treatments and homecomings that would last into a hazy future neither of us acknowledged. The voice message: *Please hurry; Ms. Weber is failing.*

Because of his incontinence, Sirarthur spent his nights in a basement room with a tiled floor. This morning, clapping and shouting "Sirarthur, hey!" didn't rouse him. The hairs on the back of my neck lifted. I pushed, but the door didn't yield.

Heart failure, they said at the hospital—Susan had fought hard, but the strain of her treatments had taken its toll. Sheeted to the chin, she lay alone when I arrived, breathless. Her wig was backwards, and I shifted it into place above her smooth brow. Her parted lips seemed about to chide—the wig? my lateness? Eyeglasses and dentures in a cup waited on the nightstand. She would never again see me or say my name.

Because the husky's body blocks the louvered inner door, I enter Sirarthur's room from outside. His open eyes, mismatched blue and brown, never intelligent, are empty—there is a great distance between simple-mindedness and death. His tongue lolls through his open jaws as if he's tasting the floor. But his mass is ambiguous: he is neither furniture nor art, but he is definitely here.

Susan suggested modeling. She saw an ad. "'No experience necessary,'" she read. "It's at the college. You're great at sitting and doing nothing." I like watching old movies. Sometimes I read. "You need to get out," she said.
"I walk Sirarthur," I said.
"That doesn't count," she said. "You need to see people."
"I walk him twice a day."
"The neighbors stay away from the two of you. He growls. You never trained him."
"He doesn't like people."
"See about modeling."

"Would you mind taking off your shirt?" the instructor asked. I offered the rest of my body. "I'm at the mercy of time and gravity," I warned. At the end of the session the instructor praised my "gift for stillness." She passed my name on to other art teachers.

Sirarthur must be removed, but there are problems: first, I have not yet achieved sufficient objectivity to touch him; second, his weight will make transporting him a challenge. The flesh should disappear with the life. Leaving it behind is like littering: the dead's irresponsible final gesture.

Half an hour. At Susan's bedside that's how long it took to divide the life from the body, to transform the first into a memory and the second into an object. A nurse entered and touched my elbow. I rose and a dull fluorescence followed me like a cloud down the hall to a desk where arrangements were discussed. I needed to get home to walk Sirarthur.

We'd owned two other dogs, Krishna and Watson, adopted after children proved impossible. Little dogs, coddled through long lives ending with somber, responsible trips to the veterinarian's. Then we saw a movie featuring huskies, and their beauty and vigor touched us. "They can be willful," the breeder said. "Walk him for an hour a day. Two, if possible." Sirarthur was handsome, powerful, and untrainable. Having a name seemed irrelevant to him. He was impossible to allow off-leash and only intermittently housebroken. During his first epileptic seizure I tried to comfort him; temporarily blind, he bit through my thumb. Medication reduced his seizures but left him perpetually ravenous. He spent more and more time in his basement room, where I tuned his television to the classic movie channel. And so passed the duration of his hard-to-love fourteen years.

Susan was diagnosed the week of our thirty-eighth wedding anniversary. She died a month before what would have been our fortieth. We had hoped to travel more than we did after our retirements, but kenneling Sirarthur became an impediment. "He howled all night," said one proprietor. "I can't take him again." Another he bit. One ran a kennel on her farm, and we managed two week-long vacations, one to Key West where it rained almost every day and another to London. Where it rained. Our vacation pictures catalogued humid deluges and chill drizzles. The kennel-woman told us after our second trip that on his walk Sirarthur had grabbed her rooster by the throat and shaken him dead. Then he wouldn't let go—she'd paraded him around the yard, screaming at him, while the bird hung from his jaws. Only when more chickens crossed their path did he drop his kill for a lunge. London was our last vacation.

Legions of former colleagues and students attended Susan's memorial service. A young man to whom she'd taught geometry and who became a state senator spoke. The afternoon following the service, Sirarthur followed his usual routine when brought upstairs: he barged through the door; checked for food on the dining room table; checked for food on the kitchen counters; checked to see if the garbage can was locked; checked for food in the den; drank from the toilet. Then he lumbered to my seat, dropped his heavy paw on my thigh, dripped toilet water on my lap from his open jaws, and demanded petting. He did not look for his mistress. If he had, he would have found her silver urn on the mantle, where it still sits like a trophy.

I am bleached of vanity. What, I wonder, do the art students see in my sagging flesh? Do their brushes and pencils and charcoals reanimate the surfaces youth has deserted? Tufts of colorless hair gather on my shoulders, above my nipples, in my ears, over my penis, and upon my scrotum. The students' eyes crawl over my membranous skin, collecting data, transferring it, their interest not in me, but of me; they translate me into their own languages on paper and canvas, mingle me with themselves.

Thirty minutes to objectify the body before I attempt to remove it. The veterinary hospital does not provide this service. "But we're so sorry," a young woman says. "Bring poor Sirarthur here and we'll take care of everything. We're so, so sorry for your loss." I wait and watch a movie on Sirarthur's TV, peeking at the carcass now and then to see what's changed. It's a musical. Fred Astaire and Ginger Rogers dance in each other's arms. Sirathur's tongue is frozen to the floor. Finally, I expect nothing from his vacant eyes.

The movie is *Top Hat*. Astaire wears one. I maneuver the body with a shovel. The carcass moves as a piece, hindquarters to head. I pry Sirarthur's rear quarters from the floor and slide the open end of a forty gallon heavy duty black plastic contractor's bag beneath his stiff legs and tail. It slips frictionlessly over and under the black and white fur I brushed yesterday. I try to hurry. The animal hospital waits, and at the art class there is no accounting for my absence. The bag accommodates Sirarthur's forelegs, but forty gallons are not enough. His head protrudes from the bag like a wall mounting. I keep the box of contractor bags in our bedroom. I have filled several with Susan's clothes: dresses, blouses, robes, skirts, stockings, outfits that she wore to synagogue, to parties, to dinner, to bed. I don't really fill them. I keep her closet closed. But I imagine the sleeve of her red sweater reaching from a black bag, and I remember Sirarthur shedding on it as Susan petted him. Straddling his carcass, I tug a second bag over Sirarthur's head, and it shimmies like gown to his hip.

When I model, I decline breaks, though they're offered at regular intervals. "I meditate," I tell instructors, and they allow their students to continue capturing my essence. But I don't meditate; I replay movies in my head. Entire scripts. I see the action. I hear every line of dialogue and the music. I keep still: the movies play in a private corner deep within my brain. I don't allow the tragic or comic to excite my heart. I breathe serenely.

Moving the carcass—where do I grip? Can I wrap my arms around it like Fred held Ginger? I spread a canvas tarp, push and tug with the shovel, and coax the carcass into its center. *I'm just putting on my top hat, tying on my white tie, dusting off my tails.* I turn off the television. I'll envision a different movie while I drag the loaded tarp out the door and uphill along the side of the house to the driveway where I'll somehow hoist it into the trunk of my Taurus.

Halfway up the hill, and *Of Mice and Men* absorbs me, the oldest version with Burgess Meredith and Lon Chaney, Junior. My back aches, and every two steps I adjust my grip on the corners of the tarp bunched into my fists. One-two, pause. One-two, pause. *Tell me about the rabbits, George.* It's a black and white movie, but I see it with a sepia tint. When I drop the tarp and straighten, my back crunches. My neighbors have pulled their pickups side by side in the road at the end of my driveway and chat through open windows. Their engines run. I'm in too much of a hurry for explanations and stoop back to my task, grasp the corners of the tarp, and, leaning back, straining hamstrings, quads and glutes, drag the bundle to the black-topped driveway, one-two-three, one-two-three, all the way to the trunk of my car. *The fatta the land.* I leave it there, ignoring my neighbors, cross my lawn, ascend my porch steps, and pass through the front door into my living room.

I sit on the radiator cover at my front window, peering from behind the curtain. I wait for the men in the street to drive off so I can gather my pet one last time in my arms and dump him in the Taurus's trunk. At the veterinary hospital the staff will take over. They will have a gurney. While it's rolled away, someone will attempt to distract me by patting my arm and offering a tissue. There'll be a question about ashes and I'll choose the cheapest option; when they're ready I'll keep the box on the mantle next to Susan's urn. But if my neighbors leave soon, I might make it to art class after the vet's, and the students will be happy to have me to copy—unless they've already devoted themselves to the still life I fear has taken my place.

Boy Strangling Goose

As the Uber stops across from the entrance to the emergency room, the bloody kitchen towel drops from five-year-old Danny-boy's damaged face. The sweaty driver's eyes bug at the revelation.

"Geez, look at that. Don't worry about the blood. There's been worse back there. I get a lot of drunks. Vinyl cleans up easy."

"Thanks," Reilly mutters, "a swan bit him. He got too close."

"I know, a swan, you said that." Reilly feels the driver reassess him in the rearview. "People don't usually have a swan at their houses."

"We have a pond. A flock landed last night, and they were still there this morning. I took my grandson up close to show him." Reilly pats the floor of the SUV for his cane and grips its shaft. How many times will an explanation be necessary? Not just for emergency room doctors and nurses, but for the boy's mother—his daughter Millie, and for his wife, Iris, off together on a "bucket-list" European vacation. When they find out—there is no way to escape blame. Reilly suspends his arm over the rigid child. The bloodstained dish towel has slid to Danny-boy's chest. *Come have a close up look at something beautiful in our pond.* Beauty? What about Danny-boy's? What if the swan-bite leaves a hole in the middle of the boy's face—a permanent reminder of Reilly's failure to protect him? Reilly plucks up the towel and stuffs it in his pocket.

"He's lucky it's the nose. My girlfriend's brother lost an eye to a dog bite—just one of those little cockapoos. It didn't want to be cuddled. Robbie's glass eye doesn't move with the good one."

Reilly shudders. A narrative—he will be a prisoner of this story for the rest of his life. He stares out the window—there's thirty feet of black asphalt between the SUV and the emergency room entrance, and it reminds him of the pond under the gliding bodies of the swans. He'd hurried to rouse the sleeping boy. *Come see something special.* Not the usual ducks or geese. *They picked our pond. It's a gift.* But the terrifying, breathtaking, span of those spread wings had stopped Reilly dead—he couldn't even raise his cane against the wild thing's attack. Now he can't lift his arm to open the car door.

The SUV idles in the shade cast by the hospital building. The sky above the roofline is a painful blue. "You want me to get a wheelchair?" the driver asks. "You don't look so hot yourself. Sit tight, I'll get two."

"Thank you," Reilly whispers. Danny-boy moans something when the driver's door slams shut— was it "Momma"? The driver crosses the blacktop as if he's walking on water. *The women*: a wife who is celebrating being cancer free; a daughter celebrating what—a few weeks of freedom from single parenthood? The women had gambled that a one-footed old man could keep a child safe for two weeks.

*****

It was just last night that Reilly had sat on his deck sipping a glass of wine, waiting for the first crickets to notice the fading daylight. Danny-boy watched television inside. Next would come a bath and bedtime story, and then Reilly would have a second glass of wine during his turn with the TV before dragging himself to bed.

This is the gloaming. The trees and hills beyond the pond dissolved into shadows. Reilly reeled in his gaze—it stopped on the loafers he'd propped on the deck rail. He curled the toes inside the right shoe, then concentrated on the left, which was filled by the plastic wedge of his artificial foot. There'd been no sign of a phantom limb in the year since he'd lost the original. Was there a statute of limitations on ghost feet?

Then, as if granting a wish, twenty or so swans tumbled from the dull sky and splashed into Reilly's half-acre pond. Geese, he'd thought, until the swans settled on the black surface, and the shock of their whiteness sucked the breath out of him.

Reilly stared at the birds until they became pale blurs in the darkness. The first stars appeared, and soon the sky was thick with constellations. Yet he still saw the swans, if only by faith.

"Pops? Is it bedtime, Pops?" Danny-boy called from his side of the screen door, and at the sound of his grandson's voice Reilly realized he'd let time slide by. Cartoons were over— maybe the boy was retreating from something unsettling on grownup television. They skipped a bath because of the hour, and then, like every night for the last two weeks, Reilly pretended to "lose" his grandson in the big guestroom bed. The giggling boy huddled in plain sight while his grandfather poked and probed pillows and sheets with his cane. "Where are you, Danny-boy?" he called. "Did wizards shrink you to the size of a peanut? Oh—there you are!"

If Danny-boy was large or small for his age, Reilly didn't know. He'd lost perspective. Millie had been average, and still was. And the boy's father, who knew?

"We understood that having a baby wouldn't save a failing marriage," Millie confessed, "but Yolanda and I tried anyway. And now I have Danny-boy." Since Millie was to bear the child, she'd let her wife choose the sperm donor. "The only thing Yo insisted on was religion—we had to pick a Jew." Then Yolanda had run off to Arizona before Danny-boy was born, leaving only a document waiving all custodial privileges to the child.

"I guess I'll raise him Jewish," Millie shrugged to her parents. "Christmas is a fraud anyway. At least Danny-boy won't be a third generation lapsed Catholic. He won't confuse Santa Claus with God, like I did. I'll send him to classes. Maybe he'll find out why I stomped on that glass at my wedding."

In spite of Reilly's desire to tell his grandson about the swans he pictured slumbering on the moonlit pond with their heads tucked under their wings, Reilly held his tongue. If he promised the boy "something miraculous," and the swans flew off before dawn, the empty pond would be an unkept promise. In the morning Reilly would make sure the birds were still there, and then surprise his grandson.

But couldn't Reilly nibble around the edges, whet the boy's appetite for swans without actually revealing the birds' near presence? There was the poem, Yeats, wasn't it— a god disguised himself as a swan. But it was about a rape. Reilly recalled only "a shudder in the loins" and "Agamemnon dead" before he thought of the Hans Christian Anderson fairytale.

"Do you know the story of the ugly duckling, Danny-boy?"

"Yes. It's a BS ghosty."

"'BS ghosty'?"

"Mommy says there are stories and things I have to know because they're famous and smart people have to know them. But they're BS. BS stands for "Boo-sheet." What a ghosty wears. The Boo-sheet is a disguise that covers bad messages."

Reilly frowned. "But the baby duckling that everyone in the story hates turns out to be a beautiful swan. He was better than all of them."

"Mommy says it was bad that everyone was mean, but his beauty didn't make him better. She says beauty is in the eye of the beholder anyway. And what did the swan *do* to make himself special? He *had* to be a swan, he didn't *earn* it. Mommy says we don't have kings anymore because there's no such thing as royalty. The ugly duckling is BS—Boo-sheet."

Some things *are* objectively beautiful, Reilly thought, but he didn't want to contradict the child's mother. If the swans were still there in the morning, Danny-boy could be his own beholder, Boo-sheet be damned. The child snuggled

against Reilly, who warmed with pride—such a smart kid—
how much of that was due to an anonymous donor?

"Pops, can I see your foot? Can you take it off?"

"Not tonight. It takes too long to get it back on, and I
don't want to hop out of here." Reilly remembered the first
time he'd put weight on his artificial foot— it had been like
stepping into the Grand Canyon.

"You have your cane."

"I'd still have to hop. Remind me tomorrow when
I'm not so tired."

"I can't tell which foot is real and which isn't because
your shoes are the same." Danny-boy said.

"If I don't move, I can't tell either." Reilly pictured
Millie's wedding, the moment his daughter, wearing a white
tuxedo, brought her foot down on a linen-wrapped glass.
Everyone clapped, including Yolanda in her tulle ball gown,
and then the newlyweds kissed.

They wound up reading *Make Way for Ducklings*,
Danny-boy's choice.

"So this story's not Boo-sheet?" Reilly asked when
they finished.

"A little bit." Danny-boy yawned. "Mommy says Mr.
Mallard isn't very nice— when he takes a trip up the river by
himself after the babies hatch, he leaves all the work to Mrs.
Mallard. But the good part is she shows she can do
everything on her own."

"She's independent."

"And I like that Mr. Mallard comes back at the end.
Tomorrow you'll let me play with your foot, right?"

"I'll let you look at it. I don't know about 'playing.'" It
was time for Reilly to leave the boy, but he couldn't budge.
The most he could manage was wiggling the toes in his right
loafer.

"There's a famous picture of me with Mrs. Mallard
from when I was little," the boy said. "I've got my arm over
her back. She's a statue. I'm wearing my Red Sox cap."

26

"It was just last spring," Reilly said. "You weren't that little. And then we want on a swan boat, just like the one the Mallards see in the book. Remember?"

Danny turned away from Reilly and shifted toward the wall. "No. Oh, yes, a little. Grandma held me on her lap."

Grandfather and grandson lay still. *Get up*, Reilly ordered himself, but he still couldn't move. He saw himself sitting on the toilet lid in his bathroom, sweating with headache and fever, dabbing ointment on a foot and ankle swollen with infection to the size and color of an old galosh. When Iris, who'd just turned the corner in her breast cancer battle, poked her head through the door and saw Reilly's condition, she'd screamed.

The diagnosis was *necrotizing fasciitis*—a "flesh-eating" bacteria. "It's spreading fast," the doctor said. "If we don't amputate, you'll be dead by tomorrow."

The bacteria had ambushed Reilly in his pond, where he'd stood, ankle deep in mud, digging out cattails that spoiled the view from the deck. During her recuperation from chemo and radiation treatments, Iris lay for hours up there, under an umbrella, gazing at the dark water. Hot, thirsty, and breathless, Reilly paused to consider the pond's smooth surface, imagining, at the moment the deadly microbe was invading his tissue, that a school of piranha had sniffed him out. He pictured the frenzy of an attack: the water splashing around him like scattered diamonds; pain like the bites of a thousand hornets; his picked-clean skeleton half-submerged in the shallows.

Though Reilly lost his foot in the service of his sick wife, he would never draw attention to this fact. And while Iris's recovery was rightly looked upon as a triumph, around Reilly's loss lingered the suggestion of personal neglect.

Danny-boy stirred. "Tell me about my other mommy," he whispered to the wall.

"Yolanda?" Reilly saw the wedding again, the newlyweds dressed in white, the descending foot, the kiss. "She left before you were born." *And she gave you up.*

"Like Mr. Mallard?"

"At least he waited until his kids hatched." What would Reilly say if the boy asked about his father?

Danny-boy rolled back toward Reilly. "When's she coming back, Pops?"

How do you say *never* to a five-year-old? "Nobody knows. You'll have to ask your mother."

"That's what I mean," Danny-boy said. "When is Mommy coming home?"

"Oh—" Reilly grunted. "In a couple of days. Thursday, late."

*****

Reilly shut his laptop and slid it to Iris's side of their bed. Under the sheets, his left leg was noticeably shorter without his fake foot. He wiggled his toes and felt the usual five—but there was something unusual going on with his left stump, a strange pressure, as if strong fingers massaged the outside while something pushed back from the inside. Something a tadpole growing new limbs might feel.

He'd found a different Yeats swan poem, one not about rape: "The Wild Swans at Coole." He memorized a few lines for Danny-boy: *They drift on the still water . . . mysterious, beautiful.* Swans were not boo-sheet ghosties. While he studied the poem, Reilly's stump throbbed with the external kneading and internal pushing. What if frogs took the next step and sprouted wings? He remembered the "famous" picture of Danny-boy in his Red Sox cap hugging Mrs. Mallard. Did the mother duck suspect that one of her ducklings would run off and become a swan? Which one—Jack, Kack, Lack, Mack, Nack, Ouack, Pack or Quack? Reilly put his money on Ouack.

And where were Millie and Iris while Reilly lay on the cusp of sleep surrounded by flying frogs and duck mommas? Were they still in Rome? The few texts they'd sent assured him that they were fine and having a ball. They loved and missed him and Danny-boy. Their meals were incredible, they wrote—*like nothing we've ever experienced. Heavenly.*

Reilly heard his own voice in a dream. He was talking to teenage Millie, who'd just asked a favor—a ride to a party— and he'd responded with a demand.

"Sure honey, no problem— but I'll need a roast swan in return."

"A roast swan? There's no such thing."

"Check the frozen poultry section at the supermarket. Right with the chickens and turkeys. Or catch your own, pluck it, and roast it fresh. Ask Mom for my favorite recipe."

Millie saw he was joking and frowned. "Roasting swans is mean. They're too beautiful."

Reilly edged out of sleep, grinning—so there was a time that Millie recognized that superior beauty was a natural gift. He hoped the swans pardoned his jest about being baked—but of course they had—otherwise, they wouldn't have come to his pond. He imagined a swan couple, beak to beak: their graceful necks formed a perfect heart.

Startling musical chords burst from the laptop across the bed, and Reilly rolled toward it, conscious of the lesser weight of his shortened leg. He opened the computer, and there, like a pair of trapped genies, were his wife and daughter.

Reilly! Dad! Did we wake you? What time is it there? We're in Paris!

He squinted at the screen clock. "It's 2:12. Danny-boy's asleep. I was sleeping, too."

The women looked at each other. "I told you," Iris said.

Millie cocked her head, then faced Reilly, who discovered himself in a little square in a corner of the screen. "I thought it was the other way around—that we were six hours behind."

Reilly watched himself shake his head. "Nope."

"Well, sorry and *bonjour,*" Iris said, more amused than apologetic. "We're going to take a boat on the Seine this morning after breakfast. We went to the Louvre yesterday afternoon and the Eiffel tower last night. It was all lit up. From the observation deck you could see the city all lit up, too."

"Paris is the City of Lights," Millie said. "How's Danny-boy? How are you?"

"We're fine," Reilly said. "We're doing great." He stifled a yawn. "How's your hotel?"

"Lovely," Iris said. "It comes with this laptop. Look at our room—"

The picture lurched from the women's faces. Fuzzy walls and leaning doorways spun by. Reilly focused on the tiny image of himself. He tested a smile. "Nice," he said. "And you're okay?"

"This has been wonderful," Iris said. "I feel ten years younger. And the food—"

She kissed her fingertips with very red lips. She did look younger. Had she dyed her hair?

"You're frowning," Iris said. "Are you sure everything's alright?"

"It's all fine. It's just late, that's all. We miss you. Danny-boy has been a good boy. We read *Make Way for Ducklings* tonight." He almost told about the swans, but held his tongue. What could he say that could compete with Paris? If the flock stayed put, the women might see for themselves.

"Oh—" Millie bowed off the screen, then popped back in, her phone in hand.

"What?" Iris asked, looking over her daughter's shoulder.

"Remember the boy and goose sculpture, Mom?" Millie thumbed at the phone. "I want to show Dad. I've got the picture here somewhere, speaking of *Make Way for Ducklings.*" She shook her head and gave up. "I can't find the picture. I'll have to send it later. So at the Louvre we saw an old Greek statue of a chubby little naked boy standing next to a goose. The boy's clutching the goose's throat, like he's choking it. It reminds me of the picture of Danny-boy with Mrs. Mallard. At the Public Garden. Remember, Dad?"

Reilly blinked. "Hey, he and I were talking about the same—"

"I don't think the boy is choking the goose, dear," Iris interrupted. "He's just holding it by the neck to keep it from running away."

"No, Mom. The statue's called 'Boy Strangling Goose.'"

"I thought it was 'Boy Struggling with Goose.'"

"No, definitely 'strangling.' Dad doesn't want to listen to us argue. But wait until you see this picture, Dad. I swear, all the chubby boy needed was a Red Sox cap." Millie paused, and Reilly realized from her narrowed eyes that his daughter was studying him. "You sure you guys are okay?"

"We're having a ball, no worries." *And when the sun rises, we'll be seeing swans.*

"Hm—I looked up about the statue on my phone. Wikipedia says that maybe it's an allegory for how humans have to learn to tame their natural wildness—like the superego battling with the id."

"Then the name could be 'struggling' or 'strangling'" Iris said. "But we've got to hurry or we'll miss our boat tour. You get back to sleep, Reilly. Oh—if you need to get in touch, use Millie's phone. I left my charger in Rome. Mine's dead. Love you—we'll be home in a couple of days."

"Yuch," Millie sighed. "Love you, Dad. Sleep tight. Give Danny-boy a kiss."

"Love you, miss you," The little picture of Reilly hovered on the blank screen before winking out. As he closed the laptop he noted the time, 2:22, and remembered that he had to set his alarm for 6:30.

*****

A very lucky young man, the emergency room doctor who has tended to Danny-boy concludes. "The nose," he says, "is very flexible. Just cartilage and skin. And there aren't any exterior lacerations. Davy will have those black eyes for a few days, and the swelling will last for a bit, but we should be able to remove the bandages in a week. For now, just make sure you clean the blood out of his nostrils so it doesn't clot up. Use cue tips and lukewarm water—it will probably sting a little, but you're a tough one, aren't you, Davy? Next time don't take on Big Bird —try somebody your own size." The doctor stoops for a last look at Danny-boy. The crossed white bandages over the child's nose contrast horrifically with the livid bruises around his eyes.

"It's 'Danny,'" the child corrects, breathing though his mouth. "And it was a swan."

The doctor stands upright, folds his arms over his chest and addresses Reilly. "He shouldn't need more than a double dose of ibuprofen every four hours. He'll be a little sore. Try not to let him sleep face down—No sleeping on your face, Davy!"

No one asks about wheelchairs as grandfather and grandson make their way out of the hospital, where an Uber should be waiting. Reilly waves his cane at the automatic door as if he's a magician. He grips Danny-boy's elbow with his free hand—to comfort the child, but also for balance.

"This way," he says. When the boy looks up at him, Reilly scowls, then tries to smile. His hand is sweat-slippery on the cane's silver knob. Just last night he'd been searching on the web for swan-headed canes.

A white SUV driven by a young woman whose hair is tucked up under a Patriots cap awaits the pair in the pick-up/drop-off zone.

"Woo," the woman says, catching a glimpse of Danny-boy's face in her mirror as grandfather and grandson slide into their seats. She turns around for a better look. "What happened here?"

"Just a silly accident," Reilly says. "He's going to be fine."

The driver makes a face. "Looks like somebody punched him."

"Not exactly, but something like that." Danny-boy flinches when Reilly reaches for his shoulder. The driver shakes her head and turns back to the steering wheel. Reilly folds his hands on his lap. The boy will still be bandaged when Millie and Iris come home. The driver fiddles with the GPS and pulls out of the hospital lot. Reilly gazes through his window as buildings, trees, telephone poles, and light posts scrape a colorless sky.

"There's been another one," the driver says. "Did you hear?"

"Another—?" Reilly discovers that his artificial foot is stuck under the seat in front of him. He bends over and pulls it out with his hand.

"An explosion. You know, probably a suicide bomb, though they're not saying for sure yet. Paris again. Lots of casualties."

The news hits Reilly's chest like a cannonball. "Paris?" He glances at Danny-boy. He hadn't told him of the late night call, had he? This morning everything had been about the swans. Reilly catches the driver's eye in the rearview, inclines his head toward Danny-boy, and shakes his head. The young woman nods and switches on the radio. She hums along with a pop tune. Reilly sits back and slides his cell phone from his pocket with a trembling hand. No messages.

*****

It's late afternoon. Danny-boy is in his bedroom, maybe asleep. Reilly lies on the den sofa, his back to the muted television. The last time he'd looked out the den window—five minutes ago—the swans still occupied his pond. He reviews his responsibilities with Danny-boy: examine the boy's bandages, unclog his nasal passages, fix him a milkshake for dinner like the doctor recommended. Reilly has seen what there is to see on TV: it's raining in Paris;

strobe lights from police cars and ambulances flash like pulse beats off the wet pavement; police and rescue workers in yellow slickers mill about in front of a crushed building. Damp-shouldered correspondents front the video loops showing sheeted bodies loaded onto ambulances, dazed survivors leaning on rescuers, and fire trucks blasting jets of water at smoldering ruins. From time to time there's a shot of a phosphorescent Seine, the Eiffel Tower glittering in the distance. A permanent "Breaking News" banner at the bottom of the screen keeps track of the rising totals of dead and injured.

Reilly peeks out the window: the swans dot the pond like a pox. He checks and rechecks his phone, punches in Millie's number. Reilly left the same message until the voicemail box filled: *Just calling to make sure you're okay.* Exhausted with worry, he lets his eyes shut. His phone, plugged into its charger, rests on his stomach. His arm dangles from the sofa, and his fingers brush his artificial foot.

If he opens his eyes, he's afraid he'll see the faces of his wife and daughter on the TV screen, pleading for attention. Who should Reilly contact for news? Who might contact him? What can he ask the computer?

When the reporters speak, the closed captioning covers the casualty totals. Three times he's read that in late summer most Parisians leave the city for vacation, so the numbers could have been worse. No mention of tourists. Can Danny-boy read? Reilly thinks hard, but he's not sure. But even if he can't, he's smart—he'll look at the screen and at his worried grandfather and know something's up.

*****

That morning, Reilly woke at the sound of his alarm, clearheaded and full of purpose, prepared for a miracle. He swung off his bed, and hopped to the bedroom window, bracing himself on the sill. The swans drifted on the pond, pure white against dawn's muted colors. Their long necks curved like question marks: *Where are you? We're waiting—bring us the boy.*

"There's something you've got to see," Reilly coaxed as he tugged Danny-boy from sleep, led him through the house and out the door to the deck. They descended to the lawn in pajamas and robes.

"The grass is wet," the child croaked. "Did it rain?"

"It's dew," Reilly whispered. "Keep your voice low. We don't want to frighten them. Look ahead at the pond."

Danny-boy stood tall, squinting. "Geese? I've seen geese." His gaze fell to his slippers. "My feet are soaked."

"Shh— not geese. Can't you see? Swans!"

Danny-boy looked again at the pond. His mouth formed an O. "They're wearing masks—" he murmured. Reilly took the boy's hand. The swans floated together in pairs. "They're so big—what are they doing here? They're so white."

"They chose our pond," Reilly said. "Aren't they beautiful?"

Danny-boy dropped his grandfather's hand and dashed toward the closest swan. The attack began and ended in seconds: the silent bird's wings spread as wide as a bed sheet as it launched itself, neck stretched, at Danny-boy. The sudden blow knocked the child backward onto the ground. Before Reilly could exhale, the huge bird was back in the dark water, settling itself beside its mate. It folded its wings, and the couple slid indifferently toward the center of the pond.

Reilly hobbled to his grandson, who sat in the mud, and bent over him. "You okay?" he asked. Then he saw Danny-boy's face: its center looked like a crushed fruit. Blood leaked like juice over the boy's mouth and chin.

"It bit me," he nasaled, his eyelids fluttering.

"Oh," Reilly groaned, "that nasty thing." He somehow hoisted his grandson to his feet, and together they staggered back to the house. "Sorry, sorry, sorry," Reilly repeated as he limped along, his cane pinned under his elbow as he tried to stem the flow of blood with the sleeve of his robe.

*****

Reilly's hissing snort wakes him. He discovers the phone on his belly; dreadful facts seep into awareness one by one, slowly drowning the faint hope that the day has been all dream. No new messages in the hour that's passed. It's dusk. He takes a deep breath through gritted teeth and winces toward the television: happy oldsters waltz silently—it's a commercial for a drug with life threatening side effects. In a minute the rain-slicked streets of Paris will reappear. Reilly considers what he can control: sitting up, for one. He hefts himself upright. And caring for Danny-boy—he needs to find the child and take hold of him—protect him from whatever's to come. Is the boy still asleep? Reilly scans the room, sensing his grandson's presence—has Danny-boy been watching him sleep? Another commercial—a red car chases a sunset over a black road.

"Danny-boy—" Reilly calls. By now the boy's nose will need attention. Reilly glares out the window—there's the murderous flock—how long will it haunt his pond? The TV screen reflects in the glass—Paris is back, the Seine and Eiffel Tower. *Iris*, he whispers, *Millie*. The burden of the swans is nothing compared to his worry over his women.

Then he sees Danny-boy out on the lawn, marching toward the pond. Reilly tries to stand, loses his balance, and drops back to the cushions. With a frustrated growl, he paws the floor and finds nothing: no foot, no cane.

Danny-boy nears the pond. He's swinging something like a sword—what else could it be but Reilly's cane? The dark thing tucked under his grandson's arm must be Reilly's foot. What's the boy have in mind? Revenge? Against the swans or his grandfather? The hair lifts on the back of Reilly's neck. Even with the cane Danny-boy can't match the speed and strength of an adult swan. The boy's only chance might be if he could get his hands around the creature's throat . . .

Stuck between the histories playing out behind and in front of him, Reilly holds his breath and stares, paralyzed, as Danny-boy reaches the water's edge. A swan breaks away from its mate and sails toward the child. Its wings spread wide as it makes land, and it descends on the boy like a blizzard.

"Danny-boy," Reilly cries.

Danny-boy lifts the cane—and plants it like a flag in the mud. The swan, nearly upon him, stops. Silhouetted against the great bird, Danny-boy drops to one knee. The wings fold back. As Reilly's pulse hammers in his ears for ten, twenty beats, bird and boy face one another, still as statues. Abruptly, both pivot. Danny-boy leaves the cane behind as he strides back toward the house, his bandaged face raised toward Reilly's window. He waves, and Reilly, still seated, lifts his arm from the back of the sofa. The swan floats to its partner's side. An object the size of Reilly's foot falls from its beak. There's not enough light to see a splash.

Something stirs—ripples—in the emptiness below Reilly's stump. But before he has time to marvel, the phone in his hand vibrates, once, twice, its screen lit with his daughter's name.

Cat Calls

We're sorry; you have reached a number that has been disconnected or is no longer in service. If you feel you have reached this recording in error, please check the number and try your call again.

When Tyler drifted into consciousness, eyes still closed, there was a peaceful, dark moment before the stab of what he mistook for a hangover headache. A list of questions piled up: Where had he been and with whom? How did he get to his bed—or was this his couch—or somebody else's? As if he were tuning an old radio, voices rose and fell.

"Two hundred pounds at least, maybe twice that. An old eagle's nest. If he'd been hit a bull's eye, it would have killed him. But there was a big limb just over his head and the nest hit that first and broke up. He still got hit by a pretty big chunk. He's not in a coma, is he? We're insured—*J and J Tree Removal* is insured. Shouldn't he be up by now?"

A clipped, professional voice: "He's sleeping. He's been in and out. No damage to the skull or spinal cord. Just a concussion and the broken arm, which we've set. We'll do more precautionary tests when he wakes up. An eagle's nest?"

"It was the size of a kiddie pool, Doc, maybe bigger."

These were answers, but not to Tyler's questions—they only raised new ones. He'd been "in" before this? Broken arm—which one? He couldn't bring himself to move. *Eagle's nest?*

Gizmo was a Siamese. She spit and scratched. The kids hated her, but they cried when she ran off. They hung up signs on telephone poles. My kids have kids of their own now. No cats, though.

Mr. J of *J and J Tree Removal*, insured or not, was obviously relieved when Tyler woke up for good. The tree-boss stood just inside his employee's peripheral vision. Tyler had worked for *J and J* for only a day. The company was contracted to clear the land by the river for the new casino that was going to save the city. Tyler remembered staring up into the canopy of a huge oak on the bank of the river, the only substantial tree on acreage overrun with scrub brush. He didn't remember getting hit.

"What part of 'Stand back!' didn't you get?" Mr. J asked.

"All I heard was, 'Whoa,' so I came to look."

"Jerry yelled 'Stand back'—that's standard safety procedure. I heard him myself, even over the chainsaws and wood chipper. But you're lucky. The doctor says so, too. Of course it would have been luckier if you'd stood back."

Mr. J shook a plastic grocery bag. "So guess what was in that nest—cat collars. When it hit the limb over your head it broke apart, and these cat collars went flying all over. We collected them to show you. The eagles were feeding cats to their babies. *Cat food*—that's Jerry's joke."

A nurse fussed around Tyler's bed. "Cat collars? Yuch. Poor little kitties."

"Law of nature," Mr. J said. He tugged a strip of blue cloth from his pocket and swung it over Tyler's bed. "This one is special." A rusty tag dangled from the filthy collar. "This guy's name was 'Mr. Lucky.' Just like you."

Mr. J might have been presenting the Medal of Honor or the key to the city. Tyler reached for the collar with his left hand—his right arm turned out to be the broken one—and he squinted at the tag crusted with dirt and rust. "'Mr. Licky,'" he read. "Not *Lucky*. It says 'Mr. Licky.'"

"What?" Mr. J snatched back the collar, "*Licky*? They spelled their own pet's name wrong?"

"That's a silly name for a cat," the nurse said. "'Mr. Licky" sounds more like a dog's name."

My first wife hated Fluffy. He left mice on her pillow. Another time he left a dead hummingbird —can you believe he actually caught one? It looked like a flower, the way it lay on the satin pillowcase with its wings spread.

The day Tyler left the hospital, he decided to wear Mr. Licky's collar as a bracelet. The nurse made a face as she buckled it over his ID band. "Not very sanitary," she said. The home he returned to was the cottage where he grew up. He inherited it from his mom when she passed, and he'd moved back because the things he'd tried in other places—jobs, women—hadn't worked out. The house stood about two miles up the same river where he'd been clearing land for the casino with *J and J* when his accident happened.

His arm healed quickly, though after the cast came off it was pale and withered and not up to heavy lifting. Tyler got enough of a settlement from *J and J*'s insurance company so that he didn't have to worry about a job for a few months. Soon he noticed that the collar, which he never took off, had a definite taint. He thought at first that it was his food that smelled bad when he lifted his fork to his mouth. His showering had rinsed off most of the collar's visible crud, but who knew how long the thing had been stewing in cat blood and eagle shit? He decided that his Mr. Licky bracelet and the whole bag of collars he'd brought home from the hospital needed a thorough cleaning. Sprucing them up could be a hobby, something to do while he listened to *The Price is Right* and sports.

When Tyler unknotted the plastic bag, the rotten-meat stench nearly floored him, and he almost trashed his new hobby then and there. But he opened his window for some fresh air, and through the tree branches caught a glimpse of the river. It sparkled like somebody had scattered jewels across a black mirror—so beautiful he wondered that he'd never really noticed it growing up, even when he'd paddled on it or fished in it.

A fresh breeze blew into his room, and the sun through the maple trees tossed dancing leaf shadows on the uncut grass. By now the casino site would have been cleared and construction started. The big tree would be long gone. Tyler pictured an eagle soaring in the blue sky over his stretch of river, heading upstream toward a nest it wouldn't find.

Maybe a cat, still thinking of the mouse it had been about to pounce on, swung under the bird like someone riding a parasail.

He sniffed his Mr. Licky bracelet, then peeked back into the grocery bag and the tangle of filthy collars and tags. He could tolerate the odor. A person can get used to anything. His bedroom walls were bare after years of moving out and back. If he cleaned up all the collars and hung them on a big board it might lessen the emptiness and make an interesting conversation piece.

A few of the collars disintegrated in his fingers, but fifty-two were salvageable— forty-four cloth, eight chain. Thirty of the collars had tags. He soaked the cloth collars in a bucket of detergent, then rinsed them under the bathroom sink faucet, one at a time, gently wringing out the soapy water. White vinegar loosened up the rust on the tags, chain collars, and buckles, which he scrubbed with an old toothbrush. He picked the dirt out of the engraved letters and numbers with a pin, then shined up each tag with some Brasso metal polish. He found a piece of plywood the size of a movie poster in the basement and hammered rows of nails into it for hooks.

After a week, his project was finished. He hung all the collars on their nail hooks, propped the board on his desk, and looked at it—the cloth collars were bright stripes of color, like exclamation points, and the tags and chains gleamed. The neat rows of collars reminded him of the rows of tombstones in a military cemetery, but, as far as he could tell, he'd gotten rid of the smell of death. He felt a little like he'd memorialized the cats and resurrected them at the same time.

No, you're wrong. My husband buried Mittens in the backyard. He marked her grave with a little stone. It's still there. Who is this?

The casino wasn't due to open for months yet, but the community college had started a six-week certificate program in "Hospitality and Casino Management." The cost was three hundred dollars, plus another fifty for books. Tyler's arm was still not strong enough for manual work, so he signed up. The half dozen required courses had names like "Casino Operations Management," "Security and Surveillance," and "Gaming Rules and Regulations." Each class met for an hour, five days a week. Mostly the classes were packed with kids ten or fifteen years younger than he was, all of them shimmery with hope, although the rumor was that the lion's share of casino jobs would go to experienced workers brought in from other sites around the country.

The instructor in charge of "Gaming Rules and Regulations" lectured in a goose-honking monotone that made Tyler's eyes water, and, assuming that everything would be in the textbook, he sat at his back-row desk, laced his fingers together like he was praying, and faded off into dreamland. His gaze dropped to his wrists. He looked at Mr. Licky's tag, then at the arm he'd broken, and thought of his father, who he'd last seen when he was fourteen. His dad had been about to leave on a sales tour—he booked hotel conference rooms where he motivated smokers and the obese to buy self-hypnosis CDs he recorded at home.

Tyler' dad's last words to his son had to do with the boy's wrists. His old man was lounging in his recliner, wincing at the TV news after a dinner no one but he knew would be the last he'd share with his family. As Tyler passed by, his father reached for him.

"Shake, buddy," he said. He gave Tyler's hand a quick, hard squeeze to let him know who was boss. He didn't let go. He inspected Tyler's arm.

"You know," his father said, "it's a well known fact that guys with skinny wrists have little dicks." Then, with a frown of condolence and disappointment, he released his son's hand. Tyler spent the rest of the night eyeballing his forearm under his desk lamp instead of finishing his homework. By morning, his dad was gone forever.

A voice from the next seat startled him.

"That's a cool wristband. Is that your dog tag or something? Are you an Iraq vet? Afghanistan? Thank you for your service."

The instructor stopped mid-sentence and peered between turning heads at the rainbow-haired woman who'd spoken to Tyler. She blinked big, pale-blue eyes. Tyler slid down in his seat and shook his head. "Shh," he whispered. "Not a vet. It's a cat tag, not a dog tag."

"A what? '*Cat* tag?'"

"After class," he hissed.

We're sorry; we are unable to complete your call as dialed. Please check the number and dial again, or call your operator to help you.

Nadine was her name, and she picked a bar instead of Starbucks, where they sat on stools and drank beer and ate peanuts for lunch and decided to skip the afternoon sessions. Like Tyler, she was no kid, but in the bar's amber light, she had a pretty enough face. Pastel shades of blue and green and pink streaked her blond hair. While he told her about the eagle's nest and the cat collars, she flipped the tag of his collar-bracelet back and forth, and he got goose bumps from her slim fingers being so near his skin. He told her that some people thought Mr. Licky was a dog's name.

"Definitely cat," she said. "Did you ever wonder if your Mr. Licky was trying to tell you something?" She leaned over and put her ear on the collar. Her cheek was cool and soft on his wrist. Tyler resisted an urge to pet her rainbow hair. "Your cat says, '*Watch out for hungry eagles.*'" She straightened up on her stool. There were faint crow's feet around her eyes.

"I've got fifty-two collars," Tyler said.

"Cool. That's a lot of voices—cats have nine lives, right? Do they keep you up at night?"

Did they? Not really. "Nope. What I did is string up all the collars on a board. Like a collection."

When Tyler told Nadine he lived close by, she asked if she could see the collars, and she followed his pickup in her rusted out Sentra, waving whenever she saw him check his mirror. He felt excited, like he had once when a stray pup had trailed him home from school. But his father said they didn't need a dog and had taken it to the animal shelter.

Mom's blind. When Sebastian disappeared we bought her a substitute cat. She doesn't know she's on her third Sebastian. She thinks he's forty and wants us to call Guinness's Book of Records.

They sat at Tyler's kitchen table, his display board of cat collars laid out flat between them. He opened fresh beers. It turned out he and Nadine had gone to the same high school, way back when, even been there at the same time. She told him he looked familiar.

"You too," he lied. The bright afternoon sun lit up the kitchen. Nadine remarked on the view through the window; the glare from the river was as sharp as a knife and showed lines and hollows in her face then he hadn't seen in the bar. He supposed his face looked more beat up to her, too. They swapped a few stories of their failures, the usual top layer of things. She'd gone out west to college, flunked out, waitressed, danced a little. Every few years she'd wind up back in the place she'd grown up, just like Tyler.

"Can I touch them?" Nadine asked about the collars. Some had come loose on the board.

"Sure. If you see one you like, you can keep it."

"Really?" Her long eyelashes fluttered as she bent forward. He looked at her cotton candy hair, half-wishing to taste it. Her hand passed over the collars like she was working a Ouija board, then her fingers dove to a tag. "'Peanut,'" she read. "What if one of the baby eagles had food allergies?"

"Survival of the fittest. I've got a few others with food names. 'Cupcake'— the pink one with the bell. It doesn't jingle anymore, too rusty. And 'Oreo,' over to the left—the blue with rhinestones."

Nadine made a little sound. She gave Tyler a quick smile and flashed her pale eyes. "It's hard to choose." She handled several collars and read their polished tags. The lines in her forehead deepened with concentration: "Mittens, Gizmo. . . Angel—that's appropriate." She blinked at Tyler. "Do you ever think about what they looked like?"

"The cats? I guess. I match them up with their names. Like Oreo is white and black, and Mittens has white paws, and Tiger has stripes—*had* stripes."

Nadine shook her head, her eyes fluorescent slashes. "No—I mean what the *scene* looked like—when they got to the nest."

"Oh—sometimes. But I try not to. It seems disrespectful."

One of the chain collars hung from Nadine's fingers, and she thumbed it like a rosary as she read the name on its tag: "'Oliver—'" She swung the glittery collar back and forth like she was a hypnotist, and he thought of the CDs his father sold on the road. He recorded them late at night, right at this kitchen table, while Tyler tried to sleep in his bedroom down the hall. "Listen to the sounds of your body," his father said into his microphone, and Tyler would pretend his father sat on his bed, telling him a story.

"I'm taking this one, okay?" Nadine asked.

Tyler shrugged. "Sure. That's a nice one."

As she fastened the collar around her wrist, Tyler noticed a pair of raised red lines on its under-flesh that stood out like an "equal" sign. She drew the tag close to her face. "Oliver," she whispered to it. "Ollie—I bet you put up one hell of a fight, didn't you? I bet Papa Eagle was sorry he brought you home."

Eagle? Yup. My brother and I were traumatized when it plucked Chauncey off the lawn, right under our noses. Then it rose up a mile high with him and disappeared. . .

Their hips touched under Tyler's sheets, just a reminder, nothing more, of the comfortable sex they'd shared. While they talked after, his eyes roamed the collar display he'd set back up on his desk. His gaze kept slipping back to Oliver's vacated spot the way a tongue pokes into the hole left by a missing tooth. Just to hear Nadine talk—because it was nice to have a voice so close while his head was on his pillow—he asked her if she was worried that there might not be any casino jobs.

"There's no point in worrying," she said. "I don't get my hopes up about anything. There are other jobs in other places. There's always Vegas. There are lots of things you can do there." She shifted, and her hip pushed away from his, and when he lost contact he was suddenly afraid to move, as if he'd just woken up and found himself lying on a diving board above an empty pool.

"There's a story my mother told me," Nadine said, "—or maybe I read it in school. It was a about a guy who got a magic piece of donkey skin— he could make wishes on it, and they came true—he wished for fame and for riches and for women, and he got them all. But every time the magic skin granted a wish, it shrank. He wished and wished, got more and more stuff, and the magic skin got smaller and smaller. And when it disappeared, he died. So you don't wish, and you don't hope."

Tyler lay quietly, wanting to feel her against him again, to reassure him that he wasn't hanging out in space alone.

"Hey," she said sharply, and he stiffened. Nadine was looking at the Oliver tag on her wrist. "Did you ever call any of these phone numbers on the tags? Maybe the people who owned the cats would want closure. Then again, all these collars are really old. They don't make pet collars with metal buckles anymore. Now they've all got plastic clasps."

Despite the time and care Tyler had given to cleaning the collars and tags, he hadn't thought of either of those things. Of course Nadine was right about the collars being old—there was no plastic on any of them. The eagle's nest might have been abandoned for decades. But calling the cat owners? Wouldn't they have made peace with their losses after so much time had passed?

"I never thought to call."

"Mmm," Nadine sounded tired, as if her own thoughts bored her. "Probably you wouldn't get in touch with too many people. Those phone numbers are probably all old landlines. Nobody has those anymore." She yawned. "And people move. And they die."

Soon she was breathing easily. Tyler kept still. He thought of Mr. Licky: he'd always pictured him as fat and yellow. What had the cat's first moments in the eagle's nest been like? When did he realize he was in trouble? Did he feel the beat of Papa Eagle's wings behind him? Did cold-eyed Mama Eagle look him over while her giant chicks squawked for dinner? Maybe Mr. Licky glimpsed a few empty collars lying around the nest and checked in vain for an escape route. Tyler thought of the marks on Nadine's wrist. Maybe she'd been fooling around with a chainsaw, accidentally lopped off her hand, and a brilliant surgeon had reattached it. And maybe Mr. Licky put up the kind of fight Nadine had imagined for her Oliver. More likely, the fat yellow tomcat just gave up, staking his hopes on the old wives' tale about extra lives.

Tyler fell asleep. He dreamed he was sailing through the air, so high the river below looked like a thin black vein, the farmland like the old patchwork quilt on his bed. Wind rushed through his ears. Something held him by the shoulders, and he kicked his feet in space. A polished disc that shone like a mirror slapped his chest—a big tag. Its smooth surface reflected his frightened eyes. The tag was clipped to a tight band around his neck—a collar.

"Your collar is made of donkey skin," a deep voice warned. "Don't you dare wish for anything, or it will shrink!"

He woke up. Sunlight poured through the bedroom window. Nadine was gone. Tyler listened, hoping she was in the kitchen, but heard nothing. His hand rose to his throat.

. . . Did I say an eagle? No, the thing that got Chauncey was even bigger, more like a pterodactyl . . .

Nadine didn't show up for any of their classes the next day, or the day after that. There was a rule about not missing too many sessions, and Tyler asked the instructors, one after the other, if they knew what happened to her. He didn't know her last name. The instructors consulted their class lists and shook their heads. "No Nadines here," they said.

. . . Come to think, that giant bird must have been a Phoenix, because it burst into flames, way up in the air. Chauncey burned up with it. There was a fireball, like a second sun, then it rained ashes.

The Eagle's View Casino opened on schedule. Its impact on the city was yet to be determined, but Tyler's certificate from the community college program had landed him a job with security surveillance. He wore a tie and a blazer with the casino's name and logo on the pocket. When he walked the red carpet with his headset, he scanned the faces of the patrons milling around the gaming table, ready to report anything suspicious.

Most of the time, he sat in an office watching a bank of monitors blink from shot to shot, exposing a hundred different interior angles: tables, slot machines, restrooms, bars, entrances and exits. He looked at a thousand faces a day. He'd been trained to ignore the hopefulness painted on them, to stare through it for something darker. But he knew that the patrons' hope was really the thing that could strangle them.

Every ninety seconds one of the monitors flashed to the casino's exterior. It captured the gigantic sign for Eagle's Crest Casino perched atop a tower that loomed over the interstate almost a half mile away. On the sign the eagle wings of the casino's logo flapped slowly in shifting colors. When they flashed yellow, they looked to Tyler like cat's eyes, and often he would think of the big tree the casino replaced, of the nest, of the collar he never removed. On certain nights he watched the cars on the interstate pass under the casino sign—headlights approaching from the east, taillights burning red on their way west. Because he wanted to keep breathing, he tried hard not to think of Vegas.

We're sorry . . .

Mister S, the Mysterious

Raymond Walchuk came home from an exhausting day of shooting multiple decapitations for his latest project, *Headless*, unprepared to find his six-year-old son smiling at a pencil-thin snake in a glass tank on the granite kitchen island.

"I named him Elvis," Carl said. "He's a cornsnake."

"Nice," Raymond said. The snake lay in an S on bare astro-turf under a bright lamp. Raymond's wife Christine chopped vegetables at the counter. "Your idea?" he asked.

"It will teach him responsibility," she said. "It's something living that will require his constant care."

Raymond nodded. "Remember *Swallow*? It reminds me of Gus the anaconda." He stood next to his son, bent over and tapped the glass. The snake didn't move. Its eyes were tiny beads.

"Your movie, yes. I don't think Elvis will eat an entire family, though, member by member. He'll eat pinkies. For now."

"Pinkies?" Raymond frowned. The word hid something chilling. Christine's gaze followed the flash of her blade as she chopped.

"Frozen baby mice—the size of an eraser."

"They're tiny, like this, see?" Carl held up one of his new school pencils and pinched its end.

"You dunk them in a cup of warm water to prepare them," Christine said. "It will be a good project for the two of you to share." Her smile was so hard her lips seemed blue. "Father-son. You can make a movie: 'The Walchuk boys raise a snake.'"

His wife knew Raymond had an aversion to rodents—the care of Elvis was an obvious test. She was inventing ways for him to disappoint her. He could read her thoughts—*You make horror movies. Human beings are savaged in them in every way imaginable—you don't deserve an irrational fear.*

"I love Elvis," Carl sighed. The tank was at his eye level, and the boy's breath fogged the glass. Raymond galvanized himself. In a marriage that had become an uncomfortable fit, he would now be measured by a phobia.

*****

"Elvis is as long as a yardstick already. I stretched him out," Carl told his dad. Less than a year had passed. Raymond watched the snake swallow the pink gumdrop babies his son had defrosted in a steaming mug. His teeth ached from wincing a grin. As the bulge of the snake's meal slid down its length, Raymond wondered if "squeamish" and "terrified" were opposite ends of the same continuum, or entirely different species. *Aren't you the expert?* Christine would ask. "Art is cathartic," he imagined answering. "Life just hurts."

*****

Raymond hoped that his three weeks away in the Arizona desert filming zombie mutants would kindle fondness in Christine's heart. But Christine barely acknowledged his return; she didn't rise from her computer.

"Carl has something to tell you about your sinewy friend," she said. She meant Elvis, Raymond realized, and "sinuous," not "sinewy."

"We keep running out of pinkies," Carl told him a few minutes later as they admired the snake. "Elvis eats too many—six at a time now."

From the half-dozen pet stores Raymond called came the same message—snakes Elvis's size couldn't subsist on pinkies. They required full-sized mice. Raymond's bowels quivered at the news.

"I can't have live mice in the house," he confessed to Christine, drawing his line in the sand.

"Let me make this clear," she replied. "For the last six years, while you've been bathing in blood and tossing around heads, I've been raising your son." Were those sneering lips the pair he used to kiss? "I don't want to hear about 'making a living out of dying.' And don't dare tell me what you do is 'art.' I'm running a magazine now. Have you noticed? *MindGames*? I may be working from home, but I'm not going to be available for your 'crises.' Do *not* disappoint your son. Do *not* teach him fear."

"We'll work it out," Raymond said. That night, while Christine slept beside him with indifferent ease, he dreamed he was filming the impossible interior glow of a coffin from the point of view of the smothering victim locked inside. "Spiders!" Raymond shouted with sudden inspiration. "We need spiders creeping toward his face."

"Mice would be easier," somebody said, and Raymond woke, sweating, his pulse thundering in his ears. Something scrabbled in the walls behind the headboard.

*****

Carl was not in favor of feeding his snake live mice either. He handed his father a pamphlet— "Know Your Cornsnake."

"You can read this?" Raymond asked. The boy rolled his eyes.

"It says pet snakes shouldn't be fed live mice. The mice fight back, and they scratch the skin—" Raymond pictured a string of blood-pearls laced across Elvis's snout. Rodents were dangerous food! "—The snake could get an infection and die."

The solution was frozen adult mice—but few pet stores stocked them. Raymond and Carl had to drive an hour to *Exotic Birds and Reptiles*, where they bought fifty frozen mice, bred hairless for lab experiments. On the ride home in the winter twilight, Carl lifted the clear plastic bag of mice and shook it. The little bodies—fifty tiny snouts and one hundred permanently shut eyes, two hundred retracted feet— shifted like eggrolls.

"It's heavy," the boy said and stuck the bag between his feet. Raymond kept his eyes on the icy road and thought about what Christine had asked long ago, when they were falling in love. He had told her about the plot of a movie he wanted to make someday, a twisted version of O. Henry's "Gift of the Magi." In Raymond's movie, the couple in love is so poor they resort to cutting off their own body parts as gifts to the other, a toe for a toe, an arm for an arm, and so on, year after year—until only their hearts are left. "Would you cut off something for me?" Christine asked. Certainly, he said. It was only a hypothetical question and had nothing to do with a genuine fear.

The bag of mice was sealed in a Tupperware box, marked with a skull and crossbones, and stored in the freezer. But the car heater that had melted the slush on Raymond's and Carl's shoes as they brought Elvis's new food supply home had also defrosted all the little bodies. They had refrozen in the Tupperware box and had become fused into a single giant mouse-block: fifty naked bodies, welded together seamlessly. Carl, responsible for thawing and feeding, discovered the problem and called Raymond into the bathroom. On the sink lay the frost-covered brick of solid mouse, a butter knife jammed half an inch into it.

"They're stuck together," Carl said. He pried the knife sideways until it curved like a leaping fish. Raymond steeled himself. He studied the frozen block. He made out a compressed ear here and there, a leg, something that might have been a snout. He grasped the knife with a damp hand and applied pressure at different angles, to no avail. A blue cup half full of warm water cooled under the toothbrush holder. Raymond tugged the knife again.

"It's like *The Sword in the Stone*," Carl whispered, and Raymond choked a laugh. He stepped back, then shoved the bathroom door shut. What he was suffering, he didn't want Christine to see. He looked in the mirror.

"What?" Carl asked his father's toothpaste-flecked image. Raymond stared at his son, aware for the first time of the boy's composite face: Christine's lips, without the disdainful curl; his eyes, though less wary; the nose—his arc, her nostrils. Whose sense of smell had their son inherited? And what about more deeply hidden legacies? But this scene—their faces side by side—held a Norman Rockwell poignancy. Without seeing what Raymond held in his hand, someone might have thought they were building a birdhouse together, or carving a racecar for a Cub Scout Pinewood Derby. Or maybe Raymond was passing down a family hobby, something as delicately masculine as sliding a ship through the neck of a bottle. He bent the blade again. The pressure slid the mouse-block across the sink counter.

"It's really stuck." Carl's voice echoed from the tiled walls.

"Shh—" Raymond focused on the blade's entry point. As if it were a creature embedded in an Ice Age glacier, a mousy shadow had begun to emerge. A fissure ran across its torso. "Let me do this alone. Don't tell your mother." Their eyes met in the stippled mirror, and, after a worrisome flutter of his eyelids, Carl was gone.

*****

But it was imperative that Elvis be fed. Raymond imagined that the stability of his family depended on satisfying the snake. He chipped away regularly at the mouse block, unable to dislodge an intact body. Fragments littered the sink rim. As they defrosted they formed legs, heads, half-haunches; then they bled. Raymond set each morsel on a paper towel. The lips of wound-ends sparkled under the fluorescent bathroom light. On the damp paper bloodstains bloomed like rose bouquets. From torso-sized chunks bobbing in the cup of warm water, crimson trails swirled like dissolving tablets of Easter egg dye. Raymond pretended that the limbs belonged to tiny people slaughtered in a Lilliputian holocaust—a genocide outside the domain of his phobia. He hurried into his son's room and dumped the raw chunks into Elvis's tank, where the snake struck at them instantly.

Secure in his fantasy, Raymond watched the snake as if it were an inscrutable god indifferent to the suffering of its worshippers. But when he noticed a leftover mouse head shriveling under the heat lamp, awe slipped to revulsion, then dread.

With spring came the close of the frozen naked rodent chapter. The block of protoplasmic mouse had been scraped into the shape of an ostrich egg. Raymond hid from Christine the fact that Carl avoided the chiseling, afraid she'd think he was responsible for the boy's withdrawal. Late one night, Raymond vomited while wiping up mouse blood. Three sleepless hours later, he took the Tupperware container from the freezer and stepped out the back door. The grass was soft under his slippers and the spring air thick with promise. He looked at the stars, then tossed the mouse egg over the stockade fence into his neighbor's yard.

*****

Elvis could not be permitted to confront live mice, though Raymond doubted the snake feared them or anything else. But eating was necessary, and Raymond was out of options. If pre-frozen adult mice were unavailable, he would have to buy live feeders and freeze them himself. To do so required more than bravery; with the same nimble creativity he used when filmmaking, Raymond conjured up an alternative self to do his dirty work: Mister S. He summoned Mister S with a whispery child's voice he remembered from a TV magic show—"*Mister S, the mysterious*"—and his alter ego appeared, drawn by the aroma of Raymond's irrational fear as if it were a freshly baked apple pie cooling on a window sill. Raymond drove with Mister S to the pet store and bought a feeder mouse. He stood with his doppelganger as he plucked up the creature by its tail from the cardboard container and stuffed its warm, frantic body, its scrambling legs, into the mouth of a yellow Garfield thermos. Raymond felt Mister S screw the cap tight and rush to the kitchen, where only the rubber thump of the shutting freezer door silenced the scuffling. Raymond peeked, as if through venetian blinds, at Mister S leading his life, and wondered if his imaginary companion had concocted *him* in order to sample the taste of terror.

Carl thawed the mice and fed the snake. Each large "mousecube" chilled the mug of hot water into a summer soup that smelled like a wet dog. Once, the boy gave Elvis an under-thawed mouse, which traveled a foot down the snake before peristalsis seized. "It was like a movie in reverse," the child reported. "The mouse looked like a cigar butt when it fell out of his mouth. Elvis wouldn't touch it after that, and I had to thaw another one. Now I bend them back and forth to make sure they're soft all the way through."

Raymond imagined manipulating the mouse with his own fingers. They could shake hands, father and son, while softening a small body between their palms. They would never hunt and fish together, and Carl would soon be past the age of Cub Scout racecars. Stuffing ships into bottles was unlikely; but they shared the feeding of Elvis. These thoughts felt like Raymond's, but were they really Mister S's?

An emergency arose: a mouse, curled into a C like half a bagel, was stuck inside the thermos, and Raymond responded. Probing with a butter knife only spun it around. Carl's fingers were too short, so Raymond filled the thermos with hot water and kneaded the small body himself. What if Christine had walked in on them then? Would her husband's resolve have healed the fractures between them? What if she'd known that Mister S's appetite had replaced his own?

*****

A phone call from Carl's school: the boy had been teasing a girl. He'd threatened her somehow with a dead mouse. Please talk to him and call her parents, the teacher asked. Better to nip misunderstandings in the bud.

"I told her I was going to bring in a mouse sandwich," Carl shrugged. "On rye. It was just a joke."

"But her feelings are real," Raymond said. "Some people are afraid of things." He glanced at Christine. *That* much was okay to admit, wasn't it?

"I'll call," Christine said. After, she talked to Carl.

"Your little friend had a nightmare. Some people don't like mice. You understand that it's silly to be afraid of something that's so harmless, right? But sometimes we have to respect another's feelings, even if they're irrational. Otherwise, we couldn't live together in society. So, apologize tomorrow. What?" she asked Raymond, who was scowling.

"Nothing," he said. Maybe Mister S visited Carl, too. Maybe there was an S family living under their roof.

*****

Had Mister S abandoned him? Where was he at night, when darkness shrouded Raymond's bedroom mirrors? The summons, *"Mister S, the mysterious,"* attracted only the ghosts of a hundred rodents that squirmed for warmth under Raymond's covers. He lay as if on a Mount Everest ledge; his fingers ached from stuffing imaginary bodies into thermoses of ice, but he didn't dare sleep, afraid of more horrifying dreams. He pulled his feet away from Christine's— their frosty touch might wake her and her scorn. Exhausted, the next morning he announced to Carl that their cruelty couldn't continue.

"Freezing them alive is kind of mean," his son admitted. "I try not to think about it."

"It's afterwards that's bad," Raymond said.

*****

The Walchuk boys sought an authority's advice. They visited the mall pet store, where they were directed to a back room for "EMPLOYEES ONLY!" They knocked and were invited inside, where they confessed their problem to a short, pony-tailed young man. Large tanks on metal shelves glittered with hundreds of feeder goldfish, and terrariums overflowed with crickets and meal worms. Hundreds of white mice seethed in a plastic basin. The odor of compressed life stained the air.

"Elvis? Cool name!" the young man said. He raised an empty plastic bag with the store's logo. "You got to kill the mouse quick, you don't want to freeze 'em slow. You gotta take 'em," and he picked up a jingling red ball, a toy for a small dog, "and pop 'em in a sack—" which he did with the ball, demonstrating with a shake the bag's new heft. "Then . . . you whap 'em!" He spun and slammed the bag against the wall with a violence Raymond felt in his chest. The transformed load hung from the young man's hand. "So it's dead, see?" He opened the bag. Raymond peeked in and nodded.

*****

After a few weeks what puzzled Raymond, when he thought about it, was why he had ever needed Mister S. The capacity to whap had surely lain within him. Now he whapped everywhere. He bashed mice against his car door in mall parking lots (he had to park far from others—how could he explain?), and even against the dashboard while waiting at Carl's school for his son to finish soccer practice. And Elvis ate and grew. Raymond learned to double bag after a live mouse popped through a single one in mid-swing; miraculously, he caught it in flight. He told himself he killed mercifully, that what he did was his duty to his family, but he knew better. He no longer cared what Christine thought. His nights were peaceful. The truth was, he liked the sound of whapping, the solid feel of it, the finality. It had become its own end.

*****

58

On a cool evening in early November Raymond and Carl stood beside the garage behind the rented bungalow Raymond had moved to after he and Christine had called it quits. Soon she would be arriving to pick up their son. Raymond had full custody of the snake. Carl was about to kill his first mouse. As instructed, he shook the small cardboard container to dislodge any footholds, and Raymond held the double bag close. The boy flipped the box open and reversed it over the bag: a soft plop, then a rustle.

Raymond handed his son the loaded bag. He patted the cinderblock wall. "Swing it firmly," he said.

"Un-hunh." Carl paused. "You think Mom remembered the pizza?"

"Probably," Raymond said. "Your mother rarely forgets things. But if she did, you can pick it up on the way home." The boy needed to focus, but Raymond wished he would hurry. This wasn't for Christine. But he knew that the momentum of the thing that had overtaken them couldn't be shifted.

Dead White Male Body

Laser is in bed with the mother of the girl he'd served nearly a year in prison for violating. All he'd done was tattoo the kid's eyelids per her request, though he'd been accused of more. After sentencing, he became a registered sex offender for "lewd or lascivious acts with a child fourteen or fifteen years old." He'd thought she was eighteen. The girl's mother, transfixed by his tattoos, stares at his chest.

"What's this hand?" She has eyes like her daughter's, but with long lashes that seem fake—her kid, he found out the hard way, has alopecia, and hasn't any lashes at all.

"It's Mr. Antolini's."

Her eyes buck to his. "Whose?"

"Antolini's. From a book. He's a guy who pats a confused boy on the head. That's hair under the fingers."

"Are they related?"

"They're made up. It's a book. He just cares about the kid. Or whatever." Her eyes drop back to the spot over his collar bone. Sometimes it's hard to see your own tattoos. It would not be cool to tell her that her daughter inherited her eyes. Laser's not one for lingering looks. One early spring years ago when he was a teen he'd driven to the beach, and at the shore he came upon a group of people, Hispanic, facing the water, some knee deep in the surf, some standing on the sand. Someone named Papi had slipped beneath the black waves. There were shouts of "Papi!" through cupped hands at a surface that was blank all the way out until it met the sky. Laser had stripped to his shorts and waded in up to his belly before the bone-numbing chill struck him—that and the realization that he was a weak swimmer. The undertow pulled at his hips and thighs like a pair of giant hands. Shaking his head, he'd retreated to the packed sand, where he found himself facing a young woman. The wind blew her dark hair straight at him, as though he lay on his back and she bent over him. Through her hair he could see her eyes, and they were full and empty at the same time. He'd run back to his car, shouting without looking back that he was going to call for help, which he did when he reached a diner five miles down the highway. Really, he'd only told a waitress that she needed to call in an emergency, that someone was drowning.

People try to hold your gaze either to show you their wounds or to look for yours, Laser knows. The woman reading his chest can't see the setting sun inked across his back. It's got wriggling beams made up of words, one of which is "Papi."

"You've got a thing for hands—what about these?" Dana asks.

"Which?"

"These right here, the clasped ones." Her lips and the tip of her tongue mark a spot just below his nipple, and her hair is under his chin, honey blond almost to the roots in her pale scalp and smelling of expensive treatments. If Laser hadn't been propped up on his elbows, he might have patted her head.

"From another book," he says. "Two guys on the deck of a whaling ship are kneading a tubful of spermaceti—smooth, soft stuff from a dead whale. They used to make perfume out of it. They were squeezing the lumps out, and it felt so good they took each other's hand."

"Tastes fishy." Dana smacks her lips. "I know, a whale isn't a fish." She sits back on her heals and scans Laser's body, maybe for nautical symbols. "Whales are endangered." She wears only his denim shirt, unbuttoned. Her flesh, all he can see, is white and clean. "And it's a little gay, too."

"Brotherhood," he said. "The brotherhood of man."

"What are you, a test all over? Who's this?" She squints close to read the name printed over his belly button. "'S-V-I'—how do you even say it? Did you—or whoever did it— spell it wrong?"

"I did it. It's 'Svidrigaylov.' A character. He's Russian." He doubts if Dana could tell this was the newest of his tattoos, that he done it in prison with a needle and homemade ink. He won't tell her that her daughter inspired it.

"'SVIDRI-GAY-LOVE . . . SVIDRI-GUY-LOVE' . . . Really. Holding hands, patting heads . . ."

Laser had thought the girl's mother would be smarter, or at least better educated. She was a school principal, after all, though only elementary. Most of what she's asked about on his chest was from books he'd read in high school. His body *is* kind of a test, though, and he can't really say she's failed it, because none of the women he's been with has offered more than a general "Cool!" or "I like that one," or "Those scare me," about his inkings. Only Willie Freeze, his first and only cellmate, had picked up the references, and in a heartbeat. "*Catcher*," he said about the patting hand, and "*Moby Dick*" about the clasped ones after Laser gave him the hint about the spermaceti squeezing. He'd watched Laser complete "SVIDRIGAYLOV" across his stomach.

"Dude, you're lucky you're borderline, man. If that girl you're in here for was as young as the girl that pimp Svid turned into a hooker in his dream, you'd be fucked. And I don't mean fucked, I mean dead. Child molesters here, man, they're dead-fucked. This shit you got inked all over you—you already got a dead white male body."

"Mmm." Laser was finishing the second V. There was something satisfying about the jab of the pin, the blue-black ink—something where there'd been nothing on his belly.

"Damn—" Willie Freeze wagged his big Mr. Peanut head. "Dostoevsky must have been messed up. *Crime and Punishment*. 'Do the crime, pay the time.'" Then he got excited. "Hey, man, you got to ink my eyeballs! I heard about it, but never seen it. You got to ink 'em! Scare the shit out of anybody who looks at me."

"Never did it, but I've seen it. But you don't really want that."

"You got to tattoo my eyes, man." Willie's voice and glare were iron hard.

*****

The mother of the girl he tattooed is playing with Laser's dick, which isn't stiffening, but neither of them is ready for more sex yet. She's examining it the way she's looked at his body art, like it's a curiosity, something that he has that she doesn't. Laser had tattooed Willie Freeze's eyes, turning the whites blue-black, and his cellmate had indeed been transformed into one fearsome mother-fucker: he looked like midnight had risen within him and would never leave. Willie had laughed like a demon when he saw himself in the mirror. Then, within an hour, he'd gotten knifed in the yard during a fight he'd started, and Laser never saw him again. There's also a "Willie" in Laser's sunset.

*****

Dana hates how she sounds. Like a coquette, like a little idiot, and here she is, forty, and a professional. Forty-two. But what did people sound like when they were having affairs? She has no script, but she's deeply, daringly involved in a scene with this man whose body is a museum—a library—of prompts. She's an unskilled teaser, and everything she says sounds stupid. "If it's Russian, why didn't you write it in Russian?"

"I've inked in Cyrillic. But I don't read Russian."

They'd met when she'd rushed to his tattoo parlor, furious and frantic, insisting that Laser remove the Stars of David he'd tattooed on her daughter's eyelids. Thrusting the branded girl in front of her, she screamed at the figure in the tattooing chair. He was reading a newspaper under his work lamp.

"We're going to shut you down!" She'd been hoarse, intending to be as dangerous as she tried to appear. That morning, Dana had found her daughter dressed and napping on top of her covers, as usual. The girl habitually rose at dawn to shave herself smooth from head to toe: the hair the alopecia left surfaced overnight in unsightly patches. Dana had started shaving the child in pre-school, but since the onset of puberty the girl had been doing it herself. With adolescence, her daughter had spurned the brunette wig she'd worn since kindergarten in favor of a hot pink bob. The new wig complemented a rich fantasy life that excluded Dana. But it had been a relief to roll her eyes at the superficial excesses of a daughter who, if not exactly a normal teenager, at least overlapped with Dana's idea of one.

"Up, sleepy head, time for school," Dana had called. "Missed you last night." There'd been a late PTA meeting. Then she'd seen the stars, which the girl fluttered drowsily at first, then defiantly as she realized why her mother was staring.

"Tattoos," she said, and Dana shrieked. The SUV's GPS directed mother and daughter through commuter clogged downtown streets to *Laser's Tattoos and Piercings*.

The large man with the ring through his nose and the ponytail and the ink-stained arms lowered his paper, removed his glasses and nodded at them with a frowning grin, as if he'd expected them.

*****

The minute he'd agreed to tattoo stars on the eyelids of the whip of a girl with the crazy pink wig and audacious, drawn-on brows, Laser knew there'd be trouble. But the kid was right about the stars—she needed them. He'd tried to explain to the frenzied mother that he couldn't really help.

"It's a coincidence that my name is Laser. I don't do laser removal—I don't have the equipment. There are clinics that do that. Try *Tatt-off*. It's a chain—there's one in the mall near you."

Near you. That's the thing he shouldn't have said. He'd known not to say, *Laser removal might leave permanent scars.* He hadn't said, *The stars look good, let her keep them.* He'd said *near you,* and it had come out that he'd driven the girl home after tattooing her. Given the questionable safety of his neighborhood and the fact that she'd finally admitted to being a month shy of eighteen, a ride seemed the right thing to do. He wouldn't have guessed she was only fifteen.

After the half hour drive into the suburbs, he'd passed the entrance to her gated community before pulling over—when he saw the size of the houses and the lush lawns and the clean, broad, black streets on the other side of the gates, he'd decided to let her walk through them on her own. He had to admit, anybody checking them out in his pick up might have been curious about their story—a girl in a pink wig with white gauze taped over her eyes was not your everyday sighting. But her lids had bled a little, and Laser hadn't wanted to risk infection. Blind and oblivious, the girl had chattered about pop movie stars the whole way. Thank God she knew her own address—probably something she'd been forced to memorize in kindergarten. Without his GPS, he'd never have found her neighborhood. She squeaked a little when he pulled off the tape holding down the gauze pads, but it couldn't have hurt more than the tattooing. Part of the sassy eyebrows she'd drawn on her forehead came off with the tape. He twisted his rearview mirror so she could admire herself. The bleeding had stopped. She closed one eye at a time, batted her lids at herself, then at Laser. It was twilight, and he only knew her eyes were green from memory. She was smiling.

"I'm smooth, you know," she blurted. Then she yanked off her pink wig, revealing her completely hairless scalp. "Touch it," she said, and he'd patted her bald head. It was cool and dry. "I've got that alopecia disease," she said. "Don't worry, you won't get it from touching me. I've had it forever. But I get patchy, so I shave all over twice a day to stay smooth."

"Un-hunh." Laser was used to confessions. It took a long time to ink people, and maybe something about the permanence of what was happening to them made his customers spill their crimes, infidelities, and aspirations.

Other people's secrets buzzed continually around his head. But it was hard not to look at a girl when she wanted to show you she was smooth.

"It's itchy now, because the patches have started to grow in. I didn't tell you about the other tattoo I want— I want drops of milk coming from my tit, like there'd been a baby nursing and someone pulled it away. But you can't let the drops look like blood. I want them right here—"

Before Laser could protest she'd pulled up her t-shirt, and he turned his head away a second after he saw her place a finger two inches below a little nipple that looked like a boy's.

"You need to cover up," he said, staring hard into his side mirror back toward her neighborhood's gates because his eyes needed something else to look at besides this girl's nakedness. "I don't do breasts as a regular thing. Now cover up."

*****

"—the mall near you," he'd said. Only at the *Tatt-off* clinic in the mall, where her daughter wept with humiliation and pain at the de-inking of her stars, did Dana wonder how he knew. The lasering left white lines on her daughter's lids, "which should fade, but no guarantees." In the SUV on the way home—there'd be no school for mother or daughter— the interrogation, punctuated by "I hate you! I'm going to live with Daddy!" finally yielded the story the child repeated in court, where her baldness was hidden beneath her old brunette wig: "He covered my eyes and told me he wanted to give me a special tattoo, and he lifted my shirt and touched me where he said he'd put it." Under her hand-drawn virginal brows a small band-aid covered part of a fading star.

The girl had sat with her father at the trial, a man Dana thought the shadow of an ideal parent. He'd been less than the shadow of a husband, though he hadn't actually used the phrase "better prospects" a decade earlier when he'd left the big house in the gated community, and he never ceased to provide for his ex-wife and child. With the attorney he hired, a golfing buddy, he kept a close eye on the criminal and civil proceedings. He called his daughter "Pumpkin," which made her smile and blush.

It took a year, after the civil suit and the settlement that would be held in trust until her actual eighteenth birthday, and just weeks before Laser's release, for Dana's daughter to finally change homes. While the girl stood at the front door, waiting among boxes and suitcases and rolled posters for her father, she'd confessed, "He never touched me except for the tattoos. All he did was give me a ride home. And I swore to him I was eighteen."

*****

"You're legs are as pale as all of me," Dana says to Laser "Can you tattoo me? Can you tattoo me now?" She's right about the whiteness of their bodies, all of hers, and his thick legs. Under the black hairs kinking from his thighs and shins and calves, his flesh is like a frog's belly. Except for some sun-freckling on her forearms and the brown thatch between her legs and the tits so dark they're nearly black, she's white, too, but like a satin sheet.

The second after asking for a tattoo, she blushes fiercely, the color spilling like warm soup from her cheeks down her neck to her chest. Laser had been easy enough to find. She'd learned in court that his real first name was Lazarus, and his address was a matter of public record. But she'd left her intended apology unspoken. How could she apologize for the time he'd spent in prison and the livelihood he'd lost? All she said when he opened the door to his flat that first visit was, "She's gone to her father's," as if he'd been waiting for the news, and he'd invited her in and offered her a cup of tea and a seat while he finished tattooing something on a young man's bicep. His tattooing machine was about the only thing he hadn't lost. His apartment smelled of the ink and antiseptic of his art, his business conducted now without a license and by word of mouth.

While Laser bent over his work, inking with a steady hand, she found the hum of the machine soothing until she saw the muscle of the young man flinch. Getting tattooed had to hurt. She tried to picture her daughter in Laser's chair, but remembered instead how she'd dreaded shaving the child's head each morning, hated the dark, bristled islands that would surface, despised the fresh scent and the texture of the white cream she molded over them, and cringed at the drag of the razor. But she'd been a faithful and cheerful mother, humming a made up tune like a lullaby, the only lyrics the refrain: "*Sooo*, smooth, *Sooo*, smooth." Didn't anyone see the respect due her for her endurance?

Now Dana's attention again fixes on Laser's tattoo of a hand patting a head. Who is Antolini? That very afternoon, a few hours earlier, minutes before she sent out the email canceling her faculty meeting so she could rush to her lover, she'd touched the head of a third-grader who'd been banished from class for "bothering a girl." Seth was a hard little boy to like. He was unpleasantly overweight and smelled like baloney. She'd asked him to take a seat and tell her what happened.

"I just said her name," he whined.

"Whose name?"

"Jillian's.

"How did you say it?"

"JillianJillianJillianJillianJillianJillian—"

"Okay," Dana had smiled. "But why?"

Seth's gaze had dropped to the floor, his lips rising toward his nose to form a snout.

"There are better ways to show someone you like them," Dana said. She stood and moved to the child. His head was at the height of her hip. "Ways that aren't so silly. Try writing Jillian a poem. Or, if you want to keep things private, just for yourself, keep a journal." Then she'd placed her hand on top of the boy's head. Its jelled surface reminded her of the glazed sugar crusting a pastry. After sending him back to class, she'd murmured, "LaserLaserLaserLaserLaser" like an incantation while posting the meeting cancelation.

*****

This woman in his bed examining his tattoos, back now for the fourth—the fifth?—time, is small-breasted, like her daughter. He hadn't revealed the girl's specific tattoo request in his testimony—said nothing about the drops of mother's milk, stating only that the girl had asked for a tattoo on her chest.

"Your legs are as pale as all of me," her mother says. He expects her to ask why he hasn't tattooed his legs, and he has an answer ready. "Did you ever read Dante? The *Inferno*?" he'd begin—and by now, suburban wealth, school principal and all, he knows she hasn't—"Well, at the very bottom of Hell, the worst offenders, those treacherous to loved ones, they're frozen for eternity in a lake of ice. The worst ones are up to their eyeballs. Me, I picture myself in ice up to my waist. My legs aren't available for inking." If she asks, that's what he'll say, but she doesn't.

Laser reaches toward her and cups one slight breast. It's warm, like a dove. On the back of his hand is the fierce head of a Chinese dragon, its scaled body twisting down his forearm, its stubby dog-legs clawed, its sharp, reptilian wings spread across his forearm.

"Mark me," he says in a too-deep voice. She won't know he's doing the ghost of Hamlet's father. But her clean skin suddenly goose-bumps, her eyebrows lift and her lips purse. On one of his back's wriggling sunbeams there is a pair of B's, followed by a second pair with a line through them: *To be or not to be.* He slides his hand down the woman's ribs to her hip. She's smiling—he likes the tiny lines that radiate from the corners of her eyes. Deeper creases frame her lips, and he likes these, too.

*****

"Mark *you?*" Dana mimics his tone, a contralto the lowest she can dip. "What with? Where?" Meaning covers the man who touches her, but she feels blank. She waits. An answer doesn't come, and she falls forward, her palms threatening to sear fresh prints among the symbols on his chest.

Glorious Vessel

.   My seven-year-old son Aaron sits coloring at the back of the conference room in the Mobile, Alabama, Hampton Inn. Aaron adds red to Jesus' flashing robes as He throws the moneylenders out of the temple while I stack my official Awake and Aware relaxation recordings on the table in front of him. You'd think a twenty-first century kid would be involved with a game on his smart phone instead of with a Bible coloring book, but Aaron's fundamentalist mother and new step-father don't allow him electronics. *No electronics, including TV* is first on the list of rules I signed off on a week ago so they'd trust me to watch over my own son for the summer. Shelley and Rodney are on an "Evangelical Inspiration Cruise" along the coasts of Central and South America. By the time I return Aaron to his home in Pensacola, he'll have witnessed my Awake and Aware group hypnosis sessions in nearly two dozen Southern cities.

The first nine rules I've sworn to uphold include keeping the Word of God holy, making sure Aaron says his prayers, and refraining from carnal activity. But Shelley and Rodney left a blank space after the number for a tenth rule.

"We've left you room to create a rule of your own, as needed," Shelley said when I questioned the omission. "We trust in the Lord to guide you with His wisdom."

Shelley and I met in Alabama twelve years ago. I noticed her first at a continental breakfast at the Best Western outside of Mobile, caught her eye a week later at the omelet station in the Montgomery Sheraton, and three days after that introduced myself at the make-your-own waffle griddle at the Holiday Inn off of Interstate 85 in Birmingham. She was conducting sessions for a company that packaged educational programs for parents who wanted to home school their kids.

"Mostly for religious people who are afraid public schools don't provide good Christian values," she said. "It's a job. I don't trouble myself much with the content." Shelley giggled when I told her that I hypnotized people to stop overeating and smoking. I invited her to attend my morning session for free, but she declined.

"I'll be busy right next door, Conference Room C. And I don't smoke," she said. "Do I look overweight to you?"

"No," I said, because she wasn't at the time, though I should have noticed her heavy hand with the syrup. "But maybe you look different to yourself. And maybe you're white-knuckling through an urge to smoke."

Mistaking coincidence for fate and lust for love, we slept together for the first time a week later at the Hilton in Tuscaloosa, and two months after that we were married. Shelley quit her job and moved into my cottage in Pensacola. I'd return from the road every few weeks because we were trying, without much luck, to have a child. Shelley's failure to become pregnant left her terribly depressed, and she spent the lonely hours I was away eating and poring over the Christian home school materials she formerly sold. When I returned after a month long stint in Mississippi, she met me with a gleam in her eye. I patted the belly swelling over the elastic waistband of her stretch pants.

"This is it, right?" I grinned. But the gleam had been fired up by Jesus, not a baby, and the big belly was nothing but extra flesh.

"The Lord is testing us," she said. So we kept trying. We barely left the bedroom whenever I was home. Shelley got bigger and bigger and more and more devout, but not at all pregnant. After another evening's struggle with "baby-making" (we'd stopped calling it "love-making"), I thought she was asleep and tried to plant a whispered hypnotic suggestion that she eat less.

"Close your eyes and retreat to the pure silence you felt in the womb," I began. But it turned out she wasn't asleep. She was praying.

"Don't start your hypno-tricks with me," she snapped. "Not while I'm talking to Jesus."

It was Shelley's dream that got us to a fertility specialist. She phoned me at four AM at the Hampton Inn in Biloxi, Mississippi, to tell me about the beautiful, slender woman in a flowing white robe: "She had streaming hair, dark as midnight, and eyes that glittered like a Fourth of July sparkler. And her lips looked so red and soft even a woman would want to kiss them—and still feel guiltless."

Coincidentally, there was a woman with long, dark hair and kissable lips asleep in bed next to me, an attendee from the day's session. It was not unusual for one of my subjects to require free "extra attention" for a particularly noxious tobacco addiction. My bedmate lay with her back to me while Shelley continued.

"The beautiful woman pulled out the most precious baby boy, all swaddled up, from the folds of her robe. He had my blue eyes and little dab of a nose, but your mouth. 'Go see a doctor,' the woman said, displaying the baby, 'See a doctor, and this will be your prize.'"

So Shelley flew into Shreveport, Louisiana, my next stop, where we visited the Center for Fertility and Reproductive Health. For her own reasons, she wanted the testing done as far from Pensacola as possible. The conclusion of our visit? Though neither of us was sterile, Shelley had "anatomical peculiarities" that made conceiving and carrying a child impossible.

Shelley had prepared herself for all eventualities: "But Jimmy and I can make a baby in a dish, can't we?" she asked. "And have an angel carry it who'll pass it on to us the second after Jesus brings it into this world?"

The answer to both questions was "Yes," and so it went: while an anonymous surrogate in Louisiana carried our baby, Shelley pretended to be pregnant back home in Pensacola. Shelley believed it was part of our private miracle—hers, mine, the dream-woman's, and Jesus'—that she "feel" pregnant. Her size permitted the subterfuge. She donned maternity clothes, "ate for two," and "glowed," according to her church friends.

When the time came, we flew back to Shreveport, where we took care of the necessary paperwork and the hospital staff handed over Aaron. Holding him to her bosom in her non-maternity dress, Shelley looked particularly stout—I guess I half-expected her weight to melt away with the birth of our child. We never met the surrogate, and no such encounter was planned. "It would spoil the miracle," Shelley said.

After a week back in Pensacola enjoying my new family, I needed to get back on the road. A year later, after I came home without a believable explanation for the mingled scents of tobacco and perfume that saturated my flesh, Shelley filed for divorce. Until our summer road trip, my time with my son consisted of the occasional weekends I'd hole up with him at the Pensacola Motel 6.

And now my boy gets to see his daddy at work. He looks up from his coloring book and stares out over the registration table at the rows of chairs and the podium where my lectern stands. "This is like church, isn't it Daddy?"

"A little," I say as I appraise the Awake and Aware recordings display, then lay out the registration materials, including the cashbox. "But it's not." I stride down the center aisle and mount the podium. I test the microphone.

"Hello, there, young fellow." My amplified voice crackles before achieving perfect modulation. Aaron waves. I expect a good crowd. There are eighteen pre-registrants—ten smokers, eight overeaters—and I estimate at least a dozen walk-ins. I move back to the registration table to await my flock. As usual, they slink or waddle through the conference room doors one at a time, slouching under individual clouds of failure. They register, pay what's due, and take their seats. Before the day is over, most, motivated by a host of strategically dropped suggestions, will purchase an Awake and Aware Relaxation Re-enforcement Recording at the special reduced price of $49.99.

I leave my son and make my way to the podium, from which I smile down upon the attendees. "Look around at your fellow health-seekers," I say, and neighbors blink into each other's faces. I see hope and resentment in their tobacco stained teeth and double chins—and shame, always shame. "These are your brothers and sisters," I say. "Though you've taken your own routes, you've all been on the same pilgrimage, and that pilgrimage has brought you here. Check your watches—your new lives start *now*."

Aaron colors away as I summarize the basis of hypnotherapy to those who've placed themselves in my hands: synapses will be rewired; unwanted desires will be purged. Surrender through relaxation is the key. I remind my listeners that I've been certified by the American Board of Neuro-Linguistic Learning as a Master Hypnotherapist and Master Success Coach. If my titles impress my son, he doesn't show it—his crayon work is all he's got eyes for.

I ask my subjects to inhale deeply, to hold their breath while I count to five, and to release. Wheezes and gasps—a familiar odor of burnt paraffin washes over me. "Close your eyes," I say, and I begin the entrancement.

"Imagine that you're asleep and dreaming. All parts of you melt toward your center and form a single weight, a soft heaviness. You're a baby in the womb, floating; you have no memories because you've only breathed in darkness."

Now Aaron lifts his head, his mouth open and crayon poised. I wink and blow him a kiss over my shut-eyed subjects. He bows back to his coloring.

"After I instruct you to open your eyes," I say, "I will ask you how it felt to travel back to the womb, and some of you will describe the experience. But then I will say a sentence with the word "dog," in it, and when you hear that word, "dog," you will think it's funny and you will laugh. I'll say the word "dog" several times, and each time it will seem funnier and funnier, until you won't be able to control your laughter."

I clap and direct my subjects to open their eyes. "What did you see?" I ask. They are shy and hesitate. "Who saw darkness?" A few raise their hands. "Who saw light?" More hands. A woman volunteers that she saw her child-self in a crib clutching a teddy bear.

"Very good, yes." I nod. "And did anybody see a dog?" There are chuckles. I look perplexed. "Nobody saw a little puppy dog?" There's increased laughter, and puzzled participants glance at each other, unable to explain their merriment. "It's not unusual for hypnotized subjects to picture a *dog*," I say, raising my voice as guffaws crescendo. "What if I told you that I hypnotized you to visualize a *big, shaggy dog*?" The room rocks with spasmodic laughter. Arms akimbo, I smile a knowing smile.

"And perhaps you recall," I say after waiting for the hilarity to subside—my audience becomes rapt—"that I *told* you—I planted the thought in your minds—that you would find the word d-o-g irresistibly humorous."

There's an electric silence. Faces close like fists. Then, as my subjects accept that surrendering to my will is a good thing, that it's what they paid for, foreheads uncrease and frowns relax. For the first time, they allow themselves hope. I snap my fingers. "You are now free," I say. "'Dog' is no longer funny. And now we can begin."

At the back of the room, Aaron is waving his hand. His legs dance under the table.

"Yes?" I ask with a stiff grin.

"Daddy," he pipes, "I have to go the bathroom."

It's too early for a break, but I have no choice, and I release my subjects for five minutes, assuring them we'll get to the heart of the program when they return. Aaron waits for me at the table and takes my hand. The women who file past beam at us with puckered smiles, while the men in the hall and in the restroom avoid eye contact. Aaron and I take care of business and wash up, my boy carefully mimicking me as I rub my hands under the blower.

"I didn't laugh when you said 'dog.'" He forgets to stop shouting when the blower stops, and his fluty voice bounces off the tiled walls.

"You did fine," I say.

"Why didn't you make the word 'Jesus' instead of 'dog'? You could make your people rejoice in His name every time they hear it."

"But that wouldn't be fair, would it? They should rejoice because they want to, not because I make them. And remember," I say, "what I do isn't church. Zip up your fly."

Our father-son summer passes quickly. Between cities and hotels, Aaron and I float along Interstates as if they're rivers: I-10 through Mobile, then I-65 through Montgomery and on to Birmingham. We take notice of road signs, bridges, and water towers. Sometimes we observe the travelers we pass or who pass us, and we guess if they're smokers or if they're Christians. Sometimes we decide they're both. The overeaters are obvious. When we reach our next city, we check-in, and there's dinner at Denny's or Applebee's, unless the hotel restaurant is having a special. If we find a playground nearby with a swing, we'll stop, and I'll push Aaron. I'll feel his fleeing, returning weight in the pit of my stomach as if I'm the one riding. I grab him only to shove him away, his body compact as a yo-yo, his blond hair flapping.

Some days, usually at sunset, whether we're in the car or in a park or enjoying dishes of plain vanilla ice cream at an outdoor stand, my son will lecture me about the Rapture. He'll stare toward the flood of colors at the horizon, orange and lavender, and describe how the sky will open wide and Jesus will descend amid the blare of trumpets and the fluttering wings of golden angels. "We're all to have glorified bodies like Jesus," Aaron says. "We'll be like ghosts who can walk through walls." He'll become so steeped in the narrative his face will flush pink, and he'll stammer. His enthusiasm is so visceral, I wonder if such vividness is healthy for someone his age.

Back in our hotel room, I'll read with him from his Bible comic books, or he'll color or work on one of the Bible word searches in his home school workbook. While I lie on one of our pair of queen beds making notes for the next morning's session, he'll stretch out on his, circling the names of ancient Bible places he finds in the big block of letters. "Thessalonia," he might murmur with the slightest of lisps, or "Jerusalem." Finally, when it's time for lights out, I'll heed the rules I agreed to and listen to Aaron recite his prayers. If I can't sleep, I'll listen in the dark to one of my Awake and Aware recordings through my ear buds: my own mellifluent voice merges with the sizzle of a summer rain shower and the heave and suck of ocean waves on a pebbled shore, and I'm soon asleep.

One August evening after we've settled into our room at the Embassy Suites Hotel in downtown Birmingham, the air conditioner gives a long, desperate shriek and quits. It's declared "unfixable," and, because the hotel's regular rooms are jam-packed with a hundred-plus nurses and midwives for a weekend conference on "Birthing in the 21st Century," management resituates Aaron and me "at no extra charge" in one of their honeymoon suites. Our suite features two rooms: a bedroom with a king-sized, heart-shaped bed and an "entertainment area" with a foldout sofa. I give him his choice, and Aaron picks the foldout.

It's past midnight when I look into the neighboring room and see that my boy is still awake. He's coloring on his made up bed. We haven't been this far apart all summer. I invite him up to my giant heart, and he climbs aboard with the coloring book and a fistful of crayons. He shows me the picture he's working on: a huge dinosaur with a spiny back and dagger teeth. Aaron's coloring the dinosaur blue. It towers over a half-dozen bearded cavemen with raised spears. A few spears already pierce the beast's hide, and blood that Aaron has colored yellow drips from the wounds. Little dinosaurs spy on the battle from behind the trunks of coconut-laden palm trees. The baby dinosaurs sit in half-shells like Easter chicks. A caveman with his back to the central struggle waves his spear at the babies. Aaron has colored the palm fronds purple. The picture reminds me that one of Shelley's irrefutable rules sets the age of the world at six thousand years.

"There's a life-sized dinosaur and caveman fight just like this at Creation World," Aaron says, as if eavesdropping on my thoughts. "Rodney took us there. The dinosaur moves its head and roars, and the cavemen shake their spears. Rodney knows the names of all kinds of dinosaurs."

"Rodney's a smart man," I say, though there's no rule dictating that I compliment my son's stepfather.

Aaron stops coloring and winces at me. "Daddy, what's a 'woom'?"

"A 'woom'?"

"You know—you tell the people to close their eyes and picture that they're back floating inside the 'woom'."

"Oh—'womb.' It's got a 'b' on the end that you can barely hear." I pause. What does Aaron know about babies? How much does any seven-year-old know? Have I got a rule for this? Could this be a call for Rule Ten—the blank one that Shelley says the Lord is supposed to help me with? I sniff a deep breath and wait, but there's no divine intervention. I exhale.

"A womb is where a baby grows," I say.

"Like my *bed*-room?"

I look at the dinosaur picture, at the spears in the blue dinosaur's side, and I bite the side of my cheek. Aaron is my son, too. He isn't kin to Rodney at all. I deserve some say in my boy's upbringing; Rule Ten should state that it's a father's right and responsibility to see that his child understands *something* true about life.

"Wom-*b*," I say, exaggerating the final letter. "Has your mom talked to you yet about where babies come from?"

Aaron shrugs. "Babies are miracles. They're Jesus' gifts."

"Yes," I nod. "That's true. But Jesus has to work at the miracle, and miracles aren't easy. That's why Jesus had to suffer for us, right? Okay, so—you know how there are lots of fat ladies in the world? Like a lot of the ones who come to see me? Well there are other fat ladies who get that way not because they eat too much, but because they have a baby inside—in their womb."

Aaron grins, but his brows knit. "Nobody eats babies," he says.

"Of course not. But Jesus makes it interesting. He's fixed things so a mom and a dad make a baby together. He gave dads something like a key to open up a mom. And a mom's got an egg inside of her, a little tiny one—in her *womb*, which is a big space behind her belly button that's got room enough for the baby to grow into." I hear myself purring, just like my voice on my recordings. "The dad uses his key to 'anoint' the mom's egg, or it won't start growing into a baby. That's how Jesus works it out. Once the egg is anointed, it starts to grow in the womb, bigger and bigger until it's ready to come out. It takes a long time—about nine months."

Aaron's scowling with concentration. He might be puzzling over any of a thousand particulars. *Key? Anoint?* What was I thinking?

"How's the baby get out?" he asks.

I choose retreat over graphicness. "Usually a doctor in the hospital keeps an eye on things. A doctor or a midwife."

"I bet Jesus touches the baby just like He'll touch us at the Rapture," Aaron speculates. "Babies get glorified bodies just like His, for just a while, and they pass right through the mom's skin. I bet that's the miracle."

"Something like that," I say.

Aaron puffs his cheeks, then lets them go slack. "So— I grew in Mom's womb. She was my glorious vessel, and then I passed through her and into the world."

I start to agree, but something stops me. Maybe it's the way Aaron lisped "glorious vessel." Maybe I'm mad about the rules I'm forced to follow—and maybe I'm mad at myself for promising to follow them. But I don't waste a lot of time looking for a rationale for telling the truth—I just tell it. I clear my throat.

"Your mom wasn't actually your 'glorious vessel,'" I say. "Your miracle was a little bit different." The heat of Aaron's gaze singes my cheeks. My eyes drop to the coloring book and the standoff between the cavemen and the dinosaur. "Your mother's womb—there was something wrong with it. It was broken. She had a good egg, though. Jesus helped the doctor take the good egg out of your mom. I 'anointed' it in a special dish, which turned the egg into you, and then the doctor put you inside a very generous woman who volunteered her womb for you to grow up in. With Jesus' help, of course. It was that special woman's flesh you passed through when you were born."

Aaron's mouth is a circle: he's trying to make a word—maybe "womb."

"Who?" he asks. He's as white as the bed sheets. "Who was my glorious vessel?"

I shake my head. "We don't know. Jesus has kept it a mystery. When you were ripe, you passed through the special woman's womb, and the doctor called us and told us to come get you." I wonder if Rodney knows that his new bride has fertility problems. Does he know that a dozen of Shelley's eggs—fertilized by me—wait in a Shreveport freezer? "We've got zero information. Either the woman or Jesus must want it a secret. She could be anyone. Maybe she's an angel," I add, admiring my tone. But have I gone too far? These revelations will bear consequences. "It's really late," I fake yawn. "We'd better get to sleep."

"My glorious vessel," Aaron whispers. He squirms down under the covers of the giant heart-bed. His coloring book and crayons slide into the valley between us. It would be cruel to send him back to his foldout, so I turn out the light and listen for awhile to my boy breathing before I plug myself into one of my recordings.

The breakfast buffet is packed, and I seat Aaron before waiting on line to fill a plate with blueberry muffins for us to share. My son barely registers my return. He's jerking glances from table to table.

"I'll know her, right?" he asks. "The lady I was born from?"

Something in my belly squirms. My gaze follows Aaron's: women of all ages, shapes, and sizes fill the dining room. They sip coffee, fork up slices of melon, nibble toast and chat with tablemates. "I'm not so sure," I say. "You're made up partly of your mom and partly of me. The woman who carried you was like a Fedex driver who's got nothing to do with the package she delivers. You're not part of her."

"Didn't I share her body and her blood?"

"I guess," I frown. "But finding her will be like looking for a needle in a haystack." I look at my watch. It's time to go—my session begins in half an hour. I lead Aaron between tables. Woman after woman flinches as we pass, each face stung by my boy's sudden glance.

There's chaos in Conference Room B. Eager nurses and midwives crowd the registration table, while my smokers and over-eaters shrink into the background. Who would have believed that there are two unrelated hypnotherapy sessions occurring simultaneously in the same hotel? Exasperated, I direct everyone to find a seat. The multitude surges forward as if I've started the world's largest game of musical chairs. I stand behind Aaron, my hands on his shoulders. His head wags as he sifts through the women rushing by. His home school manual is open to a word search: "Women of the Bible." "H-A-G-A-R," circled as an example, spills diagonally through the block of letters.

The crowd quiets as I stride up the center aisle and take the podium. I fasten my microphone to my lapel. There are two sessions, I explain. The one for nurses and midwives on "hypnosis techniques for childbirth" meets in suite 201 and begins in fifteen minutes. Awake and Aware attendees are in the right place. "So let's all get where we belong," I smile.

Two-thirds of the mob rises, mostly women; they shuffle out the door past my son's keen-eyed squint. About thirty remain in what might be the largest room I've worked this summer. It's definitely got the highest ceiling. My voice, as I get the ball rolling, booms with authority.

"You're dreaming of yourself deep in the womb," I intone. At "womb" I look back at Aaron—he's bent over his word search, framed by twin towers of Awake and Aware recordings. My subjects sit, some with lifted chins, others with lowered foreheads, all with eyes shut. But then there's another face—it belongs to a woman who sits in an otherwise empty back row. Her orange hair glows like a sunrise over her red track suit. She's straight-backed and bites her lower lip. She seems to feel me observing her and shakes her hair. One of her eyes pops open, then shuts. She twitches a smile. My chest feels light, as if I'm breathing helium. When I plant the suggestion that "dog" is an irresistibly funny word, my throat feels rusty.

As the induced laughter begins, the woman laughs along, but without the perplexity of her session-mates. And, after I instruct the group to listen to the sounds of their bodies, she opens her eyes and pins me with a green-eyed gaze so intense that my skin prickles.

"*Jesus loves me, this I know*—" Aaron's voice is like a little bird's. He's on his feet now behind the registration table, his attention fixed on the orange-haired woman between us. Hers is the only head that turns to find the singer. Everyone else has focused inward, mesmerized by his or her own body sounds. The woman waves at my son. He waves back and sits.

At the break, the woman lingers near the exit while I process registrations. *She knows me*, I think, but I can't place her. Is she someone I saved? Someone who's shed a hundred pounds or sworn off cigarettes and now sparkles with good health? As the others leave for the restrooms, she steps forward. She's about my age, but has freckles like a kid.

"This is your boy," she says, smiling at Aaron, whose blue eyes glisten. "He favors you in the chin and mouth. I'm Megan." It turns out she's one of the midwives who'd come to Awake and Aware by mistake. But, unlike the others, she decided to stick around. "Your session seemed like fun. You're so *earnest*." She waves at Aaron again, and his arm rises and sinks as if he's underwater. "I'll be glad to pay. It wasn't right for me to intrude. I'm sorry if I made it hard for you."

"No charge," I say. "We'll call it an introductory special. You don't have to leave."

"Oh, but I do," she says. "I'm afraid I'm spoiling your magic. Maybe I can treat you and your son—" she pauses.

"'Aaron,'" I say. "And I'm Jimmy."

"'James,' yes, it's all over your materials." She nods at my recordings—my picture is on the cases. "So—can I treat you two to dinner?"

I accept, and a few long strides carry Megan through the door and into the hotel lobby. Aaron appears at my side.

"You let her go—" He's staring into the vacated space.

"It's okay. We'll see her at supper."

"*Megan.*" Aaron weighs the name in his mouth as if it's a gold coin.

We meet in the hotel restaurant. I wear a fresh shirt under my session suit, and Aaron has tugged on his favorite John 3:16 T. Megan's green dress turns her eyes into emeralds and sets her hair aflame. She's driven in for the conference from west of the Mississippi, she says, looking for a vacation. When she describes her last few months as "rough," a shadow falls over her face that discourages pursuit of the subject. I tell her about Aaron's mom's honeymoon by way of explaining our "summer bonding tour," and she makes a face at the idea of a cruise.

"They're like prison islands, those cruise ships, aren't they?" she asks. "Like Alcatraz? And they force feed you." She cocks her head "Though I guess that's good for your business?" She asks Aaron what grade he's in, and he tells her he's home-schooled. He asks if her name is from the Bible.

"I don't know." She looks at me with a raised eyebrow, and I shake my head.

"His mom has become *very* religious since we split up," I say. "Aaron's been filling me in about the Rapture."

"Really?" Megan leans toward my son, absorbing him in eyes as verdant as any meadow Jesus blessed a lamb in. Aaron tells her all about Jesus' glorious body, and how the saved will have bodies made of air just like His when the Rapture comes. We just have to be prepared.

I'm sure my boy believes he's found his needle in a haystack—the "glorious vessel" whose flesh contained him until his miraculous birth. He might put his suspicion into words at any moment, and I should be planning an explanation. But there's a faint hum—a single lovely note— inhibiting forethought, and I've surrendered to it. I don't taste my steak, and the conversation passes into the ether, and I'm as happy as Megan and my son seem to be. When the waiter asks about dessert, I order Aaron his dish of plain vanilla ice cream. Megan wants only a coffee. "I'm not crazy about sweets," she says.

"Oh, but you'll like our suite, won't she Daddy," Aaron says. "We got a special one because the air conditioner in our first room broke. Megan can come up to see our suite, can't she?"

"How did you come to do what you're doing?" Megan's voice surprises me—she's been breathing so gently beside me I've assumed she's been asleep. I've only been awake myself for a few minutes. I drifted off for the first night in a long time without listening to myself on an Awake and Aware recording. Is it Rule 6 or Rule 7 that forbids "carnal activity"? My hip presses against Megan's. "Carnal" implies a guilt I don't feel. "Carnal" reeks of stale cigarettes and perfume, of greasy sweat. What I feel is cleansed.

"Daddy's bed is a heart," Aaron murmured after Megan and I had tucked him into his sofa bed. He fell asleep before the end of the Christian movie about righteous cartoon vegetables we found on the Gospel Network—our first television of the summer.

"A heart-shaped bed," Megan responded without inflection while I dimmed the light in Aaron's room.

I close my eyes and imagine Megan's freckles glowing under the sheets like trapped fireflies. My skin tingles as if it's been scoured. Has she just asked about my history? I'm afraid I'll compromise the present if I speak. But thinking about the past implies the future: what will we say to Aaron when Megan exits this room with me in the morning?

A muffled commotion from behind the closed door jars the silence and I half sit up. Megan stiffens beside me. "My phone," I whisper. "I left it on the table out there. That was my ringtone." We hear a high-pitched voice, indecipherable. "Aaron answered it," I say. I switch on the bedside lamp. Megan, her eyes slits, pulls the sheet under her chin. Her hair is a brilliant nest, her freckles spatter her cheeks like dried blood. We hunch shoulder to shoulder, trapped by the child's voice.

"It must be his mother," I say.

"At two in the morning? What about her cruise?"

We listen. Aaron's voice drones short and long. What questions is he answering? What is he volunteering? Then his words grow more distinct—he's approached the door.

"—right here. Daddy has his own room—no, no it's okay—we have a *suite*! I'll wake him up."

As the knocks sound there's a blur, a snapped pearl necklace of bouncing images: I jump out of bed and throw the door forward while using it to hide my nakedness; I feel a thump through the knob and curse doors that open outward. Aaron sits on the floor, stunned, one hand to his nose, the other gripping the phone, from which a voice buzzes like a bee in a jar. *He's going to cry*, I think, but before I process what this might mean, Megan, who's yanked on her dress, rushes past me, a burst of green. She scoops my boy from the floor and hands me the phone. I pull the door shut. The last thing I see is my son's face: he's caught up in Megan's arms, and our gazes lock over her shoulder. He presses his cheek into her wild hair. Blood dribbles from his nose, but he's smiling.

I press the phone against my temple as if it's an icepack. "Hello," I gasp. "Hello, Shelley?"

"What's going on there?" my ex-wife demands.

"Nothing," I say. "Aaron dropped the phone while he was knocking. We have a suite."

"You shut your door on him?"

"He slept with me the first night. But tonight I needed to listen to some new Awake and Aware recordings, and I couldn't find my ear buds. So—you're calling from your cruise?"

"Don't you pay attention to the news? We've been on the news. I know you had the TV on—Aaron said you watched a movie."

"On the Gospel Network. It was about vegetables. But that was all. We kept to the rules. What happened?"

"Some kind of bacteria got on the ship. In the food. Half of the passengers got sick. Not me, thank Jesus, but Rodney got so dehydrated they had to hook him up to an IV. They had to helicopter in medical supplies while we made our way back. I thought sure you would have called to check on us, but nope, not a single message."

"Because we didn't know," I say. "But that's horrible. You deserve better."

"Rodney says the Lord must have had His reasons, and I guess he's right. Who are we to question?" I pull on my khakis while we speak as if Shelley's about to walk through the door. "So," she continues. "Aaron's okay?" There's something coming, and I gird myself.

"He's fine," I say. "He's a good boy. He keeps himself occupied with his Bible stuff. I promise, except for tonight with the TV, we've been following the rules." I button my pants and contemplate my bare-chested reflection in the dresser mirror.

"Hm. Maybe you have been and maybe you haven't. I had a long talk with Aaron just now." Shelley's so wound up her voice shakes. "You had that blank spot for a tenth rule—for the Lord to guide you—and it sounds like you must have ignored Him. You went and told Aaron the facts of life? He's only *seven*. He's got to be twelve for that. There'll be pastor-talks and workbooks—but not until he's twelve."

If this is all she's got, I can defend myself. "A father has a right—"

But Shelley's not done. "You told Aaron that I didn't carry him?" She's struggling so hard to control her voice she must be beet purple. "You told him that he grew inside a woman that wasn't me for nine months? A 'miraculous vessel'?"

"'Glorious vessel,'" I correct. "He got the idea from the Rapture."

"So-he-tells-me—" Shelley hisses. "You know what you've got to do now, don't you? There's only one way to make this right. You know what that is?"

"No."

"You've got to put him right this very second. You're going to put your phone on speaker, and I'm going to listen to you tell him that everything you said about that 'miraculous vessel' was a lie. My boy's not going to think that his mother didn't carry him. You're going to tell him that you were trying out some new kind of hypno-something, or whatever. But you will make it clear to him that I'm one hundred percent his mother in every single way!"

I hesitate, reflecting on the circumstances. If I'm going to trade the truth I've shared with Aaron for the lie his mother demands, I've got to pry him from the arms of the woman who's got him—and me— enthralled. And I've got to accomplish that without revealing Megan's presence to Shelley.

"Okay," I say. "I'll tell him."

"Yes you will," Shelley huffs. I picture her gripping her landline receiver as if she's choking Satan's serpent into silence to prevent its offering the apple of knowledge to Eve.

"I'm putting the phone on speaker," I say and push the button. I drop to my knees. "Aaron," I call under the bed so my voice is smothered, "your mother wants me to tell you something." I count to three. "*Okay*," I squeak, holding the phone at arm's length. "He's tired," I say to Shelley in my own voice, "but he's here."

"Daddy's got something to tell you, honey," Shelley says.

"*Un-hunh*," I squeak.

"Aaron," I say, "remember the other night when I told you about how moms and dads and Jesus work together to make a baby? About how the father anoints the mother's egg, and parts of both parents join, and a child starts to grow inside the mother's womb?'

"*Yes—*" My "Aaron" voice cracks, but I lisp the "s".

"—And I said something about Mommy's womb being broken—" I hear a groan from Shelley's end— "Well, I was wrong about that. I was wrong about somebody else carrying you for nine months. There was only your Mom. She was your only 'glorious vessel.' There was never another."

"*No?*" I squeak. "*But why—*"

"Why did I tell you that? I don't know, son. I guess I was trying a new kind of hypnosis. For Awake and Aware. I used it on you because there wasn't anyone else around. It was mind control—like the way I make people laugh when they hear the word 'dog.' But let me make it clear: what I did was wrong. None of what I told you is true."

"*Not the 'anointing' either?*" The words I speak for Aaron are sticky on my lips, and the silence on Shelley's end looms like an iceberg. She hasn't bought a word of my subterfuge—she's pretending, too.

"There's a little truth to the 'anointing,'" I say, because what else can I do but keep going? "But I should have waited until you're older to tell you about that. The part about your 'glorious vessel' not being your mother, though, that's a complete and total fib. You understand?"

"*Okay*," I squeak, without much conviction. The bedroom door swings open. Megan is holding Aaron in one arm. They're cheek to cheek. She presses a washcloth to his nose. They're looking down at me where I'm kneeling next to the bed.

"Time to sleep now, Aaron," I say. "It's late. Tomorrow morning we drive all the way to New Orleans. Say good night to your mother."

"Goodnight, Mommy." The washcloth muffles Aaron's voice.

"Goodnight, precious," Shelley says and makes kissing noises. "We'll see you soon, okay. You said your prayers?" He doesn't answer because Megan has backed out of the doorway.

"He's gone," I say. "I'll make sure he does." I take Shelley off speaker. There's a curtain closed over a window of truth, and neither my ex-wife nor I touch it.

"Jimmy," she says, "You ought to bring Aaron home. Right now, this weekend. New Orleans is a sinful city."

"Can't afford to miss New Orleans," I say. "Those will be my two biggest days."

"Well," Shelley sighs, "I've got to wash the germs out of all our clothes and take Rodney some soup and crackers. He still can't keep anything inside himself." Shelley's tone is flat—she's given up something important, but she's not sure what. How much truth and how much lie are we going to let stand? "You keep to your word," she says. "Don't confuse real life with Awake and Aware. Jesus loves you."

"Yes He does. Goodnight," I say into a phone that's already dead.

That's how we leave it, Shelley and I. After New Orleans, my summer with Aaron will be drawing to a close, and I don't know if the time we've got left with Megan is only a matter of minutes or days, or if our glorious vessel will carry us toward some permanent transcendence. But there's a reckoning to come, of that you can be sure. However I phrase it, Rule Ten will require at least one reckoning.

Balance

You feel the girls cowering behind you, but you don't turn. The rusted tracks lead through the trestle's steel frame: it looks like the entrance to a giant Have-a-Heart trap. Thirty feet below, the river is slate blue, except for the trestle's skeletal shadow. The day is breezeless, the water without a ripple. Though it's October cool, you're all sweating—you've been running for almost an hour. Across the river the curving tracks disappear into a forest of scrub oak.

"Cross or don't," you say. "It's two miles back if you do, five if you don't."

"What if a train comes?" a nervous voice asks.

"They don't use these tracks anymore," you say, though you're not one hundred percent sure. "Look how rusty they are. I run this trail all the time." This is a lie. You have never crossed the trestle before. But you can see that there are wooden planks on either side of the tracks all the way to the other side. Your heart is pumping. You're sure the girls' fifteen, sixteen, seventeen-year-old hearts are pumping, too. This is something new, something to break the monotony of training. Something inspirational.

"The Wellington girls do this kind of thing every day," you say. "That's why they're champions. Who's first?" You know who'll be first, Mary, determined as a pit bull, likely to qualify for states. Of the dozen members of your cross country team, her name is one of the two you'll always remember.

"It's empty between the wooden things," somebody says.

"Railroad ties. Stay off of those," you warn. "Stay on the side boards, like I said."

"Is there room if a train comes?"

"I told you, don't worry about trains." You're challenging their trust. "Just go slow and be careful. Jog. Hold the side rail if you have to. If the boards don't look right, if they're rotten or have a hole or something, just stop. And don't bunch up. String out, spread the weight. I'll follow you. Just keep your eyes forward—down on the boards in front of you." You disallow second thoughts, theirs and yours. This crossing will be the stuff of legends.

Mary dashes past you. Her running shoes thud on the boards, and she slows, but keeps going. The twins, the skinny seniors, follow. The hoods of their blue team sweatshirts bounce on their backs. Then they're all out there, all twelve girls stretched out like a blue caterpillar. The last pair of feet belongs to Cherise, a lanky JV sophomore, who's directly in front of you. Cherise has talent—you'd run her varsity if she didn't miss too many practices because of her lead role in the school play. "World of potential," you told her mother last week after watching her win her JV race. "She tries to do too much," her mother said, shaking her head with poorly disguised pride. "Sometimes we worry that she's spreading herself too thin. We hope she learns to balance things. She's going to have to make choices." "Balance is important," you agreed. The two of you gazed at the girl, who sat on the grass, tugging on her sweatpants, sharing a post-race laugh with her teammates. At that moment you'd had a premonition that Cherise would not be remembered for running.

There's a shout up ahead, Mary's: "Stop—hole!" and the caterpillar bunches up and halts. Cherise, directly in front of you, looks up from her feet and veers to her right to avoid bumping into the girl ahead of her. She trips, grunts, lunges to her left for the side rail, misses, stumbles, and slips between ties.

What? you wonder. *Is she melting?* But you know Cherise is falling. Her hair flaps for an instant at your feet. Then there's only an arm, a hand, spread fingers. You bend over the space between ties and see nothing but shadowed water ten yards down, and only then do you shout her name. Eleven heads jerk around, mouths gaping. When they understand why you're stooping, they bleat like frightened sheep.

Your team shuffles back to you, their knuckles white on the side rail. Your jaw moves, but no words come out. All eyes are on the water.

"There—Cherise!" Mary yells, pointing at a spot downriver. "She's okay, look, she's moving. Cherise!"

Where? She's okay, she's moving! Che-riiiise! Is she climbing on shore? She's trying to climb on shore! Che-riiiise!

Faces flash towards yours, each pair of eyes a slap: *Coach? Coach? Coach? Coach?*

You watch the twisted figure bob in place just offshore, less than a hundred yards away: just a water-logged bundle of clothes, snagged on something unseen.

*****

Waking or sleeping, you relive versions of her fall. Images shift randomly, like a television with a fitful remote: you see yourself save Cherise with a steadying hand on her elbow; once, you snatch her hood at the last second, and as she sways in space between the ties, her eyes bulge up at you with confused gratitude; another time, you stand on shore, watching from a distance as she plunges toward the water like a stone.

Sometimes you slip between the ties with her, and there's a thrill in your gut as the dull water rushes toward you. You fall beside her for what seems like hours, both of you squinting and grinning against the updraft. Her hair streams skyward. She's asking you a question, but you can't make it out. Is she rehearsing lines from her play?

*****

Your senior girls take action: the twins sprint off the trestle with tear-streaked faces, looking for a house from which to call 911; Mary and another slide down the embankment beneath the trestle and make their way toward the spot where Cherise bobs; you herd the remaining girls off the trestle and tracks. They huddle together, trembling and crying silently. One vomits behind a bush. Your challenge to cross the trestle hangs in the air like burning sulfur.

Ankle deep mud prevents Mary and the other girl from reaching Cherise. Their teammates and you watch them flounder. Police cars, fire trucks, ambulances arrive. Stony faces ask question after question and you answer in a numb-lipped monotone. EMTs wrap the girls in foil blankets. An hour passes before firemen in a rescue boat reach Cherise.

*****

Once, the hair disappearing through the ties is nothing but light that stains your fingers yellow. Once, the hair pours through your cupped hands like cold, hard coins. Another time Cherise's hair turns into a waterfall of tiny goldfish as it spills through the gap at your feet. One fish misses and lies quivering on the wooden tie. You squat, flick it off, and watch it drop like a golden tear.

*****

You are never criminally charged because town records list the trestle as a "pedestrian bridge." Crossing it was perfectly legal, though now yellow barricade tape blocks the plank walkways. Your union would have been obliged to support you in a criminal case. There is talk of a civil suit brought by Cherise's parents, but it never materializes. Regardless, you resign. You don't impose yourself on friends, colleagues, acquaintances. Apparently relieved at the distance you keep, none of these seeks you out. You will never coach or teach again.

You leave town the night of the final performance of Cherise's play. Her understudy performs in her place. As you drive across the state line heading west, you picture a curtain call dedication to Cherise: actors and audience offer a tearful ovation to the auditorium ceiling.

You leave behind rumors, launched, you suspect, by your ever-faithful runners: Cherise at the time of her fall was teetering emotionally, they whisper, working too hard, in despair; she wrote "LIFE HURTS 2 MUCH" on an Etch-a-Sketch at a team sleepover, then shook the message away. They hint that the incident on the trestle was less a horrible accident than a seized opportunity. No one believes them, and these girls, your team, will eventually forget that they love you. When they grow older, marry, have children of their own, their sympathies will change. *Poor Cherise*, they will sigh as they rock their babies, *how could he have let her fall?*

*****

You punish yourself with exile to another coast, but Cherise fills the vacuum inside you: in the corner of your eye there is always a girl slipping between railroad ties, a flap of hair, a waving hand. What if you offered her fear: if you found work as a firefighter, a coal miner, a deep sea fisherman? Might risking your life daily against earth, fire or water free you from the girl you let fall? Maybe, but you lack the qualifications or opportunities for these dangerous jobs. Instead, you lie about your janitorial experience and find employment as a nightshift custodian in a nursing home.

You find a sparsely furnished flat and swear yourself to monkish isolation, but the nursing home's night security guard foils your efforts at friendlessness. He synchs his rounds to yours and follows you like a puppy from waste basket to waste basket, toilet to toilet. Jeff thinks you're intelligent because you speak in polysyllables. He pries at your history, but his own guesses bore him, and his questions are always self-referential.

"Do you have any sisters?" Jeff asks. "I don't."

"Nope," you answer. "Only child." You don't tell him that your parents are dead, that you're glad they are, because what you let happen to Cherise would have been impossible to explain to them.

"If I had a sister, I bet I'd have better luck with women," Jeff muses. "You get used to talking to girls if you have a sister. I only have a brother."

"What about your mother?" you ask as you follow your push-broom down one of the facility's many long, brightly lit hallways.

"What about her?" Jeff scurries to keep pace, an edge to his voice, wary of an insult a smart guy like you might try to sneak by him. He is an army veteran, though he survived his enlistment without leaving the country.

"Your mother's a woman, isn't she? Don't you talk to her?" As you ask this, familiar female faces appear in the gleam of the floor you're sweeping; your broom chases them away.

"Oh." Jeff ponders. "But a mom is different. Some guys have sisters, you know, who are, you know, *hot*, right?" He pauses, struggling to organize his thoughts.

"Yup," you reassure. "I get it." Did Jeff see your head snap as if you'd whiffed the undiluted ammonia you use for toilets? Had you ever thought of Cherise as *hot*? You increase your pace with the broom. The click of Jeff's heels on the linoleum behind you speeds up. You reframe your memory: *Cherise might have been hot someday*—if you hadn't let her fall.

Jeff leaves to check on the other wings. He will ogle the night duty nurses without speaking to them. After mopping, dusting, and scouring, you doze on one of the love seats in the common room. You hear your runners' feet echoing on wooden boards. Where is Cherise? Tracks and trestle emerge from a bright fog. You glance down between your legs, thinking of hair being spun into gold. *Rumpelstiltskin*, someone whispers in your ear, but in the fairytale it's not hair being spun, it's straw. A shove in the back jolts you awake.

"Caught you," Jeff chuckles, "red-handed." Your heart pounds.

The security guard stares into space, suddenly attuned to the snores growling from every open doorway. "Listen to that racket," he mutters. "Good thing they're all too deaf to hear each other."

You hold up a finger, as if testing the wind. "Room 107," you announce, nodding down the hall. "Mr. Johnson has stopped snoring."

Jeff cocks his head, listens, then squints at you. "Bet?"

"Five dollars," you say.

Jeff hooks his thumbs in his belt, strolls to room 107, and ducks his head inside the door. When he pulls it out, he's shaking it. "You got great ears," he concedes when he rejoins you. "That's a beer on me."

You lick your finger and mark a one in the air. What you don't tell the security guard is that Mr. Johnson never snores.

*****

You take your first run in your new town, and you have a plan. You jog past apartment buildings like your own, noting trees with unfamiliar bark and leaves. Soon you turn onto the main drag: a mile stretch of small businesses, coffee shops and convenience stores. It's been a long time since you've run in place at a red light. The first bridge you come to crosses the Interstate. The bridge is part of your plan.

The sidewalks on both sides of this overpass are empty of pedestrians. The guardrails are hip-high, metal, the top rail flat, the approximate width of a gymnastics balance beam. Once on the bridge, you discover that the highway below is traffic-free: there's not a car, truck or bus heading in either direction. There doesn't appear to be any construction underway, and the six lanes seem fine; it's their emptiness that's disconcerting. At work you'll ask Jeff about it. But the absence of witnesses is probably better for your plan.

It should be simple: you will take a deep breath, and, without breaking stride, leap atop the guardrail and balance yourself. Then you'll jog a few steps along the rail and hop back down to the sidewalk. You'll commit yourself to this risk on every run. You'll test the rails of every bridge and overpass in the city, come rain, snow, or wind. Every precarious step will be dedicated to Cherise.

But at this moment, on this overpass, you hesitate—you jog back and forth half a dozen times. You rehearsed for this last night by jumping on and off the back of your sofa for ten minutes. A city bus pauses beside you, and you wave the driver on. You stare through the windows as the vehicle glides by; none of the passengers looks back.

You grasp the railing and, releasing a deep breath, peer down at the vacant highway. Cherise fell no further, though you'd strike pavement instead of water. You don't trust the Interstate's emptiness: what if you survive a fall only to be crushed by a truck? But the contemplation of such consequences—this is exactly what you're offering Cherise, isn't it? You turn and lean against the top rail, which cuts across the small of your back. You find the rail with your hands, hoist yourself up, and set your bottom on the steel. Your feet hover six inches above the sidewalk. Behind you, nothing.

You grit your teeth and pivot. Your feet dangle out in space, and you resist looking down. You focus on a tall uptown building you think is a hotel. When you pull up your legs so that your feet are under you on the top rail, you fight an impulse to sob. Awkwardly perched, chin on knees, you look up at a chalky blue sky.

You remind yourself that when you rise you must keep your center of gravity back. And just when it seems like you'll never pull the trigger, *you are up*! One-two-three, chest pressed against space, arms spread . . . and then something yanks you from behind like an invisible hand. You pretend it's Cherise, but you know it's your fear. You're on your knees on the sidewalk, but you're not praying. Caught between triumph and terror, you reject both: you can't do this again, even for Cherise.

*****

99

It's been weeks, and you haven't laced on your running shoes since the day you mounted the railing. You're gaining weight. On this Saturday evening you sit on a tall chair at a high table in a popular neighborhood bar. It's your first night out with Jeff, and under the table you pinch your soft belly. He's paid off his beer debt and then some for your correct call on Mr. Johnson's snoring.

"We're night workers," he hoots over the din of juke box music and chatter. "The later it is, the sharper we get." He sloshes beer from a third pitcher into his glass and yours. "It's science." He burps and lifts an eyebrow. "Physics?"

You're only half listening. "English, not physics. I taught English. I told you that." You're still not drunk enough to tell him that you also coached. Then you reconstruct his question. "Yes, physics. F=MA: Force equals Mass times Acceleration. I'm in training for the midnight toilet cleaning Olympics."

Jeff, glassy-eyed, nods and glances around the bar. Four laughing young women crowd into a booth across from your table, and he smiles toward them as if he's in on their joke. He takes a swallow of beer and blinks at you with heavy lids. "If I had a sister—" he starts, and you expect him to repeat himself about knowing how to talk to women, but he doesn't, "she'd be smarter than me. Like you."

You raise your glass to toast the compliment. Jeff thrusts out his jaw.

"What's the shittiest thing you ever did?" he asks.

"What?" The question knocks you off balance, and you look away. One of the young women catches your expression, rolls her eyes, and turns back to her friends.

"The worst thing," Jeff repeats. "I'll tell you mine, then it's your turn." He rubs his chin. You notice for the first time that he's missing the last inch of his pinky finger, and you try not to stare. Did something bite it off, or was he born that way? Your brain feels like a snowball being squeezed into a ball of ice—your worst thing? Really?

"So listen," Jeff whispers gruffly, peeking around like he wants to be overheard. "When I was a kid, I was playing in the backyard with my brother. He's not too bright, and even though he's a year older than me, I kind of always bossed him around. He still lives with my parents. Anyway, we were throwing around a ball or something when a little bird shot between us, and bang!—it hit the house—the window—it must have been fooled by the reflection." He pauses, checks to see if you're following, and you bow your head.

"The bird was on the ground. It was bright blue, a bluebird, I guess, bluer than any bird I ever saw. The color of that bird's feathers is what I picture when I think of 'blue.' The little thing was quivering. 'It broke its neck,' my brother said, and *I* said, 'We've got to put it out of its misery.' I'd heard that from somewhere, about putting suffering animals out of their misery. It seemed very important, like a religious law or something. The bird stopped quivering, but its tiny beady eyes were flicking around. Neither of us wanted to touch it, but I had an idea. It was my job to mow the lawn, so I knew we had a full gas can in the garage—I figured we could soak the bird in gasoline and light it on fire. I guess I'd seen it in a movie, where some foreign people in white robes build a pyre and burn up a body. We could put the thing out of its misery and give it a funeral all at once."

You keep nodding. *Like a phoenix*, you think, but don't say, because Jeff probably wouldn't get it.

"So we do it. I get the gas can, and my brother gets a box of matches from the kitchen. Now the bird's eyes aren't moving around anymore, but they're still open. We thought maybe it was dead, but neither of us knew if a little bird like this one had eyelids. I mean, how small can eyelids be?" Jeff frowns at you like he expects you to know, but all you do is wink. "Dead or not," he continues, "we'd already made up our minds to burn it up, so I tipped the can over it and soaked it good. The bird didn't move, but its wet feathers turned almost black. We both wanted to drop the match, but my brother said he was older, so he should." Jeff sucks in his lips, eases back in his chair, and lets his gaze fall on the young women, who are showing each other pictures on their phones. He finishes off his beer and sets the glass down.

"Then things got hairy," he says. "My brother dropped the match, and *floom*, the flame jumped up right in our faces, and we fell back on our asses." He laces his fingers around his glass, and you pour the rest of the pitcher into it. The pinky stump reminds you of a bald man's head. "That bird was on fire," Jeff says, "but it suddenly started flapping its wings, and then it took off, like a little fireball. It flew about ten feet past us, then dropped to the grass. By the time we got to it, the fire was out, but the bird was scorched black, still smoking. It couldn't have been alive, but who knew?" He reaches across the table and gives your forearm a squeeze; the stubby pinky pokes the knob of your wrist and you shiver. "So I stomped on it," he says. "Put out the fire, put it out of its misery, ended the funeral." He releases you, runs his hand through his hair, and sits back. "I'll never forget the crunchy squish of that charred little body under my foot. I still get jumpy when I step on stuff I don't expect."

Jeff closes his eyes and folds his arms across his chest. The women at the nearby table are quiet. They stare at their drinks—two hold beer bottles, the other two have twined their fingers around the stems of big cocktail glasses. Maybe they heard the story, maybe they didn't. Jeff's eyes pop open, and the way he's smirking makes your stomach churn, because you know what he's going to say next. A waitress comes by, picks up the empty pitcher. She shifts a look between the two of you. "Another?" she asks, and Jeff nods without looking at her.

"Your turn," he says. "What's the shittiest think you've done?"

And then you're talking, too fast at first, until you get into the rhythm of the story you've chosen to tell. There are facts in it, enough to hide behind, but it isn't really the truth.

You tell Jeff you were an early reader— you practically taught yourself, you say, by looking at the comics in the newspaper. Then one day you found the obituary section, and you asked your mom who all the people with little pictures next to their names were.

"Dead people," she said. She told you to skip that section, but you didn't.

"After that," you say, "I turned to the obituaries every day after the comics. It was the little photos I liked, the headshots: new photos with old faces, old photos with new faces, once in a while a new photo with a young face. So, I'd look at each face, and then I would decide who was going to go to Heaven and who was going to Hell."

"*You* decided?"

"Absolutely. Most of people got sent to Hell. I guess I was a mean little kid, but that's where I put most of them. One or two a day got to go to Heaven."

The waitress drops off your pitcher. You top off Jeff's glass and your own. He seems to be buying your story.

"So you got to be like God."

"Exactly. I marked Xs with a pencil over the eyes of everybody I sent to Hell."

"And the ones going to Heaven?"

"Their eyes got stars." You think of telling him that Jews got Stars of David, but that seems too sophisticated for a little kid just learning to read. "When my dad got mad at me for messing up the paper, I quit, which I was ready to do. At some point it struck me that all the people I'd doomed to Hell were stuck there forever, and I felt guilty that I hadn't thought more about the selection process."

"You couldn't change where you sent them?"

You look aslant at the security guard, as if he's missing the point. "How?"

He frowns. He slides back in his seat. Then he shakes his head. "Nah," he says, "Your story doesn't count. Not shitty enough."

You pull your glass from your mouth—beer runs down your chin. "What? Why not? Sure it's shitty."

"God can't be shitty," he says. "God's all-mighty. Whatever God decides goes." He leans forward on his elbows. "You're not getting off that easy," he hisses, and you feel like your skin is melting off your face. "What the hell are you doing out here really? What are you running from? Got to be the shittiest thing ever."

*****

There's only an inch of beer left in the pitcher— did you drink the rest over the last twenty minutes while Jeff listened without interrupting to your trestle story? His face is a jigsaw of shadows in the dim light, and you guess yours is, too. He's let you go on for so long you half-hope he's fallen asleep with his eyes open. Maybe he hasn't retained a single word of the "shitty truth" you just shared. Most of the tables in the bar are empty now, including the booth where the young women sat. Nobody's fed the juke box, and rain hisses on the pavement outside the open front door.

"Shit," your companion mutters. He smacks his forehead with the heel of his hand. "What—so—did she have something on you? Is that why you pushed her? You pushed her, right? The whole thing, running across the bridge—the trestle, whatever—that was just a set up so you could shut her up, right? What'd you, fuck her? The kid? Make the moves at least—and she was going to tell?"

You feel like a knife's twisting between your ribs. "No," you protest. "Nothing like that. I was just irresponsible, that's all. I shouldn't have sent the girls across the bridge. Not criminal—I said, there were boards to walk on next to the tracks. It was on the records as a pedestrian bridge—"

"You said you could have grabbed her."

"I said I *felt like* I should have grabbed her." In your mind's eye you see a golden braid slithering down a hole— stepping on it would stop, maybe save whatever it's attached to, but you can't move your foot.

"You said you loved her."

"No I didn't."

"You said all the girls loved you."

"I said they *trusted* me. That's what I meant."

"You said love. You said you loved her."

You shrug twice, three times; you're shaking. "Maybe I said I loved them, like all of them loved me. I didn't say I was *in* love with any of them. With her. If I loved her, why would I push her?" You feel the thread of your argument slipping through your fingers. What *had* you said about love, exactly? You'd told Jeff you thought about Cherise every hour of every day. Is that love? Or is it more than love?

Jeff holds up his hands. "No worries," he says. "Your secret's safe with me." His eyes look closed, but there's the slightest glitter between his lids. "I don't know if I could have coached a team of girls. I wouldn't have known how to talk to them. But I tell you what—if she was my sister, I'd be after your ass. She have a brother?"

Your head flops from side to side. You feel hollowed out, like you're made of papier mache. "Don't know. I don't think so."

"Hm. You're probably okay then." Jeff clears his throat. "So it's late, even for us night owls. Time to settle up. Who wins? I think I do."

"Wins what?"

Jeff's grin warps into a leer. "Whose story is shittiest? Mine, right? Yours was an accident, right? You didn't 'push' anybody." His half-pinky mars his finger quotes. "But I set a bird on fire. I stomped on it. I made *choices*. All you did was panic. Anybody can freeze up. Even God, right?"

"But you had good intentions. You wanted to put the bird out of its misery. You did what you did out of kindness."

Jeff looks down at the table, then back at you. "Mostly," he says, "I wanted to torch a little bird. And that, my friend, makes me tonight's champion."

Champion. The word rises like smoke. Your eyes sting. You once told your team that running across a trestle was what champions did. And then one of them fell and died. You lost everything you had, moved as far away as you could—and the truth of it can't even win you a "shitty story" contest? You try to pour the rest of the beer into Jeff's glass, but he covers it. "Whoa," he chuckles. "Party's over." So you refill you own, and gulp the beer like you're trying to put out a fire in your heart. But your heart isn't on fire at all—it's a cold, hard stone, and the beer splashes over it and trickles down, down, into a terrible darkness.

"Okay," you say to your newest, closest friend, slitting your eyes to match his. "Okay, you're right. I *was* in love. I pushed the girl because she had something on me." You lift your glass like it's a trophy. You imagine cheers. "So *I* win, right?"

Knuckles

Lately, Rita only catches about half of what we're watching on television. She's busy on the sofa crocheting hats and has this idea that she's going to sell them online. So if we're watching a sitcom, say, she only hears the dialogue, but she misses the little side glances the characters give, the gimmicks and comic business, and then she says she didn't think the show, which I'm finding hilarious, is that funny. "Why don't you *watch* it, then," I ask, and she looks at me like I'm crazy, and then maybe takes a look at my drink to imply that my judgment is addled, because she thinks she's paying attention enough. TV is only worth half an effort, she'll say if we have the conversation, but really it's only her wedding dress shows and cooking programs that require half an effort. Comedy is hard, and it's sad Rita doesn't get that.

Watching and listening always require great attention, and even the most familiar things can be surprising. Like tonight, for instance, I'm watching *The Adventures of Robin Hood* on the classic movie station. I haven't seen it in decades, and guess what? The movie's in color! I had expected to see Errol Flynn and those merry men in black and white, but there's Robin Hood in brilliant green, and Will Scarlett as red as a cardinal. Then I realize that we didn't have a color television when I was a kid, and I tuck the thought of what else I might have missed away for later.

"White knuckling," Rita says. She's working on the hats, not taking in the movie at all.

"Shh," I say. "It's in color." I have to admit I'm drinking, just my usual TV beers, but if you take movies seriously, you'll know what I mean about the shush-ing.

"This is important," Rita says. "Tape it." She means "DVR it," but there's not much point in explaining. I don't even bother with telling her that breaking up the narrative flow is an insult to the director. Time is in the hands of the beholder, she thinks, and that's a big enough thought to yield to, so I do what she says. Lowest common denominator viewing is one of the secrets to an enduring marriage, and ours has lasted over thirty years.

Robin Hood and Little John have squared off on the log bridge, cudgels in hand, and so they remain. When I pause the movie so I can listen to what she wants to tell me, Rita glances at them, gives up trying to process what she sees after a second, and repeats herself. "White knuckling. That's what killed your father. That's what caused his heart attack. It was stress related. Because he was white knuckling. Dr. Oz talked about it this afternoon."

So I've got to guess which conversational thread we're picking up, although they probably all lead back to the same tangle. Mortality is a big one, and it's usually knotted up with my recreational drinking. "What's 'white knuckling'?" I ask.

"It's when someone's an alcoholic but fights it. That's what killed your dad—tension."

"Dad never had more than two drinks a day his whole life."

"Exactly! He was resisting. Wasn't his brother an alcoholic? It runs in families."

"Ralph? We never saw him." But it was what everybody said. He drank like a fish, according to my mother. "Dad made it to 75. His father was 74 when he died. The trend says I can expect at least 76. And you should blame your father."

"My father?"

"Your father's 84. He's over the average life expectancy. What's to say he didn't take a couple of those years from my dad?"

"That's just mean," Rita says. "You want my father dead? And you have more than two drinks a day."

"So then I'm not white knuckling, right?" I say. "No tension. I'm giving in to my urges. I'm relaxed." Then the telephone rings—it beeps the opening measures of "Fur Elyse." No matter what the tune, phone calls are an intrusion I can't tolerate. Why would anyone think they can barge in on my privacy any time they want? Didn't I retire as quickly as possible to get myself out of the public eye? Thirty-two years of teaching—my pension a carrot, a gift, and a prison sentence—the gold ring at the end of a ride I couldn't get off without risking my chance for peace. Rita understands what I gave and gave up, and hasn't seemed to mind working part time to supplement my pension. And she knows I never answer the phone, unless it's our daughter Bonnie, who can't believe we still have a landline.

"It's Jack," I say. I hate the calls, but I like the way the caller's name and number shows up on the TV screen—I know what I'm avoiding, not like in the old days when all phones sounded the same and rang and rang and rang. Seeing the caller's name on TV while I'm safe in my recliner gives me a warm, safe feeling, in the same family of emotions as the joy I felt when the name of the school district I taught in scrolled across the bottom of the screen on snow days.

Rita is up and to the phone, which is in the kitchen. She still moves lightly, my wife. Pilates and Zumba. She's encouraged me to join, but my weight doesn't fluctuate much, if I judge by the size of my slight belly. I've got twenty years left, by my reckoning, and I'm comfortable with my routine, even though no one ever tells me I look too young to be retired. I like the curve of my wife's neck, like a swan's. My daughter inherited it—when Bonnie got engaged, she talked half-seriously about tattooing her soon to be husband's name on her neck. "Sam" it would say, permanently, between her nape and collar. "My hair will cover it most of the time," she said. "Maybe you should be less specific," I said. "Maybe just put 'MEN.' Or, if you really want to be an object, why don't you get a bar code?" She never got the tattoo, but I'm sure my opinion didn't influence her decision.

"Jack!" Rita says. She puts the phone on "Conference," to keep from holding it close to her ear, even though no one has ever claimed that landlines will destroy your brain. Play it safe is her motto. She moves out of sight into the kitchen nook to sit at the table while she talks. I press "play" and Robin Hood falls off the log bridge into the stream, and the men of Sherwood Forest laugh merrily.

Jack works as a mental health counselor at a clinic in Brooklyn. We knew him in college, but lost touch until about a year ago. He'd been a suitemate and had moved to an off campus apartment with me and three other guys for senior year. We were friendly enough, but moved in different social spheres. He'd abandoned his political science major and law school ambitions to throw himself into the theatre program. He didn't drink and smoke pot like the rest of us, and was always impeccably groomed. But as put-together as he appeared, there was something provisional about him: too many "used to be's", "soon to be's" and "down the road's." For example, Jack was as imperially slim as Richard Cory, but we knew (because he told us, and because there was a softness to his edges) that he used to be fat, and that he'd be fat again. His hair was thinning already, which led to a new hair style every week. Before long, svelte, fashionable Jack would resemble the neighborhood butcher.

One Friday afternoon Jack found the rest of us celebrating the arrival of the weekend with bongs 'n booze in the living room. He didn't want a drink and waved off the bong. His cologne was so strong it cut through the stale stench of beer and the sweet haze of weed. One of the guys sniffed. "We smoking PCP?" We laughed, but we always felt a little uneasy with Jack, like we were waiting for something. And this time he obliged us. He took a seat on one of the wooden folding chairs we'd stolen from a campus party, sighed, and announced, "I'm having a relationship with Charles." It was no surprise. Charles was his TA for Advanced Acting. We'd met him. We sat quietly for a second before somebody said, "It's about time." That broke whatever tension there was, and Jack was relieved to laugh with the rest of us. Then Toby, a beefy guy who'd played freshman football, got up and moved toward Jack, I thought to give him a hug. He held out his hand, and when Jack took, it, Toby wrapped an arm around him. "Grab his other arm,"

Toby said, and somebody did. "Hey," Jack said, but he was giggling, and so were the rest of us. Two of us bent Jack over a couch while the other two picked up the tennis balls scattered around the room (although in my mind they were oranges, but why would there be oranges all over the floor?) and started whipping them at his ass. Jack wriggled like a puppy. "Guys," he pleaded, but he never stopped laughing. It was over in less than minute. Jack packed up and moved to his lover's apartment and we didn't see him again until graduation, where we exchanged high fives.

"Of course he's gay," Rita said that night as we lay on my mattress. "Why did you have to abuse him?" But I'd always been a little proud of the way we'd handled the news, and proud of Jack for having the balls to tell us the way he did. I always believed he trusted us completely as he absorbed the smack of each tennis ball (or orange) we whipped. Only years later did it come out that Rita thought we'd pelted him bare-assed. "It was still uncalled for," she said. But I wonder, is humiliation like cholesterol? Is there a good and a bad kind?

Jack was a safely stowed memory—until this Facebook thing. I don't play, but last year he "friended" Rita out of the blue. When I thought of Jack, which was rarely, I figured he'd become a lawyer (maybe theatrical law—he was a terrible actor), or, more likely, had died of AIDS. As unexpected as it was to hear from him at all, it was good to know he was alive. But the shocking news was that Jack had a family—a wife (female), two kids in college, one already out. He had beaten us to a grandchild! *I married Linda, my high school sweetheart,* he announced. He was indeed overweight, his picture revealed, and his shaved head was polished to a sheen.

And now Rita and Jack are buddies—they exchange emails, Facebook messages, and long phone calls every few weeks. I've talked to him a few times and mostly ask questions about his kids and listen to him tell me how lucky I am to be retired and ask how I plan to spend my time now. But Rita and I don't know and don't ask about the about-face in Jack's sexual preferences. Maybe it had to do with the World Trade Center somehow, like everything else. Maybe he made a promise to his dying mother, who was very religious.

"Isn't it hanging in the air when you talk to him?" I've asked Rita, "Because it is when I do."

"We've got other fish to fry," she tells me. Rita's in the mental health field, too, if I haven't mentioned.

Now I hear them chattering on the phone at the kitchen table, but I can't make out what they're saying. I pause the movie: the Merry Men are dropping from trees to steal the booty embezzled by the evil Prince John. I need another beer. The trick will be getting by them without Rita putting me on the phone. She thinks it's good for me to make contact with the outside world. "Jack's an old friend," she says.

"A delicate matter," I hear Jack buzz, and Rita says, "Yes, well," and shoots me a look with fortune teller eyes. I open the refrigerator. "There's often reluctance," Jack says, and then he breaks off, as if he senses Rita can't talk. She points to the phone and holds it toward me. I take a beer instead. "Just a second, Jack," she says, and thrusts the phone at me like she wants to skewer me with it. "Is that my buddy Robert," I hear. "Bob, is that you? Tell Bob I want to talk to him, Rita."

I pretend to cut my throat with my beer bottle as Rita keeps pushing the phone my way. Then I get the idea to pretend I'm juggling tennis balls, point to my mouth and the phone, but Rita doesn't get it. "Bob?" I hear. I grab an orange from the fruit bowl, bend over the counter and bounce the orange off my ass, put it back in the bowl and point again from my mouth to the phone. Rita gets it this time and stares me down. She figures I'm bluffing about bringing up Jack's reversal in "status," but I'm really on my fifth beer (since dinner, anyway), and what the hell, why not? I twist the cap off the bottle, aim a long swallow at Rita's frown, and take the phone.

"Jack, my good man," I say, "How the hell are you?"

"Remarkably well, sir, remarkable. What're you up to?"

"*Robin Hood, the Adventures of,* if you'd like it directory style, Herr director. Sword play, archery, and Merry Men." I lift an eyebrow at Rita. She shakes her head and glides into the den. I lean on the wall by the fridge.

"Un-hunh," Jack says.

"Yup," I say. "So— you've been having quite the chat with my wife. How's yours? And the kids. And grandkid."

"Fine, fine, everybody's great. Actually," he clears his throat, "I was telling Rita a story about somebody at work. Henry. And the mess Henry has gotten himself into. I'm worried about him. Henry."

"Mess?"

"Well, yes. He's fallen in love with a patient. The mother of a patient, actually."

"Is that so unusual?"

"The patient is a child," Jack says. "With nothing more serious than bedwetting issues. A simple matter of behavior modification. And there are medications. But Henry decided on the puppets."

"The puppets?"

"Yes, for a role playing exercise. Everybody wears a puppet— mother, child, and Henry. The puppets are supposed to talk about how they feel about the situation."

"Who's Henry playing?"

"That's just it—it there's no appropriate role for him to play in this scenario. There is a father, and Henry shouldn't be supplanting him."

I've moved to the doorway and lean against it. Rita is back at the sofa. She's got one of her hats on her lap, but she's just holding it. I hold my hand up like it's a puppet, but she thinks I'm saying that Jack is talking too much and taps at her ear, telling me to listen to him. I shrug.

"Okay," I say.

"So his puppet starts up with the mother's puppet. Rita, are you listening?"

"Rita went to bed, Jack." I smile at my wife who spreads her hands in exasperation. I walk back into the kitchen and hoist myself onto the counter. I bounce my heels against the lower cabinet. "What do you mean starts up?"

"Oh, well, tell her I said goodnight—I mean Henry started fondling her. I mean his puppet and her puppet. Rubbing and twining fingers—which would be the puppets' arms. Suggestive middle fingers on palms, intimate tugging. That's how Henry described it."

"Wow," I say. It did sound crazy. "What kind of puppets? Animals?"

"I think so. Some generic animals. I haven't used them in a long time."

"And in front of the kid?"

"Yes! There for bedwetting advice, and this is the vision that's going to stain his dreams for the rest of his life. But now Henry and the mother are actually involved. He's out of control."

"Sounds like it."

"The truth is," Jack says after a pause, "there's substance abuse at the root of it. I mean, Henry's drinking. Pretty heavily."

"After or before this whole mess? Is it a chicken or the egg thing?"

"No, before," Jack says. "This latest is a symptom, really. He's cut people off, too. Withdrawn."

"Un-hunh, But not from puppets."

"No, not from puppets—alcoholism runs in his family, Bob."

"So I'm given to understand." I'm not liking the direction the conversation has turned. I wriggle off the counter and stick my head into the den, but Rita's left the room.

"Frankly, I think there's been a problem for years, but he'd been white knuckling."

"White knuckling, you say."

"Mm. Resisting and resisting until finally, for one reason or another, he reached his breaking point."

"Maybe he just gave in to it," I say, and I want to kick myself, because Jack jumps in with extra vigor.

"Yes, maybe so, that's a good observation, very sensitive. But I wonder if he's aware of how much damage he's doing to those around him. He's got loved ones. Kids from his first marriage. Parents. He may have irrevocably damaged his relationship with his ex. His family should come first, don't you think?"

I've wandered into my den, plop into recliner and lay back. But my beer's empty. I hoist the bottle overhead and tip it to my eye. A drop wets my lid. "Pity," I say. The TV's muted, but there's quite a sword fight going on between Robin and the Sheriff of Nottingham—stairs, chandeliers—rapiers pointed at head and heart. How could I not have known this was in color?

"Listen," I say, "Listen, Henry."

"Jack."

"Right, un-hunh. Listen, Jack, there's something I've been wanting to talk about. I've been needing to talk about it for a while now . . . and you're the only one who can help with this."

"Yes?" He's eager. "Whatever I can do for you, Jack. Anything you need."

"I'm eating an orange now. Navel. From California. The peel is thick, but it comes off easily." Jack had disappointed me—twice. First of all, I thought he'd been satisfied with being a memory. Did I need to hear from him again after all these decades? Now that my career lies behind me like a sunken ship. Which leads me to the second disappointment—

"Un-hunh." He can hardly contain himself. "But what was it you wanted to ask?"

"I think of you when I eat oranges," I say.

"Yeeaah—" Jack draws out the word; now *he's* the one trying to figure out where *I'm* going. The second disappointment? I thought we had a tacit understanding, Jack and I: I don't bring up the "change" in his status, and he leaves me alone. No sparring. Allow things to remain unsaid. Thirty years I spent in the classroom, probably a million words spoken on the job, and not a single honest one shared about the passion—the love and the hate—that passed across my desk every day. Every day. Unspoken. That's the sunken treasure I've left behind. I don't know if I'm jealous of this Henry or pissed off at his lack of restraint. But I know I'm pissed at Jack for bringing him up.

"Back in college," I say, "what were they, oranges or tennis balls? I'm thinking the latter, but I keep seeing the former in my mind's eye."

"Excuse me?"

So you teach literature, you teach kids, and you let your love and your hate leak out. It's your puppet. And when you finally take it off after decades, there's nothing and no one left to love. The end of love, even if it's silent, leaves you broken. Is that what Jack wants to know? And Rita? White knuckling? Have a drink. Watch a movie. With full attention.

"Oranges or tennis balls?" I ask.

The phone is quiet for a while. I notice that it weighs about the same as my beer bottle, and I pretend to juggle them, but I'm really just moving them up and down, like a kid would do. Will Jack be rising or falling when he finally speaks? Doppler effect! But he waits me out, and when I hear his voice I'm holding the phone in front of my face like it's a mirror. A second before he speaks it occurs to me for the first time that maybe we went overboard when we held him down that afternoon.

"Oranges," he says.

"Really," I say. "Well, I thank you for that. I've been thinking maybe I imagined them all these years. Listen—I'm in the middle of a movie here—" Robin Hood kisses Maid Marion. She's beautiful enough to love. Deep within

Sherwood Forest, the Merry Men feast. Jack and I exchange good nights.

Maybe I crossed a line thirty years ago. Maybe Jack and I just crossed a few on the phone. What I know is that I'm on my own high wire, and crossing the lines of others is dangerous. So I don't know how much of this conversation I'll share with Rita, who sees herself as a trapeze artist, free to sail through the air wherever she wants. Let her fly, as long as she doesn't bump me off my wire. Mine is a single ring circus. I need to stay steady, keep my feet in one place, and avoid looking forward or backward. When I weigh the pros and cons of one last beer, I don't want to think too much and find out I've already fallen and missed the net.

Beast Music

When we were kids on the cusp of ten, I took it for granted that I would marry my cousin Lexi. Our parents—her father, my mother—were brother and sister. Lexi lived practically around the block, and our families spent most weekends together. But, because I was in love, I never quite lost my shyness with her. On our last night together, after we left our parents to their drinks and gossip, ran up to my room, and shut the door, Lexi gave me a look that cut my heart like a razor.

"I heard that cousins who get married are doomed to have monsters for children," she said. I winced, feeling queasy. *Doomed?* What did I know about taboos? Then she asked for my crayons. "We need to draw pictures of monster children."

The beast babies I drew were heavy-headed and thick-limbed, fanged and clawed— imitations of the creatures from "Where the Wild Things Are." Lexi drew a pair of adults—a man with a mustache and a woman with a curvy figure and a pile of red hair. Both grownups had Xs for eyes, because, she said, "Monster babies are born old and have dead eyes."

*****

The first night we sleep together, Talia tells me that the theme connecting her tattoos is that she's a gopher tortoise burrow: her body art depicts the creatures dependent on that habitat.

"So you're not the tortoise—you're its home?" I ask.

"Right," she says. She's over six feet tall and rail thin, long and naked on the bed. Her tats mottle her white flesh. "And also the home to three-hundred-sixty other species. They're called 'obligates.' They need me." She looks smug, or proud, or maybe committed.

"But a burrow is air—it's space."

"I'm solid space. I get a new tattoo each month. I've

got over a hundred already.

In another twenty years, I'll have them all."

I grip her ankle, right over the rattlesnake twined around it, while she rambles on about how tortoises and their burrows are protected in Florida. "Lots of other states, too." Talia's breasts are small, boyish. A line of tattooed ants spiral down from her nipple. Under her right breast a worm dangles from a baby bird's beak. My own nipples are like tree stumps hidden in a thicket of chest hair.

*****

Lexi and I worked on our monster-baby pictures. "We're moving," she announced without warning.

At first I thought she was starting a new game— maybe the room was a spaceship, and we were flying our monster brood to another planet. But then she clarified:

"We're moving to Wisconsin. Dad is getting a better job. They're going to tell your parents tonight."

The floor disappeared beneath me, and I was falling. Beast babies, okay, but *leaving*? Neither of us spoke. Our parents' merriment downstairs leaked under the door like a muffled laugh-track. Had the telling happened yet?

*****

Spying on Talia while she leads Book Babies for toddlers at the public library has become a regular thing for me since we've become a serious couple. I watch her through the glass-paneled wall that separates the activity room from the rest of the children's section. While I sneak to a tiny chair at a miniature table in a hidden corner, I listen to her control babies, moms and nannies with a song. At work, whatever the outside weather, she smothers herself in leggings and a long-sleeved turtle neck shirt: the library director says Talia's tattoos might spook the children, though it's probably their parents that concern her. Talia's latest tattoo, the only one that isn't a critter, is my name in minuscule gothic script across her heel: "Sinclair."

Talia is singing about hugs and the arms that give them: *Open them, shut them, open them, shut them, give a little clap.* She has a Masters in library science, but wants to be a singer. She's posted some of her original work on the internet. Her songs are kind of "goth-punk-folk." I'm a DJ, and Talia's music is not the type of thing I get requests for at bar mitzvahs and wedding receptions.

*****

Lexi and I drew in silence. If I didn't mention the news about her moving, if nobody did, maybe it would never happen. But then I had an idea:

"Maybe we could have a secret life. After you leave. We'd grow up and have our own real lives with our own families, but maybe, just between us, we could make up another one. We'd have a made up house and made up kids and made up jobs. We could take turns adding details: vacations, holidays, pets. We could invent kids and give them names like Doug and Sarah. A whole secret story of our own." My voice cracked as I grew more and more excited about my plan. I didn't lift my eyes from my beasts. I was finishing their horns and blushing so hard my cheeks felt like bags of hot soup. "We could do it forever," I mumbled. "Even if we can't see each other much."

"Pretend we had a fake life?" I looked up to see Lexi wrinkling her nose, like she smelled something rotten. "Forever? While we had our own families?" She shook her head. "That's dumb."

I bit my lip. Tears welled. Then Lexi told me to take my shirt off.

*****

I take Talia to a club downtown where I sometimes work. It's open mike night, and she wants to try out a couple of her goth-punk folksongs. But the recorder full of her backup music doesn't work, and when she tries to sing without accompaniment, she gets through only a couple of verses before some kind of fight breaks out on the street. There's shouting and breaking glass and sirens. Nobody's listening to Talia, and eventually she just gives up.

"Not my night," she says with a wry smile and moist eyes as she rejoins me at our table.

When the streets clear, we head back to her place, where I spend most of my nights. Talia curls up on her sofa. We drink wine from mugs until she drags herself to bed. I stay up with my laptop and surf the web. I drift around, searching out the names of ghosts from my past. I google Lexi for maybe the thousandth time; the search-engine cupboard has always been bare, except for a mention of her Wisconsin high school volleyball team and a church club field trip to Beloit. But tonight Lexi materializes on Facebook, and the sight of her name sets my head spinning.

Lexi either lacks the skill or hasn't had the time to do much with her profile. Her cover picture is of a starving polar bear on an ice floe. Personal photos or other information isn't available unless I "friend" her. Her only post, "liked" by her handful of friends, displays a ring and an announcement of the time and place of her wedding. "Finally!" she's written, followed by a smiley face. The wedding is in a month at a venue less than an hour away. How long has she been back in the area?

I slide the trembling cursor onto the "Friend" invitation, but I don't click. I wonder if my cousin has searched for me. I'm not hard to find.

"Sinclair—" It's Talia from the bedroom, half-awake, half-drunk. She calls me in, and I shut down my laptop. Talia wants to sing to me, and I listen to her croak her lyrics through her tears.

*****

When our parents opened my bedroom door, they found me stretched out on my back on my carpet, my arms lifted in the air as if I was being robbed. Lexi lay on her belly. Her chin dug into my ribs as she kissed my nipple. I stared at the line of scalp where her hair was parted. My mother shouted my name, and I banged my head on the floor so hard I saw stars.

*****

While I soothe Talia, I'm aching to get back to Lexi's profile. But Talia falls asleep spooned against me, my arm stuck under her, my fingers numbing. The sheet she's wrapped in hides her tattoos: she could be anybody. Drifting off, I lose all feeling in my arm, and I imagine I'm fading away, limb by limb. What if Lexi has forgotten me? What if we become a little less real each time we fall from someone's memory?

I wake before Talia, who's rolled off my arm and slipped out from under her sheet. Her spotted skin looks like blue cheese. The room stinks of hangover and disappointment.

But Lexi's profile is waiting, and I creep out of bed, eager to get to my laptop. There's a problem when I log in—everything is gibberish, impossible to follow. Somehow, I must have triggered an automatic translator, and I'm looking at Croatian or phonetic Chinese—nothing makes sense. I restart the computer and step into the kitchen to make coffee. On my way to get milk, I glance at the refrigerator message board, thinking to write something to cheer up Talia: maybe a line from one of her songs to show I'm a good listener. What had she sung to me in bed last night? *I'm hungry, a baby beast suckling up a feast./ Forgive my fancy fangs—I'm wearing them for you.* Perfect for a refrigerator note board.

But as I start the message, I freeze. I waggle the marker, not sure what to do with it. *Baby beast*, I think, waiting for reflex to kick in. *Baby beast*, I mutter under my breath, but I haven't any idea how to begin. I know that words are made of letters, but which letters do I need? I shake my head. How much wine had I drunk last night?

I hurry back to my computer. Every picture has a jumbled caption. Icons have inscrutable labels. I click and scroll, click and scroll, and soon I'm lost. On the table in front of me is a paperback with Jonathan Franzen's picture on the back cover. "I'm having a hard time getting into this," Talia had complained last night. I flip the book over. What's the title? *What is the title?*

I can't read—I've lost the ability. I'm soaked in panic-sweat by the time Talia appears in the bedroom doorway, wearing one of my T-shirts and nothing else. I've flipped through a hundred pages of books and magazines, clicked my way to a frozen laptop screen, and I've understood nothing. The "Cheerios" box is labeled with hieroglyphics.

Talia yawns and rubs mascara-ringed eyes. The tattoos on her arms and legs stand out like bruises.

"I'm a flop," she says.

"You're not," I say. I clear my throat. "You just had bad luck. You're a star."
My words lack conviction, and Talia notices. Should I tell her what's happened to me overnight? But as sick with worry and confusion as I am over my condition, my thoughts keep turning to Lexi. And a secret life. Though I haven't been able to return to Facebook, I slap my laptop shut as if I've got something to hide. Talia frowns.

"What are you doing? Looking at porn? Already? On a Sunday morning? Let me see—"

I lean over my laptop protectively. "Talia," I start. I don't tell her I can't read. The wrong confession spills out: "I'm cheating on you," I say. "It's been going on forever."

*****

Lexi sliced a last glance my way as her parents yanked her through my bedroom door. My mother's grip tightened on my arm like a blood pressure cuff. Everything ended between our families that night. We never spoke about Lexi or her parents—it was easier to pretend the family never existed. On what basis had the adults parceled out the blame? What conversations had I not been privy to? For years, whenever there was a long silence at dinner, I'd feel my parents' eyes melting over me and I'd duck my head, waiting for questions I should have known they'd never ask. If there had been more than the sins of two kids that caused the breech, no one was talking.

My father died from cancer when I was in college. I stood by my mother near his casket at the funeral home. I shook hands and accepted condolences, but my focus shifted between Dad's rouged face and the parlor door. Finally, my mother leaned to me and whispered, "They won't come. She won't be here."

*****

The doctors refer to my condition as "acquired alexia." They say if I'm lucky other parts of the brain will compensate for what I've lost. How? What do I look for? I picture myself with thought bubbles over my head, like in comic strips, but the bubbles are full of nothing that makes sense. Shouldn't my illiteracy at least *hurt*?

For someone who can't read, a library is a house of horrors, but I need to talk to Talia, and she can't ignore me here without causing a scene. I loiter in the area outside the children's section. I hear Talia singing inside. She's leading "Old MacDonald." A late-arriving mom guides her toddler toward my ex's voice, but the little boy veers off to the fish tank near the entrance. The child squashes his face against the glass and slaps it with both hands. Blue and white fish scatter, settle, and resume cruising.

"Gentle," his mother cautions. Her son jerks his hands back as if the tank is electrified, but his eyes stay riveted to the fish.

"Arf-arf," he squeaks.

"'Arf-arf,' is doggies, Elton. Fish are 'bubble-bubble.'"

"Arf-arf!"

Elton's mother takes his hand and pivots him from the tank. He blinks, still seeing fish. His mom catches me looking, and I glance away. She scoops up her son and hurries toward "moo-moo here and moo-moo there." The boy makes bug-eyes at me over her shoulder, and I swear I can see fish swimming around in his head. I wonder if he "arf-arfed" not because he was unsuccessfully mimicking a fish, but because he was pretending to be a dog. Maybe he thinks he *is* a dog.

Talia and her crowd oink for old MacDonald's pigs as I make my way to the tiny furniture in my corner. The mothers and nannies on Talia's carpet hold their babies on their laps and gaze up at the singing librarian, their faces like flowers following the sun. I squint, imagining how the clothes Talia is wrapped in would wriggle if her tattoos came to life. Hadn't her creatures crawled from her flesh to mine when we held hands or made love? The little table and chair make me feel gigantic. I spread out some picture books of trucks and trains and pretend to read them. On the wall behind me is a poster of Sendak's "Wild Things." The fur-covered beasts are looking at books. I feel the breath of the monsters on my neck while I prepare to win Talia back. I need her. My mother's been driving me everywhere lately, but I couldn't possibly tell Mom I need to get to Lexi's wedding.

"You can't *read*?" Talia whispers. She sits across from me on a little chair, her legs folded like a grasshopper's. She wears a fake smile as she glances around to make sure we're not overheard. A scorpion creeps out of her collar onto her throat. Centipedes leak from her cuffs and race over her fingers. "And you made up that cheating stuff? That was all invention? Because you 'panicked'? Why should I believe you?"

"I *did* panic," I hiss. Out of the corner of my eye I see Elton waddling out of the children's section, heading for the fish tank, his mom in pursuit. "I wanted to protect you. Finding out you can't read is traumatic. I couldn't think straight. I thought you'd be better off without me. I swear, I never cheated."

It's easy to convince someone who wants to believe you. Talia purses her lips and searches my eyes, then asks if maybe my condition is psychosomatic.

"The MRIs showed there are lesions in my brain," I answer. She wants to know the names of my doctors, and I tell her. What I don't tell her is that when the doctors mentioned lesions in "places of interest," I had an epiphany: the lesions are the scar tissue of the secret life I once hoped to live with Lexi. That life is growing on its own. No doubt monster children I don't even know clog my brain; they've already gobbled up my ability to read. Who knows what I might lose next.

"Old rhythms," I say. "The doctors told me I need to get back to old rhythms."

"I'm an old rhythm?"

"They meant routines, like work: I can't DJ with my condition, but I should seek out familiar environments, like bar mitzvahs—and weddings— where I had to understand print." The time and place of Lexi's wedding are fixed in my brain—the last things I'd been able to read.

"I got a call from a venue," I lie. "They needed a substitute DJ. I told them I couldn't do it, but maybe I should go anyway, just to watch the ceremony. The event manager told me the date. It would be healthy, right? But I can't drive. You want to be my date?"

*****

Talia and I find aisle seats in a middle row of the wedding hall's chapel. I'm not worried about being recognized—it's been almost twenty years since I've seen Lexi or her folks, and I'm wearing a full beard. Besides, Talia has commanded the attention of all the guests. In her spiked heels, she towers over all of us. Her blond hair is woven into a crown, and she's squeezed into a sleeveless black dress that stops at mid-thigh. Her tattooed arms and legs gleam like Chinese porcelain. The looks she draws rattle off her like hail.

But it's rain, not hail, that drums on the roof and runs in sheets down the chapel's long windows, blurring what would have been a lovely view of undulating pastures and distant hills. I slap my palm nervously with a rolled program, and for a moment I lose track of why I'm in this particular place at this specific moment.

"It's too bad about the weather," Talia whispers. She smells like honeysuckle. "It's good luck, though, isn't it?"

I raise an eyebrow—I don't know much about luck. There'll be no live music at this ceremony—I've spotted the DJ, no one I know, in a back corner. To cover the drone of the rain, he turns up the volume of the harp recording so high that the notes sound like jangling nerves. There's movement at the front of the chapel—an officiant in a black robe emerges, followed by two men in tuxedos, obviously the groom and best man. I can't make out their faces.

The DJ punches in the processional staple, "Pachelbel's Canon." Heads swivel in unison to the back doors. Talia's arm glides over mine like an eel.

"Your hand is sweaty," she murmurs.

A solid young woman in a lavender gown bursts like a bowling ball through the double doors and rolls up the aisle. Wearing a wreath and a gaping smile, she creates a breeze as she hurries past our row. In her wake a tiny girl appears. She's dressed in pink from head to toe and spikes fistfuls of crushed rose petals on the red carpet with each step. By the time she reaches our row, I'm short of breath— the flower girl is a miniature version of the cousin I've come to witness. She's got the brown hair and sly look I remember—though when she stops at my row I see that one of her eyes is covered by a patch with a daisy drawn on it. The child blinks her good eye at me, and I think, *Lexi?*

As if answering my thought, the child sets down her flower basket and spins to the open chapel doors, where two figures wait: a bride in white and her dark-suited escort, an old man braced on metal crutches. I strain to deconstruct the bride—is that really my cousin?

There's a brilliant flash, an explosion of thunder, and a collective gasp. The overhead lights spasm and fail. Light fades; sound, too, except for the pummeling rain. The child sobs, and there's a bleat from the chapel doors. Where are the professionals? The event manager needs to find an emergency generator. And the DJ, instead of fluttering over his dead equipment, should be making a joke.

A stab of pain—as Talia pushes past, she accidentally drives her heel into my foot. She kneels in the aisle before the flower girl and whispers something I can't hear. The little girl rests her head on my date's dappled shoulder. Talia hoists the child, steps back into our row, and sidles back to her seat. The flower girl's chiffon dress brushes my jaw.

All the guests are standing, listening to the rain as if it exposes their private histories. Then Talia begins to sing: she picks up the processional, the "Pachelbel," and her voice fills the chapel. My nape hair tingles. She closes her eyes; her mouth is a dark oval. The flower girl tucks her head under Talia's chin. I notice a pink hearing aid wedged into the child's ear.

I watch Talia's lips as she sings. The sound engulfs me like a warm ocean current. But just as I begin to believe that receiving Talia's voice may be the sole reason I stand in this chapel, I feel a shift. Talia's "Pachelbel" has released the bride—she's advancing.

Is this bride who floats to my row and pauses really Lexi? Is her crippled escort my uncle? She's drenched in white: her dress and its puddling train; the gloves that reach above her elbows; the veil covering her face. She turns to me, and I look down, busying myself with the program I can't read.

Talia sings. I peek at the bride. Her veil is a blank page. My own face feels compressed, and my vision is fuzzy, as if I've pulled a stocking over my head to disguise myself. Then I realize that this bride isn't looking at me. She's looking *through* me. Relieved, I lean back, out of the way.

"Sarah," the bride calls to the child in Talia's arms. The little girl squirms, then offers a flower petal wink.

Talia has never stopped singing, and now opens her eyes slowly as if she's waking from a dream. As she jostles the flower girl, a single note wavers. Then she faces the bride and nods to reassure her—the little girl is fine. Talia nods again, directing the bride to the front of the chapel where her groom awaits.

I look back and forth between the women. The flower girl nibbles on Talia's shoulder. The bride hesitates, then sets her empty face forward and glides off, her escort a clumping shadow.

As Talia watches the ghost-bride fade away, she offers each note of "Pachelbel" as if it's a bite of the last apple from an enchanted tree. She rocks the child, looks at me, and lowers her lids. The processional swells; finally, I hear—I feel— what Talia has been singing in her heart from the beginning: *I'm hungry, a baby beast suckling up a feast. / Forgive my fancy fangs. I'm wearing them for you.*

She is solid space. I accept my place among her obligates. Will she carry me to the reception? Will we dare to perform?

Dirt

She wrapped it up; and for its tomb did choose
A garden pot, wherein she laid it by,
And covered it with mould, and o'er it set
Sweet basil, which her tears kept ever wet.
　　　　　　—John Keats, "Isabella; or The Pot of Basil

There's a video I haven't seen in years. In it I'm an infant held in the crook of my father's arm.

"Not 'Larry.' Never 'Laaary,'" my father says to the camera. "That's a 'Three Stooges' name—we might as well call him 'Curly' or 'Moe.' It will be 'Lawrence.' Maybe 'Law' if a nickname is absolutely necessary."

"'Lore'?" my mother, the videographer, asks.

"'Lawww'" my father enunciates. "Like 'flaw,' not like 'adore.'

*****

We've been trudging through the museum for hours, my seven-year-old self and my father, and my legs ache. The figures in the paintings we pass look like prisoners in an endless cellblock. My father stops and reads aloud from the labels beside random pictures. I pay little attention as his words rise to the high ceilings. "You're so lucky to have a father who knows so much," he says.

In a small gallery my father pauses in front of a painting I ignore because I'm gazing longingly over my shoulder at the bench behind us.

"Isabella and Her Pot of Basil," he reads. "Basil—that's a kind of spice one could grow in a kitchen garden. Let's see, let's see—oh my, yes, this is a familiar story. It's a love story. Look here, Lawrence, up at the canvas. Notice the woman standing—doesn't she look like she's floating? And you see the earthen pot she's reaching for on the shelf ? That's her pot of basil. But guess what's really in the pot.

Guess what she's watering with her tears. It's from an old story that Boccaccio recorded. Keats wrote a poem about it, too. Guess what's in the pot, Lawrence." My father nudges me with his hip each time he says "Guess."

Keats? Boccaccio? I look at the lady in the tall painting. Her face is pale. She's probably been standing a long time, like me. I don't see any tears, and they'd have to fly upward to water the pot she touches with a limp finger. Love story? Love doesn't look like this on Valentines.

"Dirt?" I try. "Is she watering the dirt?"

"Ha! Well, yes, I suppose, but guess what's hidden in the dirt—her boyfriend's head! Isabella's brothers murdered him, and she dug up the body, cut off the head, and buried it in the pot. She spends her days watering it with her tears."

I stifle my gasp and stare at the ceramic pot in the painting. There's a head in there? What if my own head were buried? Everything dims. My father grips my shoulder, and I look up at him, but he's gazing at the pot. He peeks at the museum label.

"Now that I think about it," he says, "there are many versions of this painting. Isabel and her lover—her boyfriend—have been a favorite theme for melancholy romantics for centuries."

Melancholy romantics. The phrase drifts by me in a bubble. I swallow a sob. If I saw this painting without knowing the story, would I *feel* the head in the pot like I do now? How had Isabella severed the head with such a slender arm? A knife? A saw? How did she hack through the neck bones? And where is the body? Doesn't she love her *whole* boyfriend? Isn't the rest of him as important as his head? My breaths come in heaves my father mistakes for laughter.

"It's not *that* funny," he says. "But guess what the lover's—the boyfriend's—name is. It's *Lorenzo*! That's your name, in Italian. 'Lorenzo' is 'Lawrence.'"

My eyes are squeezed shut, but I hear my vomit splash on the gallery's polished floor. Dad groans something and backs me to the bench. A sour stench stings my nostrils.

"Help," my father calls toward the gallery entrance where he must see a guard. "Can we have a little help over here?"

*****

"Lore, baby," Meredith purrs, "I've got to show my face at a workshop—'Peri-Implantitis—the Ailing, Failing Patient,' I think. When I get back, maybe we'll go exploring. Why don't you go down to the fitness center? Or you could sneak into one of the workshops for hygienists—there's one called 'Adventures in Planing and Scaling.' You'd cause quite a stir."

I'm sitting naked on the edge of the king-sized bed in our room at the Billings Hotel and Conference Center, watching local Montana news on mute. Meredith snakes her tan arms around me from behind. Her breasts press into my back. As if she's reading Braille, she fingers the ridges of my six-pack abs. She's left her rings on. At work at Coburn and Coburn Family Dental she locks them in the top drawer of the desk in the consulting office she shares with her husband. The ring with the big diamond once left a gouge on my back.

It took me three years to get the hygienist license I could have earned in two if I didn't spend so much time in the gym. I love and need my muscles and work them generously, as if my body is a visitor I'm trying to impress. My face is good, too, but maintaining my head takes a different kind of hard work. After sex or a workout, all my body requires is a shower and clothes. But teeth attract seeds, ears fill with wax, and eyes crust over at night. Wherever I go, I carry a little plastic pouch with floss, Q-tips, and a portable eye wash cup.

I've got a thing about waking up next to a woman with my eyes gummed shut like a defenseless newborn bunny. That's why an affair with a married woman like Meredith is perfect—no overnights. After our dalliances, she needs to get home to her husband Walter—my other boss—and I can take care of my personal grooming in private. But now Meredith has snuck me from Boston to Billings for this three-day conference for female dental practitioners—*Scrubs and Stilettos*, it's called. I can already see I'm going to have trouble keeping my head clean over the long weekend.

Meredith rests the point of her chin on my shoulder. The TV blocks the mirror so we can only see our heads. Meredith's hair is as black and smooth as a raven's wing. My attention jumps from our faces (I flash Meredith a grin and check out my teeth) to a commercial for a guns and ammo shop. Meredith's hands glide up from my belly, caress my chest, then clasp my biceps, which I pump up for her. She lets me go, disappearing from the mirror as she leaves the bed. She passes between me and the television on her way to the bathroom. I reach for her hip, but she's already past.

"Go to the gym," she calls. "Get sweaty. Tempt the women. Later, they'll find out who you belong to."

I bare my teeth again at my reflection, run a pinky into my ear, tilt my head back and flare my nostrils, which makes me sneeze.

"Bless you. I hope you're not getting sick, Lore." Meredith raises her voice over the water she's running in the sink. "If we both have colds when we get back to Boston, Walter might have to close the office. You know, I met him at a conference. He was facilitating a workshop. I stayed after to ask questions, and that led to drinks, and, well, the rest. He was much better looking then, not so soft around the middle, and I was barely out of dental school. And he could still get it up—no ED issues yet. He told me he was married, but on the verge of separating. 'Verge,' that's a beautiful word, isn't it? Turns out Allison—his ex—didn't know about verges. Did you know the practice is mine? Technically, Walter works for me, and I pay him peanuts—his salary is less than yours—because his wife gets half. Twelve years, and she hasn't remarried. She's a bitter and childless old woman."

The shower bursts into a hiss. Meredith doesn't usually allude to age—hers is squarely in between mine and her husband's. Walter—Dr. Coburn—has been my dentist since I was in middle school—before Coburn Family Dentistry became Coburn and Coburn. In my early teens it was Lolly, the busty hygienist, who made me thankful for the bib that covered my crotch during cleanings.

During my years as first a patient, then an employee, of Coburn and Coburn, I rarely saw Meredith without her baggy scrubs, plastic hair-cover, and mask. Then, one evening, she showed up at my gym, taut and leggy in her yoga pants and tank top. She was thrilled to see me, and that very first session she invited me out for a post-workout drink. Her second session, she invited herself to my apartment.

Meredith finishes her shower and opens the bathroom door wide to let the steam out. "Walter used to rub his cock with numbing gel he took from the office, back when he was still interested in sex," she says. "He said he'd last forever, which he obviously didn't."

Walter likes me. He claims to have noticed an increase in female patients since I joined the staff. "You must really tickle their ivories," he's said, winking with both eyes behind his thick glasses. Once, when I was on top of his wife, she spread my fingers in front of her face as if they were a Chinese fan. "Long and strong, like a piano player's," she said.

Meredith emerges from the bathroom wearing a white robe branded with a Billings Hotel and Conference Center logo. She sits beside me on the bed, smelling of shampoo, and holds out a towel.

"Dry my hair," she says.

I take the towel, cover her head, and rub. She probably finds it sexy, but to me it feels like work. On TV the weather map shows a block of territory that's so unfamiliar it looks fake.

"Why did your parents name you Lorenzo?" she asks out of the blue. "It's unusual."

"Long story." She doesn't know that my first name is really Lawrence.

"Like you're named after somebody who saved your father's life in, what, the first Gulf War?"

"Something like that." Her voice sounds weird coming out from under the towel— disembodied. Suddenly I feel as if I'm rubbing a detached object, like a football or coconut. I find her neck and tighten my fingers around it, just to make sure her head is connected to her body.

"Lore!" she protests.

"Sorry." My hands slide to her shoulders. "I'm a lousy masseuse."

*****

The fitness center in the Billings Hotel and Conference Center smells new. Except for me, it's filled with women—female dentists and hygienists toning up for post-workshop socializing. They straddle exercise bikes, hike on ellipticals, jog on treadmills, fold and stretch themselves on mats and over fitness balls. I monopolize the weight bench and the rack of dumbbells. None of the women comes near.

But they watch me in the mirrored walls as I make my way through my maintenance routine. Though they avoid catching my eye, their gazes melt over me like hot chocolate. Some of these women, the younger ones—probably the hygienists—are as fit as my boss, but I focus on my own reflection as I rip and rep. Billings is a long way from Boston—Meredith knows that none of her colleagues from back east would bother with a second tier conference way out here, so we're safely anonymous.

I left my iPod in our room, and there's no music to jazz up the atmosphere. The noise of the machines in the weakly lit room is unsettling. It's like I'm in an old textile mill full of exhausted female workers. Next to my reflection in the mirror across the way, a woman in a white track suit humps a red exercise ball. When she stands and lifts the ball to her side, it looks like a red globe rests on my shoulders instead of my head. Motion in the room seems to stop. It's museum quiet. I lower my dumbbell to the floor and stare at the ball, searching for my face. All I can hear is my pounding heart.

"Lorenzo—" someone calls. Again. And a third time, urgently. Why doesn't he answer, if he's here?

A hand on my shoulder startles me, and the room comes back to life. I'm gaping up at Meredith, who's appraising me with arched brows as if I'm an abstract painting. She's wearing black jeans and a tight sweater. Her spiked heels—a *Scrubs and Stilettos* statement— sink into the mat.

"Lore," she smirks. "I thought we lost you. Get yourself showered. It's a beautiful afternoon. We're going for a drive."

*****

"Everything looks so close on a map," Meredith grumbles as we shuffle through pamphlets in the hotel lounge. But the Badlands are a day's drive east, and Mount Rushmore is almost as far. Meredith picks Yellowstone National Park, which looks to be only about three hours from our hotel.

"We drive there, catch the sunset, and get back here at a reasonable hour," she says.

"What's at Yellowstone besides a setting sun?"

"'Old Faithful'—the geyser? Hot springs. Bears and moose, I guess, and buffalo herds. Wolves. The park is thousands of square miles. We're not going to have time to see much. At least we'll be able to say we were there."

"Who will I be able to say that to besides you?"

Meredith rolls her eyes, then glances around the lobby to see if we're being noticed.

*****

"Tired from your workout? From the flight?" Meredith asks from behind the wheel of our rental car. We've been on the road for half an hour, and she's right, I haven't said much since we left the hotel. I'm not good at small talk, and this isn't like our flight, where I could plug in my iPod and zone out. Car trip etiquette requires chatting.

"The flight, I guess—I couldn't get comfortable." My father was never at a loss for words until he had a stroke a few years back—not long after my mother passed away from breast cancer. He's wheelchair bound now. This trip with Meredith will keep me from my weekly visit to his nursing home. He gets speech therapy, but the only word he can say is my name, which comes out as "Low."

I twist open a flat pint bottle of peach brandy. I bought it at the Billings liquor store next to the convenient mart where Meredith tried to buy bread and cheese for our picnic. Instead, she wound up with a bag of potato chips and a couple of water bottles.

"They didn't have French bread," she said, with a sidelong glance at my brandy.

I tipped the bottle at her. "Makes me feel like a cowboy." Meredith doesn't drink. I try to treat my body as a temple, but sometimes I forget.

We cruise down the empty highway through a prairie that's flatter and broader than anywhere back east. The late autumn sun flashes from Meredith's dark glasses. Her forehead and cheeks match the brown of the terrain. I can't tell if she's smiling or frowning. She holds the wheel with just her left hand—the big diamond on her ring points our way.

I sip the brandy. It's super sweet, but warms my head, which I rest on the cool window. What's the outside temperature? I can't recall any of the digits I saw on the weather map back in the hotel room. Mountains loom in the distance—how far away they are depends on their size, which I can't begin to estimate. Closer things rush by—road signs, boulders, clumps of scrawny trees— but the car seems like it's stuck, even though the speedometer reads 80. Meredith has stopped trying to get me to talk. Her lengthy silence suggests I'm failing some kind of test.

"Sleep is funny," I offer hoarsely and clear my throat. "Our bodies shut down, but we still dream. Something cuts the connection between head and body. What if we tried to *do* everything we dream?"

Meredith's lips pinch. "Sleepwalkers?" she asks without taking her eyes from the road.

"That's the body acting on its own. Like a chicken with its head cut off. I'm pretty sure if you wake a sleepwalker he wouldn't know what he was dreaming."

"You wake up when you have to piss. That's something your body tells your brain when you're asleep." My ears might be clogged, or else Meredith is whispering. I left my Q-tips at the hotel. I wouldn't use them in front of her anyway. Meredith glances at me. "Do you have to piss? Should I pull over?"

"I'm good—maybe at Yellowstone. Old Faithful will inspire me. I'll piss into the Grand Canyon."

"The Grand Canyon isn't at Yellowstone. Get your national parks straight."

I suck on my brandy and feel it burn down my throat. "We never left Boston for vacations when I was a kid. 'Plenty to see right here,' my father said."

Meredith's rings click on the steering wheel. She tosses me a look of sympathy. Or maybe I've got something on my face. My eyelids cling when I blink.

"It's too bad Mount Rushmore's so far away," she says. "Walter likes to read biographies of the Presidents."

Her husband's name sits between us like a stone. Talking of sleep has made me drowsy, and I lean on the window again. "We're missing the Badlands, too," I yawn, "whatever they are."

*****

I doze—I wheel my father through the Museum of Fine Arts. We pass through a long hallway, with galleries on either side. When we look in the doorways, the figures in the paintings lean out of their frames and stare back at us: there are dancers and nudes and portrait-sitters with amazing hats; at least a dozen Jesuses have climbed off their crosses to give us the eye. Then we turn into a gallery that feels familiar. My father and I have switched places—I'm in the wheelchair, and he's pushing me. We roll up to a painting. I can't see it clearly, but I know it's "Isabella and her Pot of Basil." With the muted shock of dreams I realize that only my head is set on the wheelchair. My stomach sinks, though I'm body-less.

"Low," my father gurgles behind me, and I understand it's not my name he's trying to say, but "gigolo." Something drips on my scalp—am I being watered with tears or drool?

*****

"Lore—Lore!"

My head snaps up. Have we landed in Billings? But this isn't a cramped airline seat I'm buckled into. Everything is the dull blue of dusk. I blink gummy lids and look through the windshield—a narrow road, pine trees on one side and a rock wall rising on the other.

"I dropped off. Sorry," I mumble. "Where are we?"

"You've been out a while. How much did you drink?"

I jerk a glance around my seat as if I've dropped a lit match and find the flat bottle, nearly empty, pinned between my hip and the door.

I bite a numb lower lip. "Not much."

"We turned off twenty minutes ago." Meredith chokes the wheel with both hands. "The GPS said this is the shortest way, but we're driving up a mountain. No guardrails. I haven't even seen a place to turn around. Yellowstone is still fifty miles away, and it'll be dark long before we get there. Is there any point in continuing?"

"To say we were there, right? To finish what we started. Do you want me to drive?"

"Not after you've been drinking."

139

I brush potato chip crumbs from my chest. When did I eat them? My mouth feels pasty, but the water bottles are in the backseat, too hard to reach. I shift my back toward Meredith, uncap my brandy, and finish it off with a quick swig. Gaps between the trees and rocks expose limitless space.

"What's that, some kind of gorge?"

"This is real mountain, Lorenzo, not like back east." Meredith's slitted eyes don't leave the road. "I'd make a U-turn if I could be sure nobody would run into us."

"I haven't seen anybody, have you?"

"All it takes is one."

"Maybe the road is supposed to be closed."

"There'd have been a sign when I pulled on—and the GPS would have said something. You want to be helpful? Keep me alert, okay? Stay awake. Talk to me."

"Sure." But I can't think of anything to say, and after a minute or two, I feel my head nod.

"Dammit, Lorenzo."

"Sorry, sorry, sorry—" We should never have left Billings. We could have stayed in the room, had sex, ordered room service. Or I could be in the gym, pumping iron in my scrubs, enjoying the feel of the sleeves tightening on my biceps while I absorb the admiration of every female dental worker in the Rocky Mountain time zone.

"I'm not kidding. I need talk." Meredith's a silhouette in the darkening car. "You said you stayed in the city for vacations when you were a kid. Where'd you go?"

"Museums." The rock walls sliding by remind me of crumbling Greek temples. "I still take my father. He's in a wheelchair."

"He was wounded in the war?"

"Stroke." Have I mentioned a war? And what would happen if, instead of a museum, I took my father someplace he didn't want to be, like to a baseball game? When he spat my name, would it sound any different? Would his eyes bulge more or less?

"Maybe I should take my father to a Red Sox game," I murmur.

"Being out in the fresh air would be nice in the summer."

"He'd hate it. Baseball's a dead game."

My head is loose. I let it flop from side to side as Meredith guides us around another switchback. I must have neglected to strengthen my all-important neck muscles: the vertebrae that protect the nerve to my brain and connect my skull to the rest of me need help. And inside the neck there's also a throat for breathing and swallowing and an adam's apple that gives me my voice. I put my hand under my chin and hum, feeling the vibration.

"Sing me something," Meredith says.

"Sing?"

"Sing anything. Don't just sit there."

"*Badlands—you got to live it every day—*" My voice tickles my palm and throbs in my ears. I'm not much of a singer. "*Let the broken hearts stand as the price you got to pay—*" I hold up a fist. "Bruuuce!" I open my hand and examine my long fingers. *Tickle the ivories.* "That's all I know. Springsteen isn't my era."

"He's Walter's era," Meredith says. "We should have tried the Badlands. I could have told him that the conference offered a side trip with a night's stay. We could have stopped at Mount Rushmore."

"*Badlands—*" I start the song too high and quit.

"We had four parakeets when I was a kid," Meredith says, "—blue ones. When all four lined up on their perch, somebody would shout 'Mount Rushmore!' like it was good luck. They were identical. We never named them. We called them all 'Budgie' or 'Pretty Boy.' We had them for years. They died, all of them, one right after the other, within a week. Probably a disease. Dad disposed of them. After he got rid of the cage, it was like they'd never existed."

"I thought kids gave their pets funerals."

"Not us. You didn't have any pets?"

"My father didn't believe in them." We had a memorial service for my mother, who was cremated. Some distant cousins and a few of my father's colleagues came. Also, my middle school guidance counselor, who I avoided.

"Maybe Mount Rushmore isn't just heads," I say. "Maybe all the Presidents are standing inside a snowbank that's buried them up to their necks."

Meredith hesitates. "No—it's just their heads. Definitely just heads."

"Or maybe they're stuck in old volcanoes. Because their bodies have to be somewhere, don't they?"

*****

Meredith hunches forward, her arms bent like a praying mantis. Our conversation has shrunk to grunts and yawns, but, though we haven't discussed it further, we hold steady for Yellowstone. I flex my pectorals and watch the fabric of my sweater rise and fall, but my chest feels hollow. The stars that cover us like a silver cloth do nothing to illuminate the road. Our drive has begun to feel like a permanent affliction—an amputation—a handicap that can't be ignored. Weaving and braking rocks the car in an irregular rhythm, and I close my eyes, shutting out my pecs, the road, and the stars.

Meredith's voice slashes through the silence: "Walter and I have been arguing about you."

"He knows about us?" My nostrils dilate, but my lids won't lift.

"Not specifically. Walter gets that I have a life on the side: I've got needs he can't satisfy, and he wants me to be happy. And when I walked into your gym, there you were, like a big, buff gift that had been sitting right under my nose, unwrapped. Exciting, right? A secret office romance. But lazy—too easy. And too hard to keep up, especially when Walter likes you so much. He likes you *too* much."

"And you don't want to hurt him." I press my lids with my thumb and forefinger, and tiny lights explode.

"Of course not, but I'm not explaining this clearly. The problem is, you're Walter's choice. And I disagree. I disagree strongly."

"His 'choice'?"

"'I think of Lorenzo like a son,' Walter says. 'He'd be perfect.' But you're not perfect, Lore. No offense, but beauty's not enough."

I peek at Meredith, and a spark from my private lightshow escapes and lands on her cheek—unless it's a tear that glitters there. Or a droplet of sweat. I try to picture Walter calling me perfect, but all I see is a generic old man in a wheelchair with a plaid blanket on his lap. The droplet runs down Meredith's jaw. I try to pluck it off, but accidentally pinch her chin.

"Hey!" The car swerves. Gravel spits under the tires. I yank my hand back—when I was little, I burned my finger on a Fourth of July sparkler. "That's what fire does," my father said, while my mother applied ointment.

Meredith steadies the car. She shoots me a bug-eyed glare. "That hurt—what the fuck are you doing? What if we were on a switchback?"

"Sorry."

"It'll probably leave a mark. See, this is just the point. Walter doesn't know your limitations. I tell him the donor has to be anonymous, but what I mean is he has to have *brains*. Walter's stuck on looks, but he needs to think about the whole genetic package. I swear, he's got some kind of man-crush on you. He won't even look at the catalogues. I tell him he'll be in his eighties eating mush when our kid's in high school, and I'll be pretty much a single parent. 'My opinion should count double,' I say. I don't remind him that it's not my fault his sperm count is so low—that would be cruel."

I'm struggling to retrieve one fact at a time. *Donor. Catalogues.* "Walter wants me to be the father—?"

"Not 'father,' don't say that. This is about sperm. And you're not going to be involved, that's a guarantee. My biological clock is ticking: this trip is the end for you and me, Lore, I decided back at the hotel while I sat through my workshop. 'Peri-implantitis' made me think of fetal implants. This—you—are my last hurrah before I focus on becoming a mommy. Oh—you're going to have to leave Coburn and Coburn—I'll find another practice for you. You'll tell Walter you need a change of scenery. He'll forget about you quickly enough. We both will. You'll forget me, too."

If I could think of anything to say, the words wouldn't get past the lump in my throat. My cheeks sting as if I've been slapped. Meredith rounds a turn—we're so close to the edge of the mountain there are stars *beneath* us, as if we're belted into a space capsule heading for the moon.

Jarring music—a muffled ringtone. The notes hang in the air between Meredith and me like frost on a window.

"That's *Walter*," she rasps. "How are we even getting service up here?"

The ringtone repeats.

"Lore, I've got to take this—he'll wonder why I'm not answering. I can't let go of the wheel—get the phone out of my pocket and hold it up to my ear."

"I'm not doing that." I shake my head, which feels empty as a balloon. "No way."

"Of course you are—get the phone, and then keep quiet, for god's sake."

I've slid my fingers into Meredith's jeans before, but never while she's driving. The phone, wedged in her front pocket, resists extraction like a cornered animal.

"Hurry up," Meredith urges. I finally pry the phone free—the ringtone clamors like a fire alarm.

"Push the talk button and hold it to my ear," she whispers. She straightens up and regrips the wheel, and I do as she says. "Hello, Walter?" she coos. "Walter, I can hardly hear you—people have been having trouble with the phone service here at the hotel. Billings is really in the boondocks.

144

Have you been trying to reach me? I've been down in the lounge, trying to be social. Wine and cheese, you know."

Walter's tiny voice chirps in my hand. My thumb slides to the button that puts him on speaker.

"—*lonely here without you. I recorded 'Chopped' so we can watch it together when you get back.*"

"Thanks, honey—we can get that On-Demand, you know." Meredith snarls silently at me to get the phone off speaker while she tells her husband she misses him, too. "It's pretty boring·here," she says.

We enter a switchback. Meredith slows to a creep and leans toward the wheel. I follow her ear with the phone, leaving it on speaker.

"*Maybe you should rent a car and take a day trip to visit the sights,*" Walter says. "*Skip tomorrow's sessions—what the hell.*"

"I thought about it, honey, but everything out here is much farther away than you think. And I can't imagine sitting in the car for hours with any of the people I've met." She frowns savagely as she wrestles with the wheel. "They're all pretty superficial," she hisses.

I pull the phone away, switch it to my right hand, and hold it up against my window. Meredith, her face contorted with rage, over-corrects a turn, and we skid to a stop in the middle of the road.

"*Maybe you expect too much—but their conversation couldn't be as scintillating as mine,*" Walter says. His wife snatches at her phone, but her safety harness holds her back. She chops at my shoulder with the heel of her hand.

"That's right," she grunts, "'Scin-til-lating'—"

I don't yield the phone. I'm as cool as a bullfighter. Meredith unbuckles her harness, and I unbuckle mine. As she hurls herself at me, I open the door, wave the phone just out of her reach, and step out onto the pavement. It's uneven, but I'm grateful for the solid ground. I take a few steps away from the car before the cold hits me—it's refreshing, but threatening—as if I'm a baby being born into a freezing sea. Out in the open Walter's voice flutters in my fist like something caught in a jar. I hear "*breaking up*," and assume he means the reception.

"Hold on, Walter, I dropped the phone—" Meredith shouts. She vaults over my seat and follows me out of the car, stumbling in the heels she's been wearing the entire trip. My brandy bottle falls out with her and strikes the ground with a glassy thud. Meredith kicks at it but misses and staggers toward me. The car's headlight beams illuminate a lone pine tree, but everything else that's rock, vegetation, or pavement is impenetrably black—except the sky. The Milky Way spreads above us, as white as a wedding canopy. I raise the phone to it.

"Recalculating," the GPS's female voice announces. We've lost Walter's signal. The car sits where we left it, engine thrumming, a hazard to every ascending or descending vehicle. Meredith's shadow-figure dives toward me, and I shuffle backward a step, still holding the phone up like it's the Statue of Liberty's torch. "Sonuvabitch," she growls. I have the urge to talk to Walter: *Hi, it's Lawrence*, I'd say if he were still connected. Meredith throws herself at me again, and I retreat another step. A glance over my shoulder reveals a million soundlessly sparkling stars, and I set my feet.

Do I toss the phone at Meredith or is it her final lunge that knocks it from my hand? Whichever, it and she are past me and gone before I can react. I turn and bend over the edge, listening with all my might— there's just the silent waterfall of stars and the hum of the car engine. I suck huge breaths—through my nose, through my mouth. The mountain air washes my eyes and ears clean. I stamp my feet so hard I feel pins and needles in my ankles. It's all so fresh.

Explanations will be required, and I'll have them. People may suffer—maybe me, maybe not, if I keep my head on my shoulders. I squat, then sit and let my legs dangle into the void. I kick my heels against the side of this mountain. I fill my lungs again, release the air, and hug myself. I'm not going to Yellowstone. Maybe I'll try the Badlands. To get there, I'll have to circumvent Mount Rushmore and its buried

Presidents. Far to the east, my father will be waiting for his next museum trip. And Walter will be waiting for his child.

Diorama

He's proud of the diorama concealed in the back of his tractor trailer. Is it art? Maybe. It's got to be something more than the stolen contents of a brother's apartment.

He's stuck in traffic now, stopped dead between Boston and Springfield in an eastbound lane of the Mass Pike. People are getting out of their cars and trucks, peering over vehicles lined up as far as the eye can see. And across the median the westbound lanes are empty enough for touch football or a picnic: whatever happened ahead is bad enough to have stopped the flow of traffic in both directions.

Next to him on the passenger seat sits Puck, the little poodle mix he took from the apartment along with the furniture. The dog's giving him the eye, and he slaps his knee, though he knows Puck's too old and timid to make the leap over the gear shift box. He picks up the dog, leashes it, tucks it under his arm, and swings out of his truck's door onto pavement rubbed shiny by millions of tires—but his boots are probably the first to touch this exact spot. The smells of asphalt and exhaust rise through the cool March air. Puck tugs like a fish too small to keep, making for the dirty snow on the highway's shoulder. A girl with a blond ponytail pokes her crimped face out of the driver's side window of the car they're behind.

"Hey," she calls, "you know what's wrong?"

He shakes his head, unprepared to speak. The dog scrapes at the pavement, eager for the snow. "Nope," he says. "Nothing on the radio. Got an I-phone?"

"It's out of power, and I don't have a car-charger," the girl whines, like a kid who has yet to learn about real trouble. She yanks her head back into her car without another word. He notices the college sticker, "Framingham State University," on her rear window and guesses that she's late for class, then squints up and down the highway at the sun-glared roofs and windshields. Everybody is missing something. He follows Puck to a crust of snow and watches the dog squat. If the young woman were to join him at the rear of the truck, her face would uncrimp when he revealed the diorama. She'd forget about missing whatever she's missing and lift a hand to her open mouth. She'd insist that he invite the multitudes stranded on the highway to behold the display.

Puck finishes, and he leads the dog to the back of the trailer where he stands and stares at the roll-down door as if he's penetrating it with X-ray vision. He reads the phone number printed after the question, "How's My Driving?" He knows the number has been disconnected because he's tried it.

The diorama replicates the brother's apartment as seen for the last time before it was emptied. He considers the contents repossessed, since most of it originally belonged to his parents. It's furniture he grew up with. He's never seen the old dioramas from the natural history museums, but he's heard about them—how they're full of dead animals shot long ago in Africa—antelopes and rhinos and wild dogs. He's heard that behind the panes of dusty glass you can see hundred-year-old bullet holes in some of the stuffed carcasses. There aren't any bullet holes in any of the furniture laid out in the back of this truck, but would it be so surprising if there were? Puck is sitting on the asphalt, showing a pink tongue the size of a postage stamp. If dioramas included living things, maybe the dog should be in it, curled up on the rug his mother spent decades braiding out of clothes her kids had outgrown.

There's a tall bookcase in the diorama, its shelves jammed with familiar paperbacks. Beside the bookcase is a formica-topped kitchen table he and the brother had sat at for thousands of childhood breakfasts. On the table are a few liquor bottles and shot glasses, super-glued into place so they won't roll off when the truck turns corners or bounces through potholes. One of the bottles is filled with water to look like vodka, another with tea to look like whiskey. Also on the table is a yellow legal pad, its wrinkled pages covered with writing.

He'd considered hanging framed apology-letters on the inner walls of the truck behind the furniture, but that would have been inauthentic: a diorama should represent a creature's natural habitat, and an abuser attempting recovery would have mailed his apology letters out, not displayed them. Then he'd had the idea of filling a legal pad with rough drafts of apology letters that he could leave on the table as part of the display. He'd used a template:

Dear {Recipient},

I am writing to you today because I am making amends to people I have harmed as a result of my addiction to {substance}. Specifically, I know that I harmed you by {state action}. For this, I am deeply sorry.

I know that sometimes apologies are more of a burden than a blessing, but I would like the chance to apologize to you in person. This will allow us to discuss how I harmed you and what I can do to make things right. If you do not feel that you wish to forgive me, or you do not wish to have any contact with me, I understand. However, please know that I am deeply sorry for what I have done to you and would like to do whatever I can to repair our relationship.

If you would find it acceptable for me to make amends in person, please contact me at {phone/email}. Otherwise, rest assured that this letter will be my only attempt to contact you, because I do not wish to impose on your life.

Sincerely,

{Sender}

As he copied the template letter, inserting "alcohol and drugs" for "*substance*" and "irresponsible behavior" for "*action,*" he didn't try to imitate the brother's handwriting. He addressed the first letter in the pad to himself. Hadn't he been the biggest victim? The next two letters went to "Mom" and to "Dad," separate letters that could have been sent in a single envelope. Three letters didn't seem like enough, so he'd kept going. He composed the next for his own ex-wife, and then one to his daughter, who must be old enough to read by now. They'd been victims, too. These two letters would never have been sent, since the brother wouldn't have had any more idea of the address than he did.

At the last moment, to fill the pad, he'd added one final letter—an apology to the dog. It must have been unsettling to have been snatched out of the apartment by someone you weren't sure you could trust, even if his scent was familiar. He'd signed this last letter with his own name, and only now, standing at the back of his closed truck, leash in hand, does he wonder whose signature he'd used to close all the other apologies.

*****

He's dozing behind the wheel—traffic hasn't budged for an hour—and wakes to find the dog gazing at him with eyes like chocolate chips. He's been dreaming of the family furniture fallen into disrepair under the brother's care: the table supporting the bottles and legal pad full of apologies is scarred and warped; the sofa he and the brother had shared for Saturday morning cartoons now leaks stuffing and smells of kitchen grease. He's absorbed that smell, having slept on the sofa for countless nights since he's begun transporting the diorama.

He dreamt of the photograph of his uniformed uncle, his mother's brother, hanging now in the diorama behind the sofa. He'd never known the young soldier, who'd barely been out of his teens when he'd died "on foreign soil." His mother said she saw him in her children. "God gave me back the brother he took when he gave me you," she told them. "A brother means everything."

But in his dream on the Mass Pike, he's seen something else on the wall of the diorama, dwarfing the photo of the dead uncle: his own tattooed flesh, stripped off his body in a single piece and hung like an animal hide. The sight of his stretched skin lingers—he feels a hot knife pierce his ribcage, sees himself peeled from himself like wet linen. What if the brother on some lonely evening had woken from troubled sleep to find that skin stretched out on the wall, its tattoos as purple as bruises and as indecipherable as hieroglyphics? What if the brother pulled the skin from the wall and wrapped himself in it?

He winces from the bright sunlight, and, hoisting Puck to his lap, laces his fingers like a collar around the dog's neck. There are tattoos of musical notes on his knuckles, but he's unable to remember why he chose them—he doesn't play an instrument and can't read music. Maybe they're the sound of a punch. Maybe they begin a melody for the diorama.

He releases Puck's throat, cups a palm over the dog's head, and shifts his attention to the car in front of him. "Framingham State University," he reads aloud. Someday his daughter will be as old as the young woman with the drained cellphone, and maybe she'll go to college. By then she'll have made up a history that explains her absent father. If he finds her and her mother, he'll show them the diorama he travels with. He'll give them as much time as they need to study it. On the beat up table, between the liquor bottles and pad full of apologies, there is a stale, pink-iced donut. He'll tell his daughter to take it, not for eating, but because it's pretty and once was something. "This is yours," he'll say, as if to remind her of an event she's forgotten.

When traffic moves—when traffic moves again, he'll continue on to the towns south of Boston. He'll look for the cemetery where his parents rest and back his truck up to the stones engraved with their names and dates. He'll raise the door with the "How's My Driving" number and show them the diorama that displays their son's history. "Come and see your boy," he'll shout at the monuments. "Read the letters on the pad. Look at the bottles on the table and the flesh hanging on the wall." Then he'll hold up his fist and turn it slowly like a globe and listen for its music, hoping it will tell him where to take the brother's story next.

Convenience

Three years ago, when Ginger and I first brought our puppies home from the shelter, we'd already picked two names, though we didn't assign them immediately. Our plan was to call whichever one proved to be less well-behaved "Bark" and the better dog "Bite." Then we could tell people that "Bark is worse than Bite." During our dozen years together, we'd been the kind of couple who'd take on the burden of dog ownership just for a punch line. Bark earned his "worse dog" title because he took longer than Bite to be housebroken. But, as it turned out, we named them too quickly: when the dogs matured into their actual personalities, Bark had a gentle temperament, while Bite was sour and threatening. Overall, Bite was much worse than Bark. We wound up calling the disappointingly literal pair Barky and Bitey.

Our first stop after a long-weekend trip to the Bahamas was to the veterinarian's to pick up our boarded pets. Despite the blue sky, warm sun, azure sea and white beaches, the mini-vacation had failed in its purpose: we left our resort with the issue of Ginger's surprise pregnancy unsettled. The window for taking action was closing, but we'd been unable to force ourselves to broach the subject.

Children had never been part of our plans; the dogs, I thought we'd agreed, were enough family for any couple. At the resort, Ginger treated herself to spa time while I hid behind a book on the beach. At meals, in bed, even on the flight home, we mumbled over neutral topics, while our glances slid apart like magnets of the same pole. I drank heavily, while I took Ginger's avoidance of alcohol to be a contingency rather than a decision.

It was still morning as we stepped into the veterinary clinic—we'd escaped the island on the earliest possible flight. It struck me that we'd reached a crisis point. "So?" My hushed voice echoed off the tile floor.

"Here?" Ginger hissed. "*Now?*" She reached toward me as if I'd stumbled, though I hadn't moved, then dropped her arm and shook her head. "The pups are waiting."

"They'll be happy to see us," I grumbled, and stuck my hands in my pockets.

When Ginger asked the smocked vet tech behind the counter for our dogs, the young woman's smile froze. She excused herself to find the vet. We waited, too long it seemed, twitching at muffled barks and yelps emerging from behind the half dozen examining room doors. Finally, the vet, file folder in hand, appeared down the hall. Behind him yowled Bitey, who dragged the vet tech past the doctor, Ginger and me on his way to the exit. I took the leash, wrapped it around my wrist, and, yanked with a firm, "Down, Bitey! Quiet!" while the dog belly-swam over the slick tiles.

"Exuberant," I grunted over his whimpering. "He's glad to be free."

Ginger shot me an inquisitive look—where was Barky, our good dog? The vet frowned over his glasses without settling his gaze on either of us. "I'm sorry to have to tell you, but Bark passed away yesterday morning." The air felt suddenly thinner, unbreathable.

"What?" Ginger asked in disbelief. "Barky?" She looked past the doctor at the vet tech, who lifted her hands like they needed washing and stepped behind the counter.

"Gastric Dilatation Volvulus," the vet said, "Commonly known as 'bloat.' Difficult to pinpoint the cause—the intestines become twisted up sometimes when the animal is overexcited. The blood supply gets cut off to important organs, and, well—" His voice trailed off. "We can do an autopsy if you like. I caution you, it's expensive." He cleared his throat and looked at the folder he held, which I assumed was Barky's medical record. "We're so sorry. It's one of those freak occurrences. We didn't call you because it's our policy to deliver this kind of news in person."

Everything happened so fast. Still dazed by the news, we declined the autopsy. No, we didn't want to see Barky's body, which was in the freezer. The doctor shook Ginger's hand, and I gave him a sober nod. He took a deep breath, expanding and deflating like a vertical accordion, and turned to leave. Ginger stopped him with a question.

"What kinds of animals get 'bloat?' Just dogs?"

The vet blinked and resettled his glasses. "It's also common in cattle. All ruminants, actually."

"Ruminants? What other kinds of ruminants are there? Cats?" Ginger's words smoked like dry ice.

"Well," the doctor reflected, "no, not cats. Goats and sheep. Giraffes. Camels. Deer."

"*Bambi*?" Ginger folded her arms. "*Bambi* was a ruminant? Did Bambi's mother die of bloat? Oh—wait—it was 'man' who killed her, wasn't it?"

The doctor, vaguely aware of an accusation, tucked his folder under his arm, bowed slightly, and retreated down the hall. Just as he passed the nearest examining room, its door swung open, and a tiny white poodle pranced out, followed by a large man in an orange track suit. Bitey stiffened beside me, barking sharply. "Quiet!" I warned and tightened my grip on his leash, while the poodle's owner whisked his dog from the floor and clutched it to his chest.

"Sorry," I shrugged and pivoted to Ginger, who was deep in discussion with the vet tech. The young woman held what I realized with a pang was Barky's collar, which she was sliding through her fingers, jingling the silver tags. Ginger turned to me with misty eyes.

"How do we want Barky's ashes? It's fifty for mixed."

Bitey lay across my feet, his low growl simmering. "Shh," I soothed. He was waiting, I knew, for another crack at the poodle, whose owner lingered behind me.

"What's 'mixed' mean?" I asked. "Barky was a mix. Some kind of lab-hound."

Ginger shook her head. "She says 'mixed' is a scoop from all the day's ashes. For just Barky it would be— two hundred more?" The vet tech nodded to confirm the price and offered the collar, which Ginger ignored.

I glanced down at Bitey. Did he sense his companion's fate? Truth be told, the two dogs barely got along. We walked and fed them separately—when it was Barky's turn for dinner, we had to lock Bitey in our bedroom. The pair had looked a bit like twins when we'd picked them out of the puppy pen at the shelter. But gentle Barky had developed into a handsome, sturdy almost-lab, while ill-tempered Bitey had turned into something more like a coyote with measles. ("Is he sick? These will go away, right?" Ginger asked of the rash of spots that eventually marked Bitey's hide.) As he grew out of puppyhood, his floppy ears rose and stiffened like a kangaroo's, in spite of Ginger's effort to pat them back down whenever he didn't shy away from her hand. "Bitey's never actually bitten any one," was the highest compliment we'd ever paid him.

"Do we really need any ashes?" I grunted as I tried to hide the effort it took to keep Bitey from lurching toward the poodle. After a sharp jerk, he melted back to the floor with a groan. "Where would we put them? We don't have a fireplace or a mantle."

Ginger winced down at Bitey as if seeing him for the first time. Was she wondering, like I was, if fate had taken the wrong dog? We'd accepted the chaff with the wheat, but now the wheat was gone. Were we a family without Barky? Could Bitey alone claim our hearts? As I contemplated our surviving dog's role in our future life, the shadow of the decision Ginger and I had been unable to resolve in Barbados fell over me.

Ginger turned back to the vet tech. She finally noticed Barky's collar, snatched it, and handed over a credit card. "No ashes," she said.

"If you change your mind," the vet tech said as she processed our payment, "you'll have to call within the hour for the individual ashes. For the mixed tell us before five o'clock." She handed Ginger a tissue while she waited for the receipt to print. "We took half off of the boarding fee for, you know, the other one."

"Half off for killing our dog? A bargain." Ginger crushed the tissue, tossed it into a nearby trashcan, and spun away. "Good luck with your bloat," she called over her shoulder, and strode toward the exit. The poodle man gave her a wide berth. Bitey had snapped at the flight of the tissue, but now, forepaws clawing at the air, he galloped after his departing mistress. I was dragged past the poodle guy, who said something like, "Why don't you train your dog, Horatio?" Before I could respond, Bitey had pulled me through the door.

On the short drive to our apartment, Bitey careened about the car, back seats and front, howling at passersby, smudging the windows with his saliva. Shoving Bitey off our laps occupied all our attention, and it was impossible for Ginger and me to share our grief over Barky's loss. We found a parking space in front of our building, and Ginger rolled our suitcases to the entrance while I paraded Bitey around the tiny square of dirt surrounding the only tree on our block. He pissed and shat on command, his only talent. I searched my pockets.

"Got a bag?" I called to Ginger, who waited at the door. She patted herself down half-heartedly.

"Nope. These are still my Barbados clothes."

After a quick peek up and down the street, I toed the turd into the gutter and scraped my shoe on the curb.

Inside our apartment, Ginger and I flopped together onto the sofa, both of us too wrung out emotionally and physically to unpack. The television remote on the chair across the room seemed a thousand miles away, and I stared at a blank screen. Bitey settled on his bed beneath the TV, his snout on his crossed paws. He seemed to be gazing at the empty bed beside him.

"Poor Barky," I sighed. I closed my eyes and let my head drop to the back of the sofa. Ginger mumbled something in reply. I didn't reach out to her. *Six weeks*, she'd said when she told me. *What do we want to do?* There'd never been an adequate explanation of how such a thing could happen. *In between*, she'd said, flushing with an expression I at first mistook for an apology. Nothing else besides that "in between"—had the miscalculation been physical? Temporal? If there had been a miscalculation at all. So, Barbados. And back, with nothing to show but lost time and a dead dog.

"Bitey's looking for Barky," Ginger murmured. "Maybe we should have paid for the ashes, at least the mixed ones."

"So we'd be spending fifty dollars on a box of cinders that's mostly other people's dogs? Or maybe not even dogs— who knows what else died there today? You want rat ashes? An urn full of snake dust? And then what? Bitey would knock it over and we'd have to vacuum up the mess anyway." Though we weren't touching, I felt Ginger's shudder—she hated snakes. "Sorry," I said. "It's just that it's a waste. Maybe instead we'll blow up a photo of him. Or have someone do an oil painting ."

"A painting of Barky and Bitey?"

I looked at Bitey, draped across his bed. "Why include him? He's still here. Besides, it wouldn't be honest to put them together—they weren't really friends." I spoke to Bitey in my "good dog" voice: "We'll wait until you're gone to get a picture of you," I said, and he looked at me. "Maybe we'll stuff you, or better yet get a statue, like the one of Balto in Central Park." I turned to Ginger. "In Russia there's a statue of Pavlov with one of his dogs. I saw a picture of it once. Maybe close up you can see drool chiseled on Pavlov's lap. Come to think of it, Bitey, you'll probably live so long, people will be getting holograms of their dead dogs instead of ashes. When I'm ninety, I'll have to walk your hologram so it can shit little hologram turds."

"Just stop." Ginger picked up her laptop from the end table. "This is—something sad. We're supposed to be sad." She opened her computer.

I sat for a while listening to her tap on her keyboard. I tried to think about Barky, but I couldn't summon any feelings that felt appropriate. I peeked at Ginger through half-closed lids and wondered if this would be a good time for us to bare our feelings about our "situation." Instead, I decided to mention the thing that had been nagging at me since we'd left the vet's office.

"Hey—remember the guy with the poodle—the big guy wearing orange—back at the vet's?"

Ginger didn't look away from the laptop. "Not really. I was too upset—I just wanted to get out of there."

"He said something to me while I was following you out. He said, 'Why don't you train your dog, Horatio?'"

Ginger glanced at me, then at Bitey. "He's right. Why don't you?"

"He called me 'Horatio.'"

"Is that a thing? Something from Hip-hop? I don't know, I'm out of touch." She blinked back at her laptop screen. "How do you spell 'bloat'? The regular way, or is there a special medical—?" She typed and scrolled. "Never mind, I got it."

Across from us, Bitey had stood up. He stared at the front door with eerily translucent eyes. The hair along his spine rose. For a good ten seconds he remained frozen, mesmerized by nothing apparent. Then the spell broke, he turned around once and lay down as if his attention had never been roused.

Ginger finished reading about bloat. "Poor Barky," she sighed with a frown. Then she remembered what I'd just told her. "Some stranger called you 'Horatio'?"

"I think maybe he wasn't a complete stranger," I said. "I was dealing with Bitey and never got a good look at him. But I think he might have been someone I used to know back in high school. 'Horatio' came from *Hamlet*. If it's who I think it was, we were in the play together. He got fat."

"You were in *Hamlet*? You never told me that. You were Horatio? That's impressive."

"It kind of sucks, actually. I was never Horatio. I auditioned for Horatio, but I didn't get the part. I was the 'Messenger from England.' At the end I got to say

'Rosencrantz and Guildenstern are dead.' Not much else. Nobody—guards, servants, all the walk-ons--had fewer lines than the Messenger from England. Girls playing guys had bigger parts than mine."

"Then why did your friend—the poodle man—call you Horatio?"

"Because he was a schmuck. He knew it bothered me and thought it was funny. And he was Hamlet, of course. And the other member of our threesome, this nasty guy Roger, he was Polonius. It might have been Roger who started calling me Horatio."

Ginger shut her laptop. For the first time since we got home, I had her full attention. "That's mean, rubbing it in. They were your friends?"

"Supposedly. Jerry Convenience. That was Hamlet's—the poodle guy's— name. Roger and Jerry—the two of them were especially tight. Inseparable." In my mind's eye I was trying to superimpose the face of Jerry Convenience on the guy at the vet's.

"That's a strange name, 'Convenience.' It sounds like a joke."

"I nicknamed him 'Seven,' after the 7-11 convenience shops. He said that an 'immigrant forbearer'—that was the way he talked—an 'immigrant forbearer' picked the name 'Convenience' out of a dictionary because it resembled the family name from the old country."

A flurry across the room grabbed our attention— Bitey was sitting up, scratching his muzzle wildly with a back paw.

"He's itchy," Ginger said. "And lonely."

"I should have let him bite Jerry Convenience."

"If you knew each other, wouldn't he have said more to you at the vet's than just calling you Horatio?"

"No. By the time we graduated, I wasn't even on speaking terms with him or Roger. They hated me. And the amazing thing is, the next time I saw them, they tried to kill me."

"*Kill* you?"

"Murder me, yeah." I leaned my head back and stared up at the ceiling. My eyes ran along a crack I'd never noticed before, a thin line that had been painted over. It ran nearly the length of the room. "I didn't even know it then. I figured it out a just couple of months ago, after, like, fifteen years. It just popped into my head—an epiphany."

"You had an epiphany about a murder plot?"

"When I went for my root canal. I sat in the chair, all numbed up. Dr. Stein was doing his thing inside my mouth, and I let my attention drift up to all those pictures they've taped on the ceiling to give the patients something relaxing to look at."

"The postcards and travel brochures—"

"Right—the Eiffel Tower, Big Ben, the Coliseum, ski resorts. And beautiful beaches—like the ones in the Barbados—golden sands, palm trees, blue ocean. So you can take a vacation in your mind while Dr. Stein's earning his living inside your mouth."

"Wait—but why did your friends start to hate you. What did you do?"

A sharp whimper interrupted. Bitey's scratching had gotten violent. "Hey, boy, what's the matter?" Ginger called. She set her lap top aside, pushed herself off the couch, and went to examine the dog. "Eew—his eye is all crusty. I bet he caught something at the vets. Yuch—" She hurried into the kitchen and returned with a damp paper towel folded into a square. But when she tried to wipe Bitey's eye, he growled and jerked his head away.

"Don't lose a finger," I cautioned.

Ginger sing-songed our Bitey mantra: "He's never actually bitten anyone." She stood with her hands on her hips and gazed down ruefully at the dog, who continued to scratch. She dabbed at her temples with the towel, and returned to the couch. "Dried crap all over his eyes," she muttered and flipped open her laptop. "They kill one dog, infect the other. Now I've got to look up 'crusty eyes.'" She blinked at the screen, then shot me a look. "Did you say why your friends hated you enough to want to kill you? I forget. Sorry, I'm a little distracted. I saw Barky's bowl in the kitchen."

"His bowl? Damn." I stayed silent for a respectful few seconds before returning to my story. "You know why those guys hated me? Because I got Jerry back for the Horatio thing. He asked me to write him a peer recommendation for college. For Darmouth. He couldn't ask Roger, because Roger had already gotten in there early decision with a recommendation from Jerry, and a tit for tat was against the rules. I guess I used the letter as retaliation— for 'Horatio.' Maybe for some other slights. Maybe I was just jealous."

Ginger lifted an eyebrow. "What did you write?"

"Wise-ass stuff I thought was clever— like, where they asked if the candidate was flexible, I wrote, 'Jerry's tendency to vacillate is legendary.' And he got rejected. Didn't even make the waitlist."

"Because of your letter, you think?"

"Who knows? Maybe. But Jerry must have figured out somehow that I screwed him because after the rejection he and Roger cut me off cold. Walked by me in the halls like I was a ghost. Overnight, the whole school treated me like I'd ruined Jerry Convenience's life. Even teachers who'd liked me for years treated me like shit. Graduation couldn't come soon enough." I wiped my brow, surprised to find I was sweating.

Ginger was looking at me the same way she'd looked at the veterinarian when he told us of Barky's death. "So did you feel like you got even? *Do* you feel it?"

I shrugged. "Jerry got a scholarship to some little college down South. He must have done okay. He can afford to live in this city. He's got a dog, just like us. And how do I know his life isn't better than if he'd gotten into his first choice college?"

Ginger's lashes fluttered. Her upper lip curled. "You're saying maybe he would have died in a car crash up in

New Hampshire? Or maybe he met his future wife at the college down South?" She sighed and turned back to her laptop. Her fingers hovered over the keyboard. She typed something, then sat back and looked at me mournfully. "And the murder? You said you had an 'epiphany' about it."

"In the dentist's office, yeah." My words felt heavy in my mouth, like stones. "One of those pictures on the ceiling—a surfer on a monster wave made me think of Seven."

"'Seven.' Jerry Convenience. He surfed?"

"Not that I knew. Not in high school. We were all indoor boys. After high school, I thought he and Roger had washed their hands of me forever, and vice-versa. But then came spring break senior year of college. Remember—you went down to Florida with your sorority friends, and I spent the week at home—at my parents'. Then out of the blue I got a phone call from Jerry Convenience."

"Daytona. We slept on the beach."

"Yeah, I know, you came back all sun-burned. You didn't want me to touch you. I thought we were breaking up. I thought you met somebody down there. An outdoor boy, maybe."

Ginger gazed at her laptop screen with narrowed eyes. The tips of her ears glowed red. "And what about the phone call from Jerry Convenience?"

"It was weird. He did the 'how's-it-going-long-time-no-see" thing, as if there hadn't been a rift between us. Then he invited me to go surfing with him and Roger. I said sure."

Ginger lifted a shoulder to rub her chin. Our eyes met, and she looked away. "But you don't do the ocean. You don't go in it, anyway. 'The surface is impenetrable,' you always say."

"Damn right. But I guess I was bored. I was tired of organizing my vacation days around *The Price is Right.*"

Across the room, Bitey groaned. He lay on his side now, but still dug at his eye with a forepaw. Ginger clucked her tongue.

"I've been looking it up—it says here he might have something called 'dry-eye.' Not uncommon. We can treat it with warm compresses and ointment."

"If we can get close enough."

"If. So—you went surfing? It's hard to believe we knew each other when all of this was happening. It's like I'm listening to a different person's life."

"I'm telling you now. Jerry and Roger picked me up. They barely made eye contact when I got in the car. They looked more like a pair of morticians than surfers."

"You didn't care that they hated you?"

"I guess since Jerry hadn't mentioned it, I thought maybe they forgot."

Ginger sniffed. "People don't forget things." She sat up straight and folded her arms. "You know what? I decided I do want Barky's ashes. I don't care if they're mixed. You still have time to get to the vet's before five o'clock."

"Really? For fifty dollars?" I shrug. "Fine. I'll go back. While I'm there I'll ask if that poodle guy really was Jerry Convenience."

"You can pick up some ointment, too, for Bitey's eyes. I'll call when you leave so they'll have it ready."

"Okay. So—the murder: Jerry drove his family's station wagon, and I sat in the back behind him and Roger. I leaned on a purple surfboard that stuck out the rear hatch like the tongue of somebody choking to death."

"You thought that then?"

"That's how I picture it now. We drove for miles in complete silence. We were headed toward the south shore of Long Island, to the beaches where people surf. The awkwardness was so thick my skin felt sticky with it. So I started mocking them."

"You *mocked* them?"

"Reflex, I suppose. Repartee, what friends do. If I'd realized that they were planning to kill me, I probably would have been trying to figure out how to escape. But at the time I missed all the clues. What I did was call to Jerry: "'Seven?'"

I said, 'you're way less than that. Not even six. Or three or two. You're not even zero. You're ever diminishing nothingness. King Minus, and your touch creates a void. What you are,' I said, 'is Unfinite. Unfinity is your new name. And you,' I said to that grim bastard, Roger, 'are Unfunity.'"

"'Unfinity and Unfunity.'"

"Nice, right? Since my epiphany at the dentist's, I think about the scenario all the time. I take it apart and put it back together. Everything about that ride comes back to me as if I'm watching a movie: I see the interior of the station wagon, and that surfboard—the big purple tongue. And here's the scary thing—there's a thick rope and a burlap bag and a metal pipe. Oh, and I'm pretty sure there's an ax."

"An ax?"

"I see them with the other stuff stored behind me under the surfboard. And all the time there are signs we're getting closer and closer to the beach—marsh grass, sea gulls, sand, the salt smell." I closed my eyes and saw my would-be assailant: Jerry Convenience choked the steering wheel with a white knuckled grip, absorbing my insults and trading glances with Roger. What were they imagining? A purple surfboard dipping and spinning over a dark wave? A rope strung with seaweed? A sinking burlap bag loaded with something that had the unmistakable heft of a body?

Another yelp from Bitey broke the spell. He was rubbing his muzzle frantically on his pillow.

"Oh—he's miserable. You better hurry to the vet." Ginger pushed her laptop to her knees and placed a hand on her abdomen; with a jolt, I realized that there was something growing inside her.

"Barky's ashes and Bitey's ointment. They owe us," I said, looking at her stomach.

"And see whether or not the guy who called you Horatio is your Jerry Convenience. I just googled him. There's a million entries for 'Jerry's Convenience Store,' but nothing for just 'Jerry Convenience.' Didn't you ever stalk him—even after you figured out about your murder? I bet his ears are burning now. Aren't you curious?" Her voice got spooky and mysterious—was she teasing me? "Maybe he's been stalking *you*. Maybe he's been waiting all these years to finish you off."

But Ginger wasn't wearing the look of a teaser. Her unsmiling face tilted up at me, as if she was sniffing for something, and there were shadows under her puffy eyes. Did she scent from the story of my imagined murder the possibility of an "or" life she might have lived without me? Just how attractive was that alternative?

"I poked around a little. Nothing but those 'Jerry's Convenience Stores' you found." I felt hollowed out, as if my insides had turned to dust.

"Hm," Ginger closed her eyes. Her lids looked bruised. "So—what happened? How did it end?"

"I survived," I said, worried she'd be disappointed, in spite of the fact that my presence belied any other conclusion. "Nothing happened. It started to rain—it turned out to be a lousy day for the beach. We turned around."

"And you kept mocking them?"

"No— I got carsick." The emptiness I felt gave way to nausea as I relived that drive home—the beat of the windshield wipers, the smell of the upholstery, the pair of heads in the front seats, as still as mannequins.

"Kind of anticlimactic."

"Yeah." I stood up, wobbly. I could have told more. Ginger's look reminded me of the contempt on Roger's rain-speckled face when I saw it through his window after getting out of the car. It was pouring by then. I was drenched before I got to my front porch.

"You okay?" Ginger asked. "You look pale. I can go back to the vet's, if you want."

"I got this. It's the least I can do," I added as I made my way, light-headed and stomach-sick, to the door. My eyes fell on Barky's bed. I tried to imagine my own absence—of shrinking away until there was nothing left of me. But I couldn't get myself out of the picture—I felt I would always be there, but everything around me would disappear, until I was surrounded by nothingness. Bitey got up and followed me to the door.

"I bet he thinks you're going to get Barky," Ginger said.

"I am," I said. I reached for Bitey's head. He didn't pull away. His eyes were crusted. He let me brush some of the crud away with my thumb. "I better hurry with his ointment—he's drying up. He's the opposite of Pavlov's drooly dog."

"Watch out for Jerry Convenience. That's some story."

Watch out for how long? I thought. For the rest of my life? "Some story," I echoed, my hand on the knob. I pushed Bitey back with my leg to keep him from following me out the door. "Not the kind we'll tell our kids. Not at bedtime anyway."

"What?" Ginger called sharply as the door shut behind me. I paused in the hall, listening to see if she would repeat herself, not knowing if I'd hear her.

Cupids

Twenty years ago when this happened I didn't tell how I smashed my hand; I'm not going to say anything about that now, either. I was eighteen and a dumb-ass, and I wrapped a dish towel around the hand and jammed it deep into my coat pocket. The last I'd looked at it, I saw knucklebone through a flap of skin.

It was mid-morning on a March weekday, a time when most people who had someplace to go were already there, and the stretch of Route 20 I'd made it to was bare and lonely. There was a thin overcast that hinted at nothing. The cornfields were snow-crusted to the hills, where trees looked like beard stubble. I made up a reason for hitching for whoever picked me up. *To visit my girl at the college.* If I could get a ride to the city, where the state university was, then I could walk to the garage where my cousin worked. He'd put me up for a while until things sorted themselves out.

For a while I did have a girl in a college— in a different city, and she wrote me after a month to say we were heading in different directions and that she met someone. So while I stood blowing into my cold-stiff good hand, I was wishing it was true that I had a girl waiting for me. Occasional pain shot up my arm from my bad hand to my shoulder, but I'd played football and knew about hurt. A couple of cars passed going the wrong way. Finally, a car spotted with primer was headed west and eased over after it passed me. The front passenger door opened and a thin-necked guy with a buzzcut leaned out. "Hurry up," he hollered, "it's god-damn cold!"

I got in the back. Because the inside handles were missing, I had to pull the door shut from the top and yank my hand in quick. The upholstery was torn, but the car didn't smell any worse than any other old car, a combination of mildew, oil, and exhaust.   The guy in the passenger seat turned and looked me up and down. "Where you headed?"

"To the city," I said. "The college—to see my girl."
The guy's nose looked like a vegetable an animal had chewed.
A few days of silvery growth covered his jaw. I tried to not
stare at his nose. He smiled at me with his mouth open.

"No college for you?"

"No," I said. "Working man. Taking a vacation.
Service station. I pump gas mostly." All of which was true,
but it was a lot of information he hadn't asked for.

"Hear that, Bob?" the guy said to the driver. "A
working man on vacation, just like us." The driver peered at
me in the rearview. One of his blue eyes might have dragged
a little behind the other. His copper-blond hair looked dyed
and hung just over the collar of his leather jacket.

"Un-hunh," he said. He gripped the wheel at ten and
two. Crosses were tattooed on the backs of both his hands.

"I'm Trudeau," the guy in the passenger seat said. It
sounded like "chewed nose." I told him my name. "Glad to
meet you," he said. "What're you hiding there?" He nodded
down at where my hand was stuffed into my coat pocket.

I hadn't planned what to say if I got asked about my
hand because I'd hoped it wouldn't be noticed, but before I
could say a word, Bob swore and stared in his mirror, and
Trudeau looked past me out the back window, and we were
slowing down to a stop, pebbles from the shoulder pinging
against the car's underside. I turned and saw a black state
police cruiser, lights flashing, right behind us.

"Picking up hitch-hikers is a federal offense,"
Trudeau whispered with a smirk, then looked through Bob's
open window at the mirror-glassed trooper who stooped to
look us over. I waited for Trudeau to tell him we were
working men on vacation, but the trooper spoke first.

"Morning," he said. "Heading to the Interstate?" It
hadn't occurred to me that we might be— the state route we
were on was just as direct and didn't have tolls.

"We were just deciding," Trudeau said. "We're going
to see our aunt." He was grinning.

"It's Aunty Anna's birthday," Bob said, his gaze through the windshield. He didn't release the wheel. "She's ninety-five. Folks are coming in from all over."

"She's got emphysema from smoking," Trudeau said confidentially. "Doesn't look like she'll make it to a hundred. But then it didn't look like she'd make ninety either. She's on oxygen—got a tank she rolls after her like a dog on a leash."

"Un-hunh," the trooper said. "Good wishes to her. But you've got to stay off the Interstate if she lives west of here." He paused while another state cruiser flew by, then another, both with lights flashing. "We've got a bridge collapsed, looks like from the rain and snowmelt. Broke the highway right in two just before Exit 38. Or just after if you're coming from the west."

"Christ," Bob murmured and glanced at Trudeau "That's Aunty's exit."

"Jesus," Trudeau said. "But everybody except us is coming tomorrow, thank the Lord. What's the story, officer?"

"Caved in. Got reports of several cars driving in and falling a hundred feet down into the creek. At least one tractor trailer." The trooper's lips were white and wax-smooth. His voice was somber, but excited. "I'm on my way to the scene now. Reports are not encouraging."

Trudeau shook his head. "So—there's just a big hole?"

"Opened up just before dawn. Emergency teams are down there now. We're blocking off everything." I felt his eyes on me through his mirrored glasses, so I frowned and shook my head. I worried that blood had seeped through my coat pocket, but it hadn't. "Can you imagine?" he nearly whispered. "You're driving along, and the road disappears underneath you? Maybe you're alone—but maybe you've got your family along. Jesus—" he paused again. "I spend my life on the highway." He cleared his throat. "So you boys stay off the Interstate. Entrance'll be blocked, anyway. Listen for updates on the news. Best to your aunt." And he was gone before he could have heard Trudeau's "Yes, officer, be careful, sir."

As the trooper drove off, Bob started us up and revved the engine. "Jesus," he sighed tragically, and looked at Trudeau. "Can you imagine? Road opens up, and down you go, like you're a turd that didn't know you'd been flushed."

"'Stay off the Interstate, boys'" Trudeau mimicked. "'Best to your aunt!'" He turned to me. His chewed up nose was bobbing, he was snickering so hard, and I smiled at him. "Careful boy—stay away from the hole!"

"Big mother hole," Bob said as we accelerated. "You got cars rolling in, trucks, motorcycles, kids on bicycles—" He hunched his shoulders up under his leather jacket as he took a deep breath, and grunted. "Got trains running straight in!"

"And planes—" Trudeau added through his titters.

"Yeah, planes and helicopters flying down to see what's what, they get sucked in. Noah's god-damned ark, camels, ostriches, circus clowns leaping in, for Christ's sake—"

"Godzilla, King Kong—"

"—in the hole. God-damned hole's got magnetic powers," Bob declared.

"Bob," Trudeau said after a minute—he was pinching his red-raw nose while he spoke—"We got to see the hole for ourselves. It's a natural wonder of the world!"

Bob nodded. We were tearing through farmland, patches of snow yellowed like nicotine stains. Then Trudeau's eyes were on me again, and they slipped down toward my pocketed hand, which was throbbing because of all the excitement. "You in? You want to see the hole?"

I nodded. I did, too. Who wouldn't? I wasn't worried anybody I knew had fallen in. Nobody I knew was going anywhere.

"Now, what's that you said you got there?" Trudeau asked. I could see the bumps and hollows of his skull through his buzzcut.

By then, I'd figured out what to say. "Messed up my hand," I said. "My uncle's dog got a hold of a frozen pack of sausages. I didn't want him to choke. Didn't want to lose the sausages either," I grinned.

"Kinda dog?" Bob asked. "Shouldn't be taking food away from a dog no matter what kind." He was serious.

"Husky mix. Bad-tempered, too, but I thought he liked me."

"No such thing as 'like' when you're talking about a dog's dinner," Trudeau said. "You wash it out good? Your mom ever tell you that human germs are worse than dog germs? Maybe so, but that doesn't mean a dog bite's healthy. I had an uncle lose an arm gone gangrene from a dog bite."

"I washed it good and put antiseptic on it and wrapped it up." I'd started to believe the truth of everything I said, and my hand hurt less. I was picturing the collapsed bridge, the pavement breaking off in the middle of the air, the opposite edge a cliff, like a chunk of chocolate cake, and I wanted to look down into the hole to see how deep it was, to see the glitter of twisted metal. I wondered if there'd be any visible blood.

"That's good. Safety first," Trudeau said.

"We can get pretty close on back roads," Bob said. He was talking about the bridge collapse. "We get to a certain point, we'll get out and walk. Probably be a little muddy."

"Your girl won't mind if you're late?" Trudeau asked, grinning like a panting dog.

"It's not every day you get to see a wonder of the world," I said.

Bob pulled off the state route onto a farm road, paved but unmarked, and we drove for a while in silence. The pair up front saw the van in the ditch before I had any idea why we were stopping.

"Looks like she's not going anywhere for a while," Bob said. By "she" he meant either the blue van, which was tilted in the ditch at a crazy angle, it's roadside wheels off the ground, or the young woman, who had the hatch open and

172

was sitting on the van's bumper with a fat baby bundled up in a red parka on her lap.

She stood up when we stopped, the baby's arms and legs spread stiff like a teddy bear's on her hip. Trudeau rolled down his window as she approached our car. "You got some trouble, miss?" he asked. "That's a cute little guy you got there. Don't you have a better coat?"

The girl bent down to talk, and when she did she stuck the baby in front of my window like I was watching him on a TV screen. He wasn't that fat—most of him was parka. His cheeks were rosy from the cold, and his eyes were the clear blue of a spring sky. Snot had crusted around his tiny nostrils. He barely had eyebrows, but he frowned like he was watching me, too, like I was in a fishtank. Or he was looking at his own reflection in the glass. From inside, I couldn't tell.

His mother couldn't have been any older than me. Red-orange hair poured out from her grey hoody and she had freckles, nice white teeth, and green eyes. Trudeau was right that she wasn't dressed warm enough—her sweatshirt didn't cover the arms, also freckled, wrapped around her baby's middle.

"I was in a hurry—I thought I had a coat in the van," she said. "Then when I got going it was too late to turn back. But I had the heater on and we were toasty-warm."

"Looks like you got yourself good and stuck," Bob said. "It's lucky we came along."

It didn't take long to get the whole story. Her name was Dolly, the baby was Brad Junior, or just Junior, and she was driving "like a maniac" across the state to the army base outside the city because Brad Senior, her husband, was flying in from his overseas tour. "Coming back from Desert Storm," she said. "All the way from the other side of the world. He's never seen his own baby." While Trudeau offered her a ride to the base, I watched Junior, who had a snot bubble that grew and shrank with each little breath.

When she walked back to the van to get her diaper bag and shut the hatch, Junior still slung over her hip, I noticed that she had on dressy black pants and open cork-heeled shoes. Her toenails were painted pink. She must have been freezing, but she wanted to look nice for her husband. She tiptoed back because the ground was softening into mud, then stopped short and rolled her eyes.

"Hold him," she said to Trudeau, dropped the diaper bag outside my door, and stuffed Junior through Trudeau's window. The baby floated toward his big hands like an astronaut in a spacesuit, arms and legs splayed. Then Dolly minced back to the tilted van, reopened the hatch, climbed in on her hands and knees, and emerged lugging a plastic car seat.

"It's against the law to have him in a moving vehicle without his seat," she said as she opened the door next to me, and I slid over behind Bob. There was something sticky on the ripped vinyl I shoved onto, but I didn't say anything. I forgot to protect my hidden hand and my eyes teared up from squashing it against the door which, like the other side, had only an empty socket and screw holes where handles should have been. Trudeau bounced Junior on his knee while Dolly tried to figure out how to secure the carseat. My hand issue kept me from helping.

"Those belts are broken back there." Bob was watching Dolly in the mirror. "We've been meaning to get them fixed, but first thing's first." Dolly stopped fiddling with the belts she'd been unable to match up and rocked the seat twice. Her fingernails were painted the same pink as her toenails.

"I guess it's pretty steady," she said. "There just has to be one in the car, I think. Give him here." Trudeau passed Junior, who glided like a skydiver into his mother's hands. "I'll hold him for a while. He'll probably want to nurse soon. I did his diaper before you came along, so that shouldn't be a problem for a bit. He likes to sleep in the car. You're going to meet your daddy today, little man," she said to her baby, propping him up, then folding him into her lap. She smiled over at me with wet eyes that were anxious and excited.

"I don't know how I missed the turn for the Interstate," she shrugged. "Probably when Junior was crying. It's distracting."

"Hmm," Bob said. From my new seat I had a direct line on his face, and his eyes were fine; I don't know why I'd thought one was off. "Your little boy there probably saved your life." There were new smells, like sweet talcum powder and sour pee. Maybe something milky, but I was probably thinking of Dolly needing to nurse the baby. She was smiling still, but her brow creased.

"What do you mean?"

"He means we're with the state highway inspection department, and there's a situation," Trudeau said, turning half way so his bad nose was in profile. "There's a bridge out, and the Interstate is closed. But if you'd been on that road at the wrong time, God knows how you might have wound up. There's a lot of people dead. We're on our way right now to check out the catastrophe. I'm afraid that's our number one responsibility."

"Maybe I'll set him down—fresh air made him sleepy," Dolly said, hoisting up her baby and leaning with him toward the seat between us, but still riveted to what Trudeau was saying. "You can't take me to the base? I thought you'd be able to take me there straight. Didn't you say it was on the way?"

"Well," Bob said, "The truth is, we've got to see the hole first. We've got to do an assessment. It's our job and a heavy responsibility. Just like your husband, your baby's daddy, had a responsibility to fulfill, we've got our duty, too. Let us do our job, and we'll get you to the base alright."

The baby was in his seat now. His arm was stuck toward my face. His hand was so small it looked fake. He was buried in his parka, so all I could see were his nose, a cheek, and one blue eye that didn't seem to be looking at anything.

His mother sniffed a few times, thinking. "Won't take too much time?" she asked.

"Just enough to inspect," Trudeau said. "And it'll take us a little extra to get around these back roads."

Dolly tugged the baby's hood back, exposing red curls that matched her long hair. I finally admitted to myself how pretty she was. She would have been the prettiest girl in my high school.

"You might find it interesting," Bob said. "It's tragic, but something you don't see every day."

Now that she'd settled herself and her baby in, Dolly tried to catch up. "So what exactly happened?" She was looking at me when she asked. I made big eyes, like, "Oh, boy, it's trouble." The baby was cooing, and Dolly automatically gave him a knuckle to suck.

"Bad," Trudeau said. "A bridge on the Interstate collapsed. Cars and trucks from both directions drove off to their doom." He paused and turned around, looking worried, his nose never uglier. "Your fella, he wasn't driving to the base, was he? Military convoy?"

The baby was asleep and Dolly slipped her finger from his lips. "Nunh-unh," she said, "thank God for that. Those poor people. Bradley's flying in on a transport. He's supposed to be in by five. What's it now?"

Nobody in the car was wearing a watch. If there was a dashboard clock, neither Bob nor Trudeau consulted it. "Little past one," Bob said. His neck under his dyed copper hair was burnt red. Nobody from around here would have a neck like that this time of year. I hadn't noticed their plates when they picked me up. But he seemed acquainted with the roads. "That gives us plenty of time to do our job and get you where you're going. You hungry?"

Dolly was looking over her sleeping baby at me, and I smiled. "Nah," she said. "I ate a sandwich and some Chips-Ahoys just before you showed up. Junior'll let me know when he wants to nurse."

"That's good," Bob said. "Cause we had a big breakfast at the diner where the troopers found us and told us about the bridge. The place was in a panic—some of the folks in there were worried that they might have lost people."

"Good pancakes, though," Trudeau said. He half-turned and winked at me. "And some of us got extra sausages."

We were passing through some low farm land and patches of scrub oak where water had risen from ponds and creeks almost to the level of the road. Bob chose each turn without hesitation—either he knew every road or had an instinct for it. It was quiet for a while, and I got used to riding in the car. Everything felt familiar, as if I'd known these people forever. Like we were all related. Like maybe Bob and Trudeau were my uncles, and maybe Dolly and I were a couple and the baby was our baby. And I felt a thrill when I remembered where we were headed. I don't know what I expected to see. I don't know why I wasn't more worried about Bob and Trudeau and the stories they were making up. They were like bedtime stories, and I felt if I could be part of one of them, then maybe I could be anything. Maybe it was having a baby so close that made for that kind of atmosphere.

"Little Junior's got a nice look to him, a little mischievous, even in his sleep," Bob said. He'd been watching the child in the mirror. "Kind of like one of those little Cupid babies."

Dolly smiled. Her green eyes had gotten lazy-lidded and dreamy. "Got his daddy's eyes. I have to keep reminding myself that that's where I'm going today. You think somebody from the base will help with the van?"

"No question about it," Trudeau said. "The military goes out of its way to help young wives and mothers, as I understand it." Then he slapped Bob's thigh, and Bob shot a look at him. "You know," Trudeau said, "it's not Junior that's the Cupid. It's me and you! We're the Cupids, taking Dolly to meet her knight in shining armor. We're in the business of uniting lovers." At that moment Bob half-winked at me in the rearview mirror, like we were sharing a secret, and I guess we were, but I didn't know which secret he meant—that the Cupids, unbeknownst to Dolly, were also delivering me to my lover? That none of us was a bridge inspector? Of course, there wasn't any girl waiting for me anywhere. Just a cousin, if I could find him.

"Baby's so cute, I could just eat him all up," Trudeau said, and we all looked toward Junior, who was smacking his lips and making little grunting sounds. "Your mom ever say that about her grand-baby, that she could just eat him all up?" he asked Dolly.

"Un-hunh," she said, blushing under her freckles. She fussed with the hood of Junior's parka. If I went to the prom, I thought, I would have wanted to go with her, and I would have wanted her to wear a bright green gown that matched her eyes and showed off her red hair and freckled arms. I would have worn a pale blue tuxedo and shiny black shoes.

"Why don't you tell Dolly what almost ate *you* all up," Bob said. He was talking to me, but his eyes were on the road, which was narrow and headed straight through some fields where bare stalks rose through acres of standing water. We hadn't seen any houses in a long time. The water was the color of slate, which was the color of the sky. I didn't know what Bob was talking about. Dolly was looking at me with a waiting smile. Her husband was a lucky bastard. I wondered how they met.

"Yeah, tell her about what got at your hand—" Trudeau said. Dolly looked me over. The way I leaned on my stiff arm I covered the door handle, but not the hole for the window crank.

"A dog." I cleared my throat. I hadn't said anything in probably an hour. "A husky mix."

"Think he'd know better than to try to take a bone from a dog's mouth," Bob said.

"But it was a chicken bone," I said. "They splinter up. They say they'll get stuck in a dog's intestines and kill him. I thought it was an emergency." I coughed into my good hand.

"They say a human being's saliva's got more germs in it than a dog's," Dolly said.

"That's a fact," Trudeau nodded.

"Un-hunh," Bob agreed.

"What time is it now, you think?" Dolly asked. And then the baby started wailing.

You'd have thought a police siren had gone off. Junior flung his arms and legs out straight, and his face was crushed up like a fist and turning red. He was screaming so loud the car seemed to buck, as if Bob was riding the brakes. My hand started aching, and Trudeau hung his head over his seat, his nose like the last rotten apple left on a leafless tree.

"He's a little alarm clock," Dolly said over the din. She shifted around, not meeting anybody's eyes, finally pulling down the zipper of her sweatshirt. "I'm going to have to nurse him, gentlemen," she said, and the way she added "gentlemen" put things in order before she lifted Junior out of his car seat and folded back his hood so his curls glowed at us. She lifted one side of her pink t-shirt over her plump, white breast, on which the nipple had risen into a hard brown knot. I'm pretty sure I saw a drop of milk on its tip before Junior's head obscured my view.

"Hungry little guy," Trudeau said. He gazed through the windshield. Junior slurped a little while he nursed.

"Not too long now," Bob said. "Couple of miles. You can't see it, but we're near the creek that flooded. Only thing is, we're going to be at the bottom. We'll be where all the cars and trucks wound up. Emergency operations'll be under way. Would have been nice to see it from the top."

From above— on the edge— was the only way I'd imagined the scene. I hadn't thought about being in the middle of it. Dolly, her gaze maybe out the windshield, maybe at Bob's burned neck, wasn't really curious about the news. Maybe she was thinking about her reunion with her husband, maybe she was off in the place mothers go when they nurse their babies. It seemed very quiet without Junior's screaming.

You could hear the tires whooshing along the road and the baby sucking.

"Un-hunh," Trudeau said. "But being down is better, because we can do our inspection from the car. We want to do our job, not interfere. Better if we stay out of sight completely." We came to a spot where the road crossed what looked like a lake but was really a flooded field. There was about a hundred feet of rusty guardrail on either side. Bob slowed to a stop. It felt strange not to be moving. Trudeau was staring at me, his eyes and mouth dead serious.

"Okay," he said, "since you left the clipboard with the specifications and the checklist back at the diner, you've got to memorize the extent of the damage here so we can have a complete report on all the structures in the adjacent territory." Bob had set the car in park, and he shoved his door open and stepped out. He looked over the guardrail at the endless water, put his hands on his hips and stretched. He was shorter than I'd thought he was, and some of his stomach showed beneath his leather jacket when he opened my door. It was cold outside, but not freezing. Dolly looked out the door for a second, but Junior kept nursing and she shielded him with her arm. It wasn't until then that I realized with a sinking heart that I was meant to leave the car. I wasn't going to see the hole from the bottom or top.

"Check out each weld of each bolt of these guardrails for structural integrity," Trudeau said. "They're all numbered just beneath the bolt head, so you memorize the bad ones. We'll be back in about a half hour, give or take a few minutes." He looked at Dolly, who was a passive witness to my departure. "Baby's going to see his first disaster," he said.

Bob was waiting for me to get out. He was looking up and down the road. What I did next was lean over the carseat, which was hard to do with my stiff arm and my hand in my pocket, and I looked close at the back of Junior's head. The red curls had gold in them, like coins scooped from a treasure chest. Just then he turned a little, and I saw his lips part, saw a line of milky spit connect his mouth to his mother's nipple.

And I bent down further and kissed his soft cheek, just a peck, but I felt its warmth pass into me. Then Junior latched on again, and when I pulled back, Dolly was smiling at me with the purest, most serene pride I've witnessed to this day.

Then the next thing, I was watching the car disappear down the farm road, billowing exhaust hiding plates I'd never know. I stood between the rusted guardrails and licked my lips to see if I could taste the baby, but they were too cold, and if there was anything to taste, I'd lost it.

Twenty years, and my hand still won't close tight around a wrench or a bottle. I try to use it anyway, and sometimes a hammer will slip or a glass will drop on the floor, and I've got to apologize. Did you ever wait for something without anybody knowing it? Maybe it's a pretty woman about your own age. Maybe a red-headed young man with blue eyes, and you listen to hear if somebody calls him Brad or Junior. You have thoughts that would fit in a picture you'd hang in the big empty space on your wall.

Wisent: a Love Story

Because he'd read the morning paper with his coffee, William knew that the beast he found dead in his garage was not a buffalo, but the wisent missing for three days from Saugerties Game Park, thirty miles south of his city. Wisents, according to the article in the *Journal*, were native to Europe and resembled American bison; both were protected species. Wisent or bison, this one was dead, William was sure, as he circumnavigated its body. It lay collapsed like a melted mountain on the concrete floor. Its shaggy head was braced awkwardly on one of its horns, and a slab of tongue spilled from its mouth. The initials "SGP" were embossed on its iron nose ring. Delicately lashed lids were shut under a brow that reminded William of God in the Bible comics he'd trembled through as a boy. Whoever had caused this wanted William humiliated. At this very moment the perpetrator might be tipping off the newspaper. He could imagine the *Journal*'s headline: "Stolen Beast Found Dead in Beleaguered Superintendent's Garage."

If he'd remembered to replace the batteries in his garage door opener, William might have discovered the wisent the previous evening after his return from the Boston conference on Safer Schools. Had it still been alive then? Maybe it had huffed its last breath while William tossed sleeplessly a few yards away. The dying wisent wouldn't have known or cared that William's heart had just been broken— that after three days and two glorious nights together in Boston, Marilyn, the married head of student services for the district, had ended their year-long affair. "I love my husband," she'd said, as if reading from the sign for Springfield they passed on the Massachusetts Turnpike, "and I love my child."

"Don't expect to be loved," the school board president had told William when he was hired, and he hadn't been. But he hadn't bargained on contempt, even after he'd failed to save the district money, to raise test scores, or to keep gangs out of the schools. After his second year as superintendent, an editorial cartoon in the *Journal* depicted him as an evil Santa, his half-buried sled harnessed to the city's children. The caption read "Snow day? Humbug!"

The city hated William, and he hated it back. He lived in a vacuum, daily survival his only object, until Marilyn burrowed into his life—a rash of student suicides had left her floundering, and, after she broke down in William's office, she'd found solace in his arms. Their miseries parallel, the two administrators had fallen into something that wasn't love, but seemed to be the next best thing—until Marilyn terminated their romance in the middle of the Mass Pike.

William contemplated the dead wisent. Its stench reminded him of a childhood spent at 4H Club meetings and county fairs. He sighed and speed-dialed Tony Costello, the district head of buildings and grounds. "Tony has his ways," the outgoing superintendent had told William. "Keep on his good side, and he'll be there when you need him." During the first month of William's tenure, Tony Costello had emailed him: *You are strong and sensible. The district needs you.*

You are someone I can trust, William had replied. The next day the head custodian had come to William's office to show his new boss a framed print-out of that message. "This will go on my wall," he'd said.

William was watching a fly disappear into the wisent's nostril when Tony Costello picked up.

"This is the superintendent," William said. "I'm at home, alone, and I need you here."

*****

William waited on his front walk for Tony Costello. He stared at his garage door—it was as broad and white as a movie screen. No one would guess what lay behind it. He spotted a flattened clod of what had to be wisent dung behind his car a moment before Tony pulled up in a silver SUV. William led him to the garage through the house. When

Tony saw the beast, he nodded, then shut his eyes and sniffed. The smell had grown worse. Tony stood with his hands on his hips. William did the same. Nothing moved except the flies buzzing around the wisent's head. The two men gazed at the body as if it were a sunset.

"You would like to know who did this," Tony concluded.

"It's obviously some kind of terrible, tragic joke," William said. "Could be anyone. I would prefer that the police not be involved— if the *Journal* finds out, it's just more negative publicity. Getting rid of it is the priority."

"But someone is responsible for this," Tony said. "When you get home tonight, it'll be as if this never happened. I'll change your locks. There'll be new keys in your mailbox. Go to your office and take care of the city's children. But," his frown mirrored the superintendent's, "you can't have the meat. It's gone to rot. Spoiled. Otherwise, you could have had buffalo steaks."

"It's a wisent, not a buffalo," William said. He pronounced the "w" like a "v" without knowing why. "I can't tell you how grateful I am." He offered his hand, and Tony shook it. Then the head custodian crossed his arms, waiting for the superintendent to leave.

*****

Printouts of budget figures and grant applications littered William's desk, but his thoughts wandered. What exactly was happening in his garage? Then he pictured Marilyn, as she'd posed for him in their Boston hotel bed. She'd be shocked by the wisent situation. "My goodness," she'd say, after she'd learned of its removal, after she'd forsaken her family again for William's embrace, as she surely would. He imagined the wisent's head, tilted like a curious puppy's— it seemed to be eavesdropping on his private thoughts.

*****

When he pulled into his driveway long after darkness, William knew the job had been done. There was no sign of Tony's SUV, and in his mailbox he found new keys and his garage door opener. With light-hearted daring he pressed "open": the door rose; the wisent was gone. The concrete floor looked freshly poured under the fluorescent light. The walls and ceiling gleamed as if repainted. William's lawn tools had been neatly arrayed. He stepped in and breathed deeply—the garage smelled like a pine forest washed by rain. For a moment he thought the wisent had been a dream. Tony had worked a miracle.

*****

Two weeks later, William took his seat at the conference table among the district's senior staff members gathered for their bi-monthly meeting.

"You've heard about the bull balls?" the assistant superintendent smirked.

"Excuse me?" William glanced at Marilyn, who sat across the table and didn't lift her eyes from her agenda. "Is this appropriate?"

The assistant superintendent lifted an eyebrow. "Bull testicles," he said. "One of the high school custodians found them hanging from his pickup's rearview this morning. Apparently he had an argument with you-know-who-Costello about overtime hours and wrote a letter to the regional union head. He complained about Tony's conflict of interest— your boss shouldn't be your union rep. But the letter got forwarded back to Tony, who didn't say a word about it. Instead, he made copies and posted them in the custodian rooms at every school. Then the bull balls."

"Was any of this on school property?" William asked.

"I think he switched the balls back to baby shoes before he drove to work," the associate superintendent said.

The others laughed. Even Marilyn smiled. William tried to hold her gaze, but her eyes slipped away.

"I suggest we move on," he said. "No one's come to me about it."

*****

Tony--

Your hard work as energy manager has not gone unnoticed. You are one of the district's unsung heroes. Please keep me advised regarding future issues concerning personal property.

--William

Mr. Superintendent—

Thanks for the support. We are men who believe in decisive action. There are not many like us.

--Sincerely, Anthony Costello, District Manager of Buildings, Grounds, and Energy Conservation

William appreciated Tony Costello's enthusiasm, but the custodian shouldn't have sliced through the cords of the coffee makers and microwaves three faculty members had neglected to unplug—the new policy forbidding the unauthorized use of appliances was barely a week old. William had immediately guaranteed the furious teachers full restitution. Problem avoided—the superintendent sensed in Tony's Monday morning email reply that his head custodian and he remained on the same page.

But a moment after reading Tony's message, William opened a letter from the state education commissioner and learned that the district's application for a multi-million dollar Safer School's grant, money that William had been counting on to balance the budget, had been denied. William read the letter three times. *Inaccurately reported information? Missed deadline?* Mistrusting everyone else, William had taken care of the application on his own. This failure would be impossible to explain. He was still dazed when he took the phone call from the president of the teacher's union.

"William," she said, "this can't happen."

"No," he agreed, before realizing she couldn't possibly be referring to the failed grant application.

"Bloody horse hooves, William? 'Waster' written on the paper bags they were in? Who the hell does he think he is, the Godfather?"

William's temples throbbed. "Who are we talking about?"

"For God's sake, William, who else? Tony Costello. Those teachers who had their appliances ruined found the horrible things in their mailboxes. At home! One of them lives all the way in Saratoga. Where does he even get horse hooves from?"

"You say it's their home mailboxes? I don't see how this is a district matter,"

"What if they'd sent out their kids out for the mail? Would you want one of your children finding a blood-soaked bag with a hoof in it? You've got to stop him."

*****

On the wall behind the head custodian's desk was a framed printout. William couldn't read it, but he knew what it said: *You are one I can trust.* The superintendent stood sweating in his coat. His fingers felt numb, and he clenched his hands.

"Tony, I just want you to know you're doing a fine job. Excellent reports all around. Something silly has come up—and I have to ask you about it. Have you heard anything about horse hooves?"

Tony looked puzzled. He sat back in his chair. "*Horse* hooves? Why would I know anything about *horse* hooves? Where would a person find such a thing?"

William's grin hurt. "Well, if you do hear anything, could you let me know? Give me a head's up? We can do that for each other, right, a head's up?"

The head custodian smiled. "Of course. Any parts I hear about, I'll tell you."

*****

William met the school board president and Marilyn in a diner. The president, as always, was concerned about the district's image. "Gangs and suicides are a lethal combination," he fretted. "Property values are in freefall." William sat beside Marilyn in the booth, but couldn't look into her eyes—their faces would have been too close. He watched his former lover's fingertips spin her coffee cup while the board president droned on about his concerns. He felt her thigh against his and remembered her beneath him in the Boston hotel bed the first night of the conference. She had whispered to him, nicknamed him Willy, complimented his bulk and strength, and she had been so smooth. Marilyn had the same scent—perfume and something else— she'd had the last time they'd made love. An image of the wisent arose, its shoulders and back humped like the Matterhorn, its head bowed, its short horns curved forward. He thought about mounting Marilyn from behind, and the muscles of his face slackened.

"Have we heard back about the grant yet?" the board president asked.

William shivered and crossed his legs. His cheeks tingled. "I should find out something by the end of the week," he lied. What he wanted was to be left alone with Marilyn. He'd move across from her in the booth, tell her he missed her, remind her of their Boston trip, reach for her hand—

"What's this I'm hearing about animal parts?" the board president asked.

William sighed and shook his head. "Just rumors. I've been investigating. It seems to be some kind of practical joke. Kids, maybe. Could be gang related."

"Well—keep it out of the *Journal*. We don't need people thinking we're into some kind of voodoo craziness."

"There are also animal rights activists," Marilyn said. William felt her warm glow beside him, like an incubator full of baby chicks.

"And if Tony Costello's involved—he's useful, but rein him in."

"Tony's a good soldier," William said. "I'm on top of him."

"Stay there. Plan on unveiling the grant at the board meeting next week. Emphasize the 'millions.' Marilyn—suicides?"

"I'm sending out fliers to the community with information William and I gathered at the Boston conference." William flushed when she linked their names. *Call me*, he longed to murmur—*or at least pick up when I call you*. If she did he might tell her about the wisent.

*****

The leg, from haunch to split hoof, was longer than William's desk. It was surprisingly thin, considering the weight it had once borne, and the hide was smooth, not shaggy. Dried blood stained the white cloth it had been wrapped in. The thing's smell revived the superintendent's shock at finding a wisent in his garage.

"Please shut the door, Stan," he asked the athletic director who towered before him. "Girls—" William called to the secretary and receptionist hovering in the doorway, their noses wrinkled in disgust, "—the door."

"What the fuck, William? What the *fuck*? My *wife* found this. There was blood smeared on my windshield. It's a good thing Sandy's a nurse—she kept her head. But what the fuck?" Stan's spit flew. "You know who did this, the little coward!"

"You're not going to get very far making unconfirmed allegations, Stan. If it was on your property, that makes it a police matter. You don't live in-district, do you? Don't you think you should, by the way? It gives an impression—"

"This happened because I came to you last week about keeping the gym open late for middle school basketball practice. Because I complained when he locked the kids out in the cold. Christ, he said they were 'using too much electricity.'"

"Stan, there's a chain of command. I told you to work it out with him." The men's eyes dropped to the bloody leg. "This is just a practical joke that got out of hand. Somebody shot a deer," William said, "or they found some road kill. But I'll investigate."

"You'll investigate." Stan sneered. This was Stan Chutsky's city—he'd lived in it all his life, had been a beloved athlete and coach, and William hated him for it. The athletic director placed his hand on the limb he'd flung onto William's desk. "The *police* will investigate. You can count on that. We'll see who's joking." He lifted the leg with a grunt. For a moment William thought Stan might swing it at him, and he slouched back in his seat. Instead, the athletic director threw open the door and strode out, cradling the amputation as if it were a rescued child.

Through the door William saw the secretary and receptionist watching him. The limb's taint remained; shed hairs were scattered over his correspondence. Without hesitation he typed an email to Tony Costello: *Just a heads up. Maybe an investigation. Be prepared. I'll do as much as I can.*

*****

William lay in bed, one hand holding his cell phone, the other down his shorts, cupping his balls. He shifted, and the cardboard tray from his frozen dinner slid to the floor. It might as well have sunk into a midnight sea. He despised the city that engulfed the house, and after dark only his bedroom felt safe. Tony Costello was becoming a burden. But William had a more immediate problem than his bond with the custodian. If he couldn't conjure up an explanation, tomorrow night at the school board meeting his failure to secure the multi-million dollar grant would become public. What he needed was time to think, and he'd crawled under his sheets at seven with that intent. But now the digits on his phone read three-thirteen, and he'd done nothing except worry. He hadn't even been able to frame a proper prayer.

With a thumb twitch he could speed-dial Marilyn. It wasn't fair for her to rebuff him. Right now she lay next to her husband, probably believing she'd reclaimed her virtue. But she'd always be marked. William had branded her—she'd feel it when she ran her fingers down her flesh.

No sleep until he solved his dilemma—if God helped him get out of this, William swore he'd head back to Indiana. If his mother were still alive, he'd have called her. "When you're worried and cannot sleep, just count your blessings instead of sheep," she'd sung to him when he was little. Tony Costello—he'd started out as a blessing. Now he had the wisent and was parceling it out bit by bit. It was possible, even probable, that Tony had stolen the beast and led it into William's garage in the first place. Hadn't William suspected something like this all along? A dead wisent was the perfect way to make someone beholden.

William rubbed his cock. He thought of Marilyn's pale skin under his hands, her mouth opening to his, her legs spreading under him. Again, what a delight it would be to mount her from the rear. Months ago, after fate had thrown them together, they'd been wildly indiscreet, and she'd shared this bed. As William gave in to sleep, Marilyn's figure seemed palpable. But his nostrils twitched from an unpleasant waft, and the weight of something that wasn't his lover's body compressed the mattress beside him: the wisent head. It haunted his dreams.

The next morning William dressed by reflex. Twelve hours—half a day—until he'd face the board, and neither God nor reason had provided him with a way out. Maybe if he broke down at the podium and wept over his mother's sudden death—but an obituary's date was too easy to confirm. He stared into his hall mirror. His fingers trembled at the knot of his tie. Marilyn would be a witness to his colossal failure. What if he publicly confessed their affair? But that didn't make sense, and his tiny spasm of hope dissolved. William stepped into his clean garage, touched a button, and the door hummed open. Here was his car. Somewhere else lay a mutilated wisent. He saw his mother's embalmed, waxy face, her gray curls against the white satin of her casket. *How peaceful she looks*, voices whispered, *how youthful, how like her son.*

William got into his car and sat behind his steering wheel. Reflected in his rearview were his neighbor's house, the trees, lawn, and driveway. Nothing distinguished any of it. He could be anywhere. He unpocketed his cell phone and dialed the police, asking that a detective meet him at his office in an hour. He'd give them Tony Costello. William had the cleanest garage in the world—there was nothing to trace the wisent there—the head custodian had taken care of that himself. Tony had the carcass. Any claim implicating William would only sound silly. William would be a hero! He'd spend the board meeting outlining the head custodian's wrong-doings. And in the weeks of chaos likely to ensue, wouldn't a missed deadline or two be understandable? Certainly the state would allow a reapplication under such circumstances. His heart lifted—he felt as if he'd been hoisted to the shoulders of an adoring mob.

*****

A detective was waiting at the door of William's office. "Thank you for being prompt," the superintendent said. "The matter I've asked you here to discuss concerns the safety and security of our city's residents." William ushered his guest into the conference room and sat beside him at the long table. "Lieutenant—?"

"Wilson. You called the department? I didn't know that. I'm here as part of a continuing investigation—I need to ask you a few questions about one of your employees—Tony Costello."

"Yes, certainly." A "continuing investigation"? That would be Stan Chutsky's doing—the athletic director had followed through on his threat to contact the police about the bloody leg. But William could still control the narrative. He answered the detective's preliminary questions quickly: he'd known Mr. Costello for two years; their acquaintance was strictly professional; the head custodian had a reputation for being "difficult to work with," but had otherwise been a loyal employee with years of service to the district and city—until William's recent suspicions.

"It's come to my attention, lieutenant, that Mr. Costello might have been responsible for some extremely inappropriate, even illegal, activities. At first I regarded them as practical jokes that were outside district jurisdiction, and I'd advised the parties concerned to contact the police—but I began an investigation of my own, after which I concluded—well, as I said, I called the police myself this morning. About the animal parts. The wisent parts."

The lieutenant cocked his head. "*Viz-ant?*"

William had slipped into the accent again. The detective tapped his notebook with a pen. "I'm not sure how you pronounce it," William smiled, then frowned, searching for the right expression. "It's the animal that all the parts came from."

"Hunh. What's a 'viz-ant'? We've got a deer leg. A 'viz-ant'?"

William cleared his throat, admonishing himself to slow down. "W-I-S-E-N-T. It's a European buffalo. It's on the 'vulnerable species' list. I read in the *Journal* a few weeks ago that one had been stolen, so when Mr. Chutsky—our athletic director, who I advised to call you—well, I just put two and two together."

"Your first thought when someone dropped fifty pounds of meat on your desk was that you were looking at a *viz-ant* and not a deer or a cow?"

"I grew up in farm country," William said. "I was in 4-H. There were hunters in my family. I know what deer and cow parts look like when I see them, and the leg Mr. Chutsky brought to show me was definitely neither of those."

"So your next best guess was a *viz-ant* because you'd read one was missing. You'd make a good detective."

William grinned, but his ears burned. "I told you," he held up two fingers on each hand and brought them together, "two and two. Because I remembered about the other recent incidents regarding district employees and animal parts. You know about those, I'm sure. I told my staff members to inform you."

"And you think the three hooves and the, uh, balls, were from the same *viz-ant* as the leg?"

"I told you I'm not sure about the pronunciation. I didn't see the other parts. But all of the aggrieved had been in a dispute of some kind with Mr. Costello. That's the link. I think he's been using those animal parts to intimidate our employees. And I suppose that means that he stole the wisent." William pronounced the "w" carefully. "It was valuable—and endangered, too, I think."

"There'll be DNA testing," the lieutenant said, jotting something down, "of the parts we have and everything they touched."

William felt sweat droplets pop at his hairline. Exactly how clean was his garage? "Have you spoken to Mr. Costello?"

"He's been in custody since yesterday evening. We picked him up at his home. There'll be more questions for you down the road about what we found there. We're searching all district vehicles he might have driven. We're presently going through his office. We've impounded his PC and the hard drive from his office computer. Your cooperation is appreciated."

"Of course." Had whatever remained of the wisent been found? It had to be at Tony's. William saw himself at the podium. His audience awaited: the board president; a reporter from the *Journal*; Marilyn.

"*You are one I can trust?*"

"Excuse me?"

"On Mr. Costello's wall. From an email you sent him."

"Yes—he'd done an especially fine job as energy manager."

"*Trust?*" Lieutenant Wilson flipped over a page in his notebook. "What about this one—: *Just a heads up. Maybe an investigation. Be prepared. I'll do as much as I can.* That was from late yesterday afternoon. From you to Mr. Costello." The detective's eyes were like a shark's.

William heaved a breath. He shut his eyes. He heard himself speaking, but in his mind it was Marilyn, the reporter, the board president who were listening: "So many terrible things in this city. Gangs and kids killing themselves. My mother's dead. I lost my girlfriend . . ." Then his mother's whisper: *Time to pray. Time to count your blessings.* His eyes popped open. "You're sure that message was sent from me?"

"Your computer. Your name. There's a reply, sent from Mr. Costello's personal account—from just a few minutes before he was taken into custody—maybe you didn't get it?"

William squinted. The lieutenant seemed to have joined the spectators at the imaginary board meeting. The officer sat next to Marilyn, who looked over his shoulder as he read Tony Costello's reply. The detective's voice even sounded like Tony's:

"'*Heads up*'— *Ha-ha. There's something in your attic in a large black contractor bag. A souvenir of our deal.*"

"*Deal,*" Lieutenant Wilson repeated. "What do you think is in your attic?"

Had William really slipped to his knees? The floor was cold and hard. He seemed to be nudged from behind, and then he tipped forward onto all fours. His back swayed beneath a sudden weight; something nuzzled his ear. A thrust rocked him forward. Another, and his chin met the tiles. He waited for more.

"Oh, Tony," he sighed.

Karaoke for the Deaf

Section 1.0: Cremation and Waste Ethics
(1.1) In no way can human remains be treated as waste.
(1.2) Even so . . . the environmental impact of cremation must be minimized.
 —*The International Cremation Foundation Guide to Cremation Practice,* p. 3

Gil, my neighbors' German Shepherd, is a retired cadaver dog. The Nelsons got him through some connection with the state police. Gil is in his prime—he's got thick muscles rippling under his glossy black and tan coat. I'm not privy to the career arc of cadaver dogs, so I don't know if he was entitled to an early retirement or if he screwed up and got fired. When Gil frolics with the Nelson children on their front lawn, his jaws gape with barking I don't hear—I've been deaf since the explosion at the crematorium two years ago. I'm sure you heard about it—the story hung in the national news for months. On mornings like this one when the two older Nelson children are at school, Gil lies on the family's gated front porch, and his amber eyes melt over me.

Before the explosion that deafened and neutered me, I loaded deceased loved ones into a cremator and poured the ashes into urns. I also took care of the grounds. According to investigators, the ninety-three year old former physicist I'd slid into the cremator had swallowed enough plastic explosives and detonating chemicals to pack his stomach and intestinal tract. 2100 degrees Fahrenheit set them off. The force of the explosion blew me twenty feet through a window onto the lawn I'd mowed that morning. I woke from a month's coma to find myself seared as smooth as a Ken doll between my knees and waist. A permanent forest fire now roars in my ears. My survival was hailed "a miracle." The crematorium's two other employees were trapped in the front office and burned to death.

The cremator operator is not legally responsible for checking the guts of ninety-three-year-olds for incendiaries, so I'm set for life, thanks to my settlement with the corporation that owns the crematorium. The corporation, in turn, lost their own suit against the hospital that released the physicist's body without an autopsy. The ruling determined that there's nothing suspicious about someone that old dropping dead. My ex-wife, Linda, was entitled to half of my award.

While he stares at me, Gil rests his muzzle on his forepaws, the tip of his nose poking between the railings of the Nelsons' porch. Now and then his tail lifts and falls. Linda and I had been having trouble well before the explosion. Our three year marriage had been a mistake from the start, she said. We'd met at a party, and she thought she'd overheard me say something witty, when really it had been somebody else. For years she'd quoted the joke: "Did you hear about the fire at the circus? The heat was intense!" and I'd taken credit for it. When she told me I'd grown morose and didn't say funny things like I used to, I confessed that I'd never told the circus fire joke in the first place. We argued about things like whether or not to have kids, which is something couples should get straight before they marry. I didn't see the point—if nothing else, the crematorium job I'd held since dropping out of college had taught me that all stories end with the same flammable page. Kids are no different than everyone else: potential ashes. Just add fire. Linda told me I have a "botoxed soul," but refused to explain what she meant.

Linda is a real estate agent and coordinated with federal and local authorities to find me a home in this neighborhood. These agencies don't know what to make of me. They don't really think the explosion was a terrorist attack, and they don't actually suspect that I had anything to do with the "percussive event," but since the physicist's motives have never been proven, I linger on their radar. The Nelsons' house and mine are the only two homes on this cul-de-sac. The family knows I'm the guy from the crematorium explosion. They've received detailed information about me, and I have a written report about them: husband Ed, wife Nina, and the kids, whose names I've forgotten. I learned all about Gil from the report. The Nelson's have had him for a year. Everything has to be written down for me—I can't read lips, and I don't have the patience to learn signing.

I'm not about to ask anyone, but I wonder if Gil, before his retirement, sniffed over the scorched rubble of my crematorium. Did he help collect the bits of the physicist? Would he have confused the parts of the bodies that had been lined up for incineration with those of the freshly killed—Nick the manager and Becca his secretary? Would he have caught wind of their not-so-secret affair? Maybe Gil had pawed at the ashes of my genitals and filed away my scent in his memory.

I've read about my event on the internet. Blowing up a crematorium didn't make sense to anyone. The terrorism talk flared up, then burned itself out. The forensic experts concluded that the physicist had swallowed the explosives the day before his death and that his clogged system triggered his heart attack. Circumstantial evidence suggests that he'd intended to self-detonate the following evening at a testimonial banquet given in his honor by the tech firm he'd been retired from for ages. The physicist's seventy-year-old daughter said her father had been "looking forward to the event for months."

"The reception was to have been attended by some of the nation's most pre-eminent thinkers," the director of the tech company said. "The loss would have been incalculable. And tragic."

I'm no scientist, but on sleepless nights I pretend that I'd been invited to that testimonial. There'd be a phone call canceling the event—*the guest of honor just passed away— heart attack—perhaps the impact of such excitement on an old man's system should have been considered.* Then another phone call—*an explosion!*—and sobering gossip among my fellow invitees regarding the physicist's probable intentions. I would understand what it felt like to have a target lifted from my back that I hadn't known existed. I'd ponder the vicissitudes of fate and vow to take nothing in life for granted. When I get tired of pretending, I fondle the warm piss-bag strapped to my thigh and doze off to the purr of flames.

At first I protested splitting my settlement fifty-fifty with Linda. She threatened, only half-seriously, I think, to turn me in to the FBI. "I'll tell them you always had suicidal thoughts," she said. "I'll tell them about your obsession with the 'fire at the circus.'" She forgot I'd confessed that the joke wasn't mine.

The Nelsons know I'm deaf, but the implanted catheter tube that drains into my piss-bag is information I keep to myself. Ed, Nina, and the two older children wave at me aggressively when they see me. They open their mouths so wide they must be shouting. My voice punches through my sternum when I answer "Hello." When the older boy and girl romp with the toddler, they mouth two syllables, so I think of him as "Eep-eep." Nina Nelson's bright red lips form the same syllables when she leaves the baby on the porch with Gil. Eep-eep spreads himself atop the lounging dog, his chin on Gil's head. While I rock in my chair and try to read the paper, their gazes tighten around me like boa constrictors.

This spring morning the sky is a sharp blue. Nina Nelson exits her front door with Eep-eep on her hip. She's holding a clipboard. When Gil rises to greet her, she says something to him, and he sits, tongue lolling. She steps off her porch, secures the gate, and crosses the grass between our houses. She's studying her clipboard as if it's a hand mirror. I don't get many visitors: a weekly nurse to check my equipment; grocery deliveries; a lawn service.

Smiling, Nina Nelson mounts my porch steps. She has the same china-dish complexion and blue eyes as the baby she jostles. She hands me the clipboard, and mother and child look down at me like astronauts on the moon watching earthrise. The message is printed in italics:

HELLO NEIGHBOR!

We hope you've been getting on well. We speak often to Linda, and we've tried to give you time and space to adjust to your new home. We'd like to have you over for dinner soon. Maybe a backyard barbecue in the summer.

But today the Nelson family would like to ask you for a big, big favor. We're supposed to leave in two days for Disney World—it's the children's April break, and they've never been. But last night our kennel called and informed us that they're infested with fleas, and all pet-boarding reservations have been canceled.

I glance over at Gil, who's panting at us from the Nelsons' porch. When he sees me look at him, he lifts his head. Nina Nelson, guessing how far I've read, points at the dog, grins, and nods. I pick up where I left off:

We're keeping our fingers crossed that you could care for Gil during our week at Disney. All the other kennels are full, and you're our last hope. Our other friends are on vacation, too, or are allergic to dogs.

I peek up: Nina Nelson's eyes are watery.

Gil will be easy to care for. He's very obedient. We've measured out food for his breakfast and dinner. He only needs walks around the block in the morning, afternoon, and evening. He could stay in our house or in yours—we promise, he hasn't had an accident since we've owned him! Attached is a list of phone numbers: ours, the vets, and the Disney hotel's. Also a feeding schedule.

So what do you think?

I sneak another look at Gil, then hand the clipboard back to Nina Nelson. My thumb lifts from my fist and my head bobs: my body has agreed to the proposition before I've had time to think it over. My neighbor's red lips stretch into a smile of relief.

"You need to enjoy vacations while you can," I feel myself say, wondering how much my injuries have changed my voice. Nina Nelson nods gravely and pokes the clipboard toward Gil: she's going to introduce us to one other. She starts to hand me Eep-eep before pulling him back and bounding with him from my porch back to her own to fetch the dog. The baby's eyes rise and fall with his mother's steps, but don't release me.

*****

Gil is staying at my house. It's half the size of the Nelsons'. Both homes were built within the last decade. All of my interior surfaces—walls, floors, counters—are off-white. Everything seems laminated. Gil watches me connect a fresh piss-bag before I pull on my pajamas.

"Easier than a walk around the block," I tell him. Gil's also neutered, like all cadaver dogs. It helps them stay focused on dead bodies instead of females in heat. The first night of his visit, Gil abandoned his bed and jumped up on mine. When my mattress heaved, I kept my eyes closed as the big dog settled his bulk against the backs of my thighs. I hadn't thought of marriage's casual contact for a while.

The exploding physicist didn't leave a suicide note. Nothing in his notebooks, nothing on his computer or in cyberspace. If a note had been in his pocket, the forensics experts who sifted the charred splatter of his entrails would have reassembled it. On the internet I find foggy pictures of the physicist as a young man. He holds a pipe and poses with famous scientists whose names are almost familiar. The same decade-old driver's license photo of me turns up again and again. There are Facebook selfies of my crematorium boss and his secretary. When I scroll through these pictures, I'm reminded of photographs of my parents from their wedding album: slim and youthful, they blazed with promise. Both died gently, Mom in a hospice bed, Dad a year later, stretched out on his living room carpet where I found him, white and cold as marble.

Tonight I dream of the Nelsons at Disney World. Though I've never been there, it's as easy to imagine as heaven: the family poses for pictures with Goofy and Mickey and Donald; they spin in tea cups and gawk at Cinderella's castle; they float in jungle lagoons and point at mechanized elephants and crocodiles; they crow at the escapades of Caribbean pirates. In fact, Nina Nelson texts often. "We're having fun!" she reports. "The weather is great! How's Gil?" I've replied, "Great. Nice. He's fine." My dream follows the Nelsons to "It's a Small World." The exhibit's theme song plays in an endless loop that out-roars the fire in my head and reminds me of Beethoven's last words: "I shall hear in heaven." The Nelsons and their fellow vacationers ride past frozen-faced animatronic children outfitted in international costumes. There's an explosion: all heads, human and animated, jerk up. The sky falls in burning chunks. The hall fills with smoke. Fake children topple from their pedestals. A burst of flame illuminates the shrieking face of Nina Nelson. Limp Eep-eep dangles from her arms. Everything shudders as the walls of "It's a Small World" implode. Then I'm outside, in the dark, watching from above. A cloud of glowing smoke blooms from the carnage and takes the shape of a gigantic, eyeless mouse head.

I wake to find Gil looming over me, his forepaws planted on my chest, compressing my diaphragm. "Gil—" I grunt, and pat my piss-bag—it's unpunctured. The dog sticks his cold nose in my ear, and I smell his fishy breath. Maybe he scented the Nelsons in my dream and wants to dig them out from under the plastic corpses of foreign children. Unless he's after something deeper. My smartphone flashes on my night table, and I push Gil off—he's as heavy as a boulder. There's a fresh message from Nina Nelson: "Mickey-shaped pancakes for breakfast!" Sunlight streams through my bedroom window. Nine o'clock already? We're an hour late for Gil's walk.

This morning, Gil is uninterested in our usual route and strains at his leash toward every side street. He looks back at me with eager eyes, and I imagine his voice:

"Burr-nee—" he begs. Bernie is the nickname my ex-wife gave me because of my job. I'm Ethan to the nurse who checks me for infections. She met Gil yesterday. "Nice doggy," she wrote on the dry erase board I use for messages.

She showed the note to Gil and bared her teeth in a laugh. The woman looks to be about as old as my mother was when I was in grade school—about the age I am now. She's my second nurse. The first had long legs and wore a short skirt. She knew I was some kind of celebrity. She wrote me a note after checking my catheter: "Your wound is like what some of the boys back from Iraq have. But more exotic." Her printing was childish and barely legible. "Exotic" might have been "erotic." I emailed her supervisor and requested a different nurse "for personal reasons."

My father was shot through the hand in Korea. He couldn't make a fist after, but his clawed fingers were perfect for throwing a knuckleball. One flew over my glove once when I was ten and smashed my nose. Is it south that Gil wants to go? All the way to Florida in search of the Nelsons?

"They're fine," I tell the dog. "I got a text message." But he's so insistent that I give in and follow his lead.

My next message from Nina Nelson is "Thunderstorms," followed by a sad face made of a colon and parenthesis. Here, the sky is a spring blue so crisp it makes my eyes ache. Since I stopped resisting, Gil has settled into an easy trot.

"Florida is a long way off," I say, and he flicks me a glance. We're on a quiet suburban road. Only a few cars pass, but we encounter other pedestrians, some also with dogs. A round woman with an enthusiastic poodle makes a face both apologetic and accusatory and hoists her pet to her chest. At the next corner we meet an old man, coincidentally led by a German Shepherd. The old man's dog is heavier and less handsome then Gil. We let our dogs touch noses. The guy twitches fingers at me as if he knows I'm deaf, and his hand reminds me of my father's. The night Dad died alone in his house, he called me at two AM.

"I'm all backed up," Dad whispered, as if he was sharing a secret. "I need Ex-lax."

He wanted me to go out and buy him a laxative. No, he hadn't called a doctor. Unless the woman next to me in bed was pretending to sleep, Dad's call didn't wake her—this was a few years before Linda.

"Everything's closed," I said.

"I'm going to blow up," Dad whined.

I told him I'd be there by noon the next day, which was too late.

Gil and I have walked a long way. Front lawns are greening. Yellow forsythia brighten some yards, and there are beds of daffodils in others. A few houses are decorated for Easter: cutouts of colored eggs are taped in windows and plastic ones hang from trees; an adult-sized, inflatable Easter Bunny lurks under the flaming blossoms of a crabapple tree. Soon I'll need to replace my piss-bag. I always carry a spare. The road we've been on comes to an end at a park, and Gil pulls me onto the gravel path leading into it. Around us are monuments. A cemetery? It's drawn my cadaver dog like a magnet. But I don't see any headstones, and the monuments are actually plywood silhouettes of dogs about the size and shape of Gil. Maybe this is a pet cemetery. Gil pauses at a nearby cut-out dog, lifts his leg, and pisses on it. It looks like he's marking his own shadow. As we move on, I remember what these dog silhouettes are for: they're spread around the park to keep flocks of geese from shitting all over the green space. The crematorium manager found "Decoy Dogs" like these in a catalogue once and asked if we needed them for our grounds, but I told him geese were the least of our problems.

The park's grassy fields end at a forested hill. Steel towers carry high tension wires up and over its crest between pines and budding oaks. The path Gil and I follow connects to a grassy swath beneath the rising progression of towers. The trees would provide enough cover for me to switch in a new piss-bag. It occurs to me that Gil has honed in on the scent of something dead. Maybe behind the next tree, the next bench, the next dog silhouette, we'll run into something horrible. Maybe a crow dropped whatever was left of my prick way out here. "Please, Gil," I pray as we hurry forward, "don't find a baby."

If a cadaver dog had led forensic experts to the few ashes I left at the site of the explosion, might my little pile have been mistaken for more of the physicist's remains? Maybe the experts would have found bits of a shopping list I'd had in my pocket and guessed it was the old man's suicide note: "Bread . . . butter . . . bacon . . . beer." Maybe they're struggling even now to break the code.

Abruptly, Gil stops and sits, his nose in the air: he's looking up at something. Hovering far overhead is an orange hot air balloon with a small black gondola. The balloon drifts through the cloudless sky toward the forested slope, and Gil lifts his rump and follows. The balloon seems to be descending, but perspective is difficult. I don't know if it's a full-sized balloon. The gondola looks empty.

After my nose stopped bleeding from Dad's knuckleball, he washed me up and drove us to the Dairy Queen. We licked vanilla cones in the front seat of our station wagon and listened to a baseball game on the radio. I couldn't taste the cone and resisted an urge to plunge my throbbing nose into it. We could see the car dealership next to the DQ through the windshield. Tethered to a new pickup truck was a miniature hot-air balloon, orange, with "BEST DEALS" printed across it. The balloon floated maybe a hundred feet over the dealership. It shifted in the breeze and looked like a fishing-line bobber on the surface of a lake. I'd never been fishing with Dad. He said there were no good places nearby. Through teary eyes I watched my father watching the balloon: he had tears in his eyes, too. God, he loved me.

My phone hums in my pocket—a message from Nina Nelson, no doubt. Maybe the storms have moved through Orlando, and the family has joined the others strolling down Disney World's Main Street. I envision the crowd as a battalion of black cut-outs of moms and dads and children—human versions of the dogs Gil and I have passed through.

But to my surprise the marching shadow families cast colorful reflections in the puddles I see them stepping over.

The phone stops buzzing. Gil sits again, and I almost stumble over him because I'm watching the orange balloon angle toward the wires and towers—it will miss them, at least on our side of the hill.

Sing along with the bouncing ball! That's what jumps into my head when I see the balloon so close to the wires—from musical cartoons older than my parents I watched on Saturday mornings at sunrise. A ball hopped along the words to a song played by goofy animals, and I remember joining in, though I'm not sure I was old enough to read. The music led me. But now I wouldn't hear the melody. It's tough to imagine karaoke for the deaf.

The balloon is gone. I look down at Gil, and he's squeezed his eyes shut. His ears lie back, and his jaws sip at the empty sky. *Burr-nee,* he howls—the sound buzzes through his leash into my palm like audio-Braille: *Burr-nee!*

If the balloon had fallen into the towers and wires on the other side of the hill, wouldn't there have been a flash of light? At least some smoke rising over the crest? Gil spins me around with a lunge, and I almost lose my grip on his leash. He's taking me home. We race over the gravel path and through the pack of shadow dogs. No chance to change my full piss-bag or check my texts.

"Gil—" I pant. *Burr-nee,* hums in my hand, then up through my wrist and arm to my shoulder. Whatever amount the Nelsons demand for this dog, I'll pay. If my crematorium money can't buy him for me, what good is it?

The Wild Pandas of Chincoteague

We've waited for the drawbridge to lower, driven through the deserted stretch of tourist-town Chincoteague, and passed over a second bridge leading to the refuge where the wild ponies herd. Six-month old Greta fidgets behind me in her car seat. My daughter won't remember this visit, but, even if we don't see any ponies, someday I'll present her with a memory she can treasure. When that day comes, I'll be counting on my little brother Austin, seated now next to his niece, not to contradict me.

"She hungry?" I ask, glancing in the rearview. We've been making our way south down the coastal highways for two days, following the same route I took with my parents when I was Austin's age, eleven. Austin splits his seat time— in back with Greta when she needs nourishment or entertainment, up front with me whenever she naps. When there's a diaper issue, we pull over. If this tour of Chincoteague goes quickly, we'll be at our rental in Nag's Head on North Carolina's Outer Banks by early evening, four hours from now.

I watch Austin waggle Greta's bottle over her car seat. His delicate features are set patiently, as if he's trying to tempt a big fish. All I can see of my daughter is a lock of bright hair and a red, white and blue ribbon. In the back of the SUV we've got a cooler packed with bottles and bags of frozen breast milk—more than enough, my absent wife and I have calculated, for this week-long vacation.

"She's not taking it," Austin says.

I'm the elder brother by nearly twenty years. Austin and I have two things in common: the same Mom and dead fathers. His passed away after a protracted bout with cancer two years ago; a massive coronary got mine a year later. During Robert's hospitalization, my dad lent my mother a hand with Austin, even though the child was no kin to him. When Robert finally passed, Dad moved into the guestroom of the dead man's house without anyone thinking twice about

208

it. Mom went back to work. My brother called my dad "Uncle Jim."

"Well, let her be, I guess," I tell Austin. We've entered the Chincoteague Island National Wildlife Refuge, and we're bumping along a narrow road surrounded by leafless oaks, skinny pines, and scrubby brush. Our map shows that the road ends at a beach. Signs mark walking paths and parking lots, but we won't be leaving the car: it's February, and the East Coast all the way to Georgia has been locked in a record setting cold snap.

No ponies. We get to the beach in about two minutes, and all we see is empty space: sand and sea and sky.

"They must be somewhere, "I mutter. "God-damned Misty." Misty is the wild Chincoteague pony from the book I read when I was a kid. I forget why a wild pony had a name. Maybe Austin knows. He inherited all my books. When I open them now, there's a faint odor of mildew.

"They must walk along this road," Austin says about the missing ponies. "Look at all the poop."

He's right. You'd think they'd hire somebody to clean up. "So," I say, "at least we've got *evidence* of ponies. I bet that's more than most people see."

*****

My parents divorced a dozen years ago, just after I started college. Mom waited until I was "independent" to announce to my father that she'd been in love with her co-worker for years. Mom told Dad she still loved his familiarity, but that she and Robert were "soul mates." Between Thanksgiving and Christmas of my freshman year there was a divorce and remarriage, and a new house across town where I began spending half my vacation time. Mom, ten years younger than Dad, presented her new husband with Austin, his first child, before the Halloween pumpkins had ripened the following fall. At twenty, I became a brother.

Greta, fed and diapered, is asleep in her car seat, and Austin has joined me up front. My wife, not my brother, was supposed to be on this trip. But Briggie, an emergency veterinarian with special expertise in panda bear births, got a call from the San Diego Zoo the day before we were to leave: Lu-Lu had borne a pair of twins, and, as is typical for panda moms, she'd picked one to nurse and had rejected the other. I suggested we cancel the Outer Banks vacation, but Briggie protested.

"You go. If I can fix this quickly, I'll fly to you when I'm done. Take Austin. Your mother said she's worried about him being home alone during his break. There's plenty of milk—you'll just have to be careful to keep it frozen." It's because of Briggie's "panda emergencies" that we keep a multi-week supply of her milk in the freezer. Whenever my wife's not nursing Greta, she's got a pump clasped to her breast.

Right now Austin, who didn't need a second invitation to take this trip, is reading from the AAA guidebook, even though it makes him carsick. He'll read a sentence and look out the window, and then dip back to the book.

"It says here that the legend of how the ponies got to Chincoteague might not be true," he says. "It's not likely that they swam ashore from a wrecked Spanish galleon. It says the local farmers probably used the island as a natural corral."

"Humbug," I say. "Of course there was a Spanish galleon. Farmers don't need ponies. They'd want horses or mules."

"If the farmers don't need ponies, why would the Spanish? What good are ponies?"

"Listen," I say—Greta has started to whimper, and I see a Kwiki-Mart ahead I can pull into so I can satisfy her needs— "never sacrifice a good story for a more logical explanation."

Austin goes into the Kwiki-Mart to pee and get us drinks, and I change my daughter's diaper in the back seat.

I've left the car running for the heat. While I clean her up, Greta blinks up like she's trying to place me. "It's me, your Daddy-O," I say. The milky, diaper-y smells and my daughter's Lake Geneva blue eyes remind me of her Swiss momma, and I wonder how Briggie's getting on in San Diego with the pandas.

When he returns, Austin waits outside the car for me to finish with the baby. He shrinks into his hoody against the wind and leans on the door, a drink in each hand. He's fair-haired and slight, like his father. I'm big, like my dad. We don't look like brothers, or like father and son, which I'm sure most people mistake us for. I plop Greta back in her seat when I'm done. I've got to use the men's room myself now, and, as I exit, I pretend I'm going to crush the balled up Pamper in Austin's face. He squeaks and limbos under it, then settles in beside his niece. "Entertain her," I call through the window after shutting the door.

On my way back to the SUV, I see my brother's bowed head, and I know he's feeding Greta. A passerby would probably think he's on his Gameboy like any kid, but I see him as third in a kind of dotted family line of male caregivers that runs through my dad and me. The partners at my law firm may think I'm on an extended bereavement-paternity leave, but I know I'm never going back. Briggie's well-paid for her panda expertise, and how could I be expected to concentrate on tax codes and torts when I've got a baby to raise?

*****

Austin's still reading aloud to us in the back seat from the AAA guide, though it's late afternoon and there's not much light. Whenever he pauses, Greta coos and gurgles.

"'Legend has it'," my brother reads, "'that Nag's Head takes its name from a practice of Outer Banks land pirates, or "Bankers." At night the Bankers lined up ponies with lanterns fastened to their heads along the shore. Ship captains mistook the bobbing lights for safely moored vessels. They sailed too close to the dangerous shoals and wrecked their ships. The "Bankers" plundered those wrecks, ransoming or murdering the survivors. There are houses still standing in Nag's Head today built from timbers of those shipwrecks. Often new houses are built with a plank or two of "Bankers wood" for good luck."'

"It wasn't such good luck for the people whose ships sank," I say.

"Another pony story," Austin sighs. "What's a pony say, Greta? A pony says, '*Neigh*.'"

My daughter screeches something whinny-ish.

"Good girl!" my little brother laughs. "I think she really gets it. You really get it, don't you Greta?" I glance into the mirror and watch him pluck thoughtfully at Greta's ribbon. "But this story's probably just a legend, like Chincoteague, right?"

"I don't know—murder, plunder. It's got the ring of truth."

"Maybe we'll find 'Bankers' wood' in our beach house."

"Why not? Every house has secrets," I say, my tone somewhere between wise and mysterious.

*****

My cell phone buzzes just as Ms. Smith, our realtor, welcomes us at the front door of our beach house. I've got Greta under my arm as I take the call—it's Briggie, from San Diego. Austin follows behind me, carrying the cooler of frozen breast milk. Ms. Smith looks past him, probably expecting the baby's mother.

"We just got here," I say to my wife while I smile at Ms. Smith. "It looks very nice."

"The first floor's got an open plan—kitchen, dining, big den with a view of the ocean—it's too dark to see the water now," Ms. Smith says, shifting her attention between me and Austin. My brother is already in the kitchen, where he's packing away plastic bags and bottles in the freezer. Ms. Smith is plump and round-faced. Her shadowed eyes remind me of the moon's seas. There's a black ribbon pinned to her overcoat.

"Fridge is empty, except for that liter bottle of cola and what you're loading in," she says. "Turn right on Route 158 for the supermarket. It's at Mile Marker Five. Store closes at nine. They're predicting sleet tonight, can you believe it? This is a bad weather record. Usually the ocean temperature keeps us above freezing." Her eyes flicker pink at Greta. "Cute little girl. Don't see many babies on vacation without their mommies."

I nod at Ms. Smith, but my attention is on Briggie. "It's freezing here," I tell my wife. "Record lows. And they say sleet for tonight. We're stocking the freezer with your milk. You're expressing there?"

"Mm. I'm getting leak-spots on my blouse," my wife says. "I might be able to get someone to bring the milk to a clinic—for premature babies."

"What about the panda baby?"

"Give my milk to the panda baby?"

"No, I just meant—"

"But that's the thing—my milk's no better than the formula they're force-feeding the baby. The problem is Lu-Lu. She gets aggressive when we bring her the twin. We're afraid she'll hurt the one she's feeding. She almost bit Dr. Ralston a little while ago."

I jiggle Greta near the phone. "I'm putting you on speaker so Greta can hear you. We think Mommy should nurse the panda baby, don't we, Greta?" Ms. Smith looks perplexed. "Are you doing the lullabies?" I ask my wife.

That's Briggie's trick—she's Swiss, a dual citizen now, and half by accident she discovered that the yodel-lullabies she learned as a child stimulate a panda mom's sluggish nurturing instinct. There's a video of my wife at work that's gone viral: she warbles away to a bored-looking panda mother

213

that's lying on a heap of straw. After a few minutes, the panda begins to moo and rock, then scoops up something from the straw that looks like a chicken giblet, clasps it to her breast, and turns away from the camera.

"Mommy's going to sing, baby," I say to my daughter, who smacks her lips and lolls her head toward the phone when she hears her mother's voice.

"Hello, baby," Briggie purrs. She yodels soft, Germanic syllables that fill the kitchen.

"My wife sings to pandas," I explain to Ms. Smith over the melody. "It helps the species survive. They seem to *want* to be extinct, to tell you the truth. *We're* the ones keeping them going."

When Briggie hears me, she stops yodeling. "We don't *know* they want to die," she says, "I think they're just depressed. Did you like the singing, Greta? Momma misses you!" Greta thinks Ms. Smith is the one talking and grabs at her. The realtor steps back, her lips puckering.

"I saw those panda bears on their ice floes on TV," she says. She notices that I'm looking at the black ribbon on her collar, and her eyes flare a warning for me to ignore it. "They say it's the global warming that's killing them. Doesn't feel like global warming outside now." She hugs herself. "I expected you to cancel. The rest of the houses on this street are empty."

Austin's at the realtor's side. "You saw *polar* bears," he corrects. "And *climate change* explains weather extremes like we're having. But, can you please tell me where the Banker's wood is in this house?"

"The *what?*"

"The *Bankers'* wood—from the shipwrecks the land pirates made houses from. You know—they put a piece in every house for good luck. It's in the guidebook." Austin's gaze wanders from the kitchen cabinets to the den's paneled walls. There's a huge picture window that looks as solid as a slab of black marble. All of us are reflected in it.

"Jesse?" Briggie's voice touches me like a blind person's hand. "I have to go now. Austin's okay?"

"I'm fine," my little brother calls. "We're looking for the Banker's wood!"

"Good boy," Briggie says. "Keep looking, and you'll find it, whatever it is. Bye, Jesse, bye baby. I love you. I'll call soon, maybe in the morning."

"Save the panda!" I sign off, as if I'm quoting a political slogan. Ms. Smith watches Austin squint along the den's ceiling beams. Greta's fixated on the key dangling from the woman's hand. "That mine?" I ask, and snatch it when Ms. Smith looks at me. "Thanks," I say. "If there's a problem I'll use the same number, right?"

"I wouldn't put much stock in those old Banker stories," Ms. Smith murmurs. "The same number? Yes, use that."

*****

It's a huge beach house, and we're only using the first two of the three floors. I've set up Greta's porta-crib at the foot of my bed, but my baby's with me, pressed up against my side like she would be at home. Except at home she'd be "between," and here, without Briggie, there's no such thing. There's a film of sweat where my skin touches hers—I'd turned the thermostat up high to drive the chill out of the house, and now it's too warm. Greta's smacking her lips in her sleep. She's going to be hungry soon. I lift her onto my chest, surprised as always by her slumbering weight and the size of my hands around her. My baby's wet mouth nears my nipple. I imagine her taking it, and shiver. I shift her so that her head rests in the hollow of my chest. Far away, I'm thinking, there's a tiny panda baby whose mother has left it on a straw-strewn concrete floor—a chill I hope Greta doesn't feel brushes my heart.

My mother didn't nurse me. Nobody did back then, Mom says, and it would have been difficult when she returned to her job. And she said she was too old to nurse when Austin was born. "The milk will be curdled," she said "Or powdered, like artificial creamer." I watched Robert hold his infant son in the crook of his arm and feed him his bottle of formula, their faces equally placid. Though for a decade I ate half of my holiday meals with my mother's second husband, I hardly knew him. He was polite, but quiet. Did he worry that I resented him for stealing my mother or that I saw him as some kind of hedonist because of the "passion" he'd inspired in her?

When my own dad died I lost my biggest fan, my unconditional nurturer, my favorite storyteller, my family historian. Dad had loaned himself to my little brother in the guise of "Uncle Jim." But what had Austin lost with his own father's passing? When I look at the boy's face, I strain to see the edges of buried stories working their way to the surface.

Greta squirms—it's feeding time. I pull on my robe, hoist her onto my hip, and pad into the kitchen. Before long, she's seated on my lap at the table, gulping at a bottle of Briggie's milk as we both doze, eyes winced shut against the stark fluorescent lighting. It's nearly four AM, according to the sunburst clock above the refrigerator.

I yawn, aware of a constant, muffled sizzling. It's not the ocean, which I still haven't seen, though I'd lain for hours listening to the surf pound the beach.

"Hear the sleet?"

Austin's voice startles me, but my baby doesn't miss a suck. She makes little growling sounds. My brother's head rises like a pale balloon above the back of the sofa separating the kitchen area from the den. "The lady said there was going to be a storm, remember?" my brother says. "And there's no Bankers' wood in this house. It's too new. I've been all over it—upstairs, in the basement, in the closets. Nothing." The glare of the flashlight he waves blinds me, and he snaps it off.

Still feeding Greta, I lift myself from the kitchen chair with tired thighs and join Austin on the sofa. He's right about the sleet. And beneath its hiss I hear the rumble of the surf.

The window we're staring at captures a photo-negative of everything behind us— cabinets, the refrigerator, a clock with its hands reversed.

"Probably they built it into the frame," I say. "Your wood is in the roof joists or in the frames of the walls."

"Nope." He shakes his head vigorously. "It doesn't make sense to hide your luck. Besides, I found it. It's not *inside*." He hops up, steps to the big window, and presses his forehead to the glass. He shields his eyes from the kitchen light with his hands. "There's a shed back here in the yard." he says. "It looks like it's a million years old. I bet the whole thing is made of Bankers' wood. Come look."

"I'll take your word for it, l'il bro." My baby's snug on my lap, and my legs are leaden from hours of driving. If it's four AM here, I'm thinking, than its only one in San Diego, and maybe Briggie's still up. "I'll look tomorrow when I can really see it. But a little out-building for good luck makes sense. Like a shrine or something."

"Like a hermitage."

I cock my head. "A *hermitage*? What do you know about hermitages?"

"Uncle Jim told me. He said a long time ago in England when rich guys started to like poetry about poor farmers and shepherds and hermits, some of them built tiny little houses in their gardens, then hired old guys to live in them. Like a personal hermit."

Greta's wriggling. I palm her diaper and sniff. It's full. "My dad told you this?"

"Uncle Jim, yeah. 'What a great job!' he said. But the hermits usually didn't work out. They'd get bored and wander off."

There's a hum— the lights dim, and I feel as if I'm falling. I hug Greta against my chest. Austin grunts like he's been punched. Then it's dark.

*****

"We lost power," I tell Briggie. It's nine AM in Nag's Head, six in San Diego, and my wife's been at the zoo all night. "I tried to get Ms. Smith on the phone," I say, "but there's just an 'out of service' message. I called you because my battery's low, and I don't want you to worry if I can't recharge. What about you—what's going on with the twin?"

"We're at a crisis point. Lu-Lu moved into a corner with the cub she picked. She won't face us." Briggie's hoarse. I'm sure she's been yodeling lullabies all night. "And the little one that she's rejected is giving up. It stopped taking formula. We even tried my milk, just a little from a dropper. But no luck." Briggie clears her throat. "Jesse—what *about* the milk? Will it stay frozen without power?"

"Oh—" The question catches me by surprise. I look at our daughter, swathed in blankets, napping in the porta-crib I've moved into the den. Austin stands beside her, looking out at a bruise-purple ocean. We haven't seen a sunrise—it's overcast and still sleeting. Snowflakes mix in with the pellets. Ice crusts the short back lawn and the beach that runs to the sea.

"The milk was still frozen, last time I looked. I'm sure we'll have power back soon. But it *is* getting cold in here. I've got Greta all wrapped up, and soon I'll have to make a fire in the fireplace."

"Good. But don't let the milk go bad. This might take a few more days. Or it could be over in a few minutes. Either way. I don't know when I'll be able to get there."

"We can put the milk in the shed," Austin says. He's been listening to my end of the conversation. "It's freezing out—it's supposed to stay this cold for days, remember?"

I step to the window. The shed is no more than forty feet from the house. It's about six feet square, with a flat, tarpaper roof, built low to keep from blocking the ocean view— I doubt I could stand up straight in it. Its gray walls are made of weather-beaten planks—Austin's "Bankers' wood." Next to the shed is a stack of split firewood.

"Austin's got a good idea," I tell Briggie. "There's an old shed out back where we can store the milk. It's supposed to stay cold here through the weekend. I'd leave it on the stoop or the deck, but animals might get it."

"Tell her the shed is made of Bankers' wood," Austin says. "It's supposed to be good luck."

"What's he saying about luck?" Briggie asks.

"Just that we're lucky to have the shed right here." I haven't got enough battery left for an explanation. "We have to get to the grocery store for supplies. We'll see if everybody's lost power, or if it's only us. So love and kisses, honey. Save that panda!"

*****

It's stopped sleeting. The plan was to start the SUV to melt off the ice encasing its windows while the kids waited inside, but the engine won't turn over. There's just a click when I turn the key. I check the dashboard for some button I might have forgotten to push, and I see that the headlights were left burning overnight. When we arrived I must have hurried us into the beach house without shutting them off. But Ms. Smith should have seen the lights when she was leaving, and wouldn't she have let me know?

I lift the hood and appraise the guts of my SUV without much hope. The icy wind at my back carries the boom of the surf. I wiggle a few wires. There's not much I can do except call AAA. I'll have to stand out in the cold with the attendant while he gives me a jump. I'm in awe of men who work outside in conditions like this—AAA mechanics; sailors; scavenging land pirates.

*****

Back inside, I discover that I needn't worry about shivering in the wind while the AAA guy works on the SUV—my cell phone's given out, and I won't be calling anyone. I slump on the den sofa next to my brother, Greta on my lap. We're all still bundled up for the trip to the supermarket we can't make.

"I'm sure Ms. Smith will show up soon. She must know we need help," I say without the confidence I'd hoped to show. Had our realtor honestly not noticed the SUV's lights, or had her silence been a choice?

"It's cold," Austin says, standing. "We need to make a fire. I'll bring in some of the wood that's next to the shed."

Greta's hungry again. We'll need that fire to heat up her milk—and we need to take care of the milk supply.

"I'll get the wood," I say. "While I'm at it, I'll carry the milk out to the shed for cold storage. This is what it must have been like in the good old days."

*****

My shoes crunch prints into the layer of sleet as I carry the cooler of milk-baggies and bottles out to the shed. I'm hatless, and the wind slices at my ears. The surf thunders away. There's an ax leaning on the wood pile, and the sight of it makes me feel like an outdoorsman. The plywood shed door, probably not from a shipwreck, heaves open at my first tug. I look back over my shoulder and spot Austin in the beach house window. He's got Greta propped up on the sill, and he lifts her arm to wave at me. I give the children a thumb's up and stoop into the shed with the cooler.

The interior's dark. I take one step and gasp—I'm not alone! Tucked right inside the door is a man seated on a lawn chair. I fumble the cooler, but don't drop it.

"Hello?" I say. My frosty breaths waft over the silent figure. "Excuse me—" gets no response either. The man's not dressed for the weather: he's wearing a dark suit, black dress shoes, and a white shirt and tie. Maybe he'd sought shelter from the cold in our shed. Why hadn't he tried the house?

"Hold it—" I place the cooler on the dirt floor next to a coiled garden hose and hunch over the man. His white hair is combed back neatly. His exposed skin is the color of pewter, and he seems deep in thought—his head is bowed and his laced fingers rest in his lap. "Sir?" I poke the man's shoulder. He's stiff—frozen or rigor mortised, he's obviously dead. I glance out the shed door to make sure the children at the window can't see the frozen man. For now, I'll have to leave him as I've found him. I'll worry about what to do when I'm back inside.

I step out of the shed and yank an armload of wood from the pile. I'm numb to the wind now, and it's my pulse roaring in my ears, not the surf. I trudge back to the house. If the kids weren't looking, I'd peek again into the shed to assure myself that the man is really there.

*****

It's late afternoon, and I've got a fire going. My daughter and little brother snuggle together on the sofa looking at one of Greta's animal-sound board books. The firelight's not strong enough to read by, so we've lit some of the candles we found in a kitchen cupboard. Austin's flipped through the book a dozen times, but Greta still burbles and rocks each time he howls or moos or oinks along with the pictures. I've pulled a wicker chair close to the fire "to tend to it properly," I tell Austin, but really because I can't warm up. My thoughts are stuck on the frozen man in the shed. What should I be doing? Should I have patted him down for an ID? But maybe the authorities would accuse me of tampering with important evidence. I wish Briggie were here—she's the expert on life and death. I think of the baby panda she's trying to save and close my eyes—if I concentrate, maybe I can feel its life force. *Come on, baby*, I cheer silently, but my thoughts drop like stones. "You'd think surviving would be instinctive," I said to my wife once. "For your pandas, it seems to be 'extinctive.'" "Maybe we just don't understand," my wife said. "Maybe they're just evolving into something else."

My brother and I fill up on peanut butter, bread, and cola. Greta's appetite has been voracious. Austin has figured out how to warm her milk bottles by putting them in a pan of water he's pushed close to the fire. Because my hands are so cold, I'm reluctant to hold my baby—what if she burst into tears at my touch? Austin's taught her a peek-a-boo game: he makes his fingers into eyeglasses, and she giggles in a perceptive way that I wish I could capture on my phone's camera for Briggie. But if the phone worked, I'd have already called 911 about the frozen man. What about Ms. Smith—she's in charge of this property. In my mind's eye, her black ribbon is laced around her throat like a cravat.

*****

It's been dark for an hour. I'll have to fetch more firewood soon, and Greta needs more milk. Austin's eager to see some "genuine Bankers' wood from a shipwreck" up close, but I won't let him go outside. I tell him it would upset Greta if he left her, so he sits beside her on the sofa and cuddles her. What I'd like to do on my next trip to the shed is bring a blanket to cover the dead man, but I don't know how I'd explain that to Austin. Right now he's telling my daughter a story, and she sits as still as a Buddha, her eyes glittering in the light cast by the fire and candles.

"So the ship full of pandas was on its way to America—hundreds of wild panda daddies, panda mommies, and panda babies," my brother narrates. "They were almost here when they got caught in a storm, and, oh no! The ship sank. But no worries—pandas are excellent swimmers, and, weren't they lucky? There was an island right near where their ship went down. So they swam and they swam and they swam—" Austin makes swimming motions with his arms, then lifts Greta onto his lap, facing him. He takes her hands and paddles them, and she puffs her cheeks with delight. "—

and swam and swam. And all of them made it, all the panda moms, dads, and kids! They pulled themselves up onto Chincoteague Island, where we were yesterday. And the wild pandas have lived there happily ever since."

"The wild pandas of Chincoteague?" I ask.

"That's right," Austin says, still paddling the baby's arms. "Why not? We saw as many pandas as we did ponies." He stops the game and squints at me over Greta's head, which she swivels like an owl to see what her uncle is looking at. "I hope that panda baby is okay." he says. "I hope Briggie's lullabies work."

"Me, too," I say.

Suddenly, Greta's face crumples. She starts to wail in tremendous sobs. Austin frowns and rubs her shoulders, but she twists away. He looks at me helplessly, but I'm still reluctant to subject the child to my icy hands. How will I change a dirty diaper?

"She misses her mother," I say. "She recognized Briggie's name when you said it." I get up and shrug into my coat. "And she's hungry again. Hold her for just a minute more, okay? I'll be right back."

*****

Milk and wood, I repeat like a mantra on my way to the shed. I glimpse whitecaps on the black surf and think of Austin's pandas struggling like soggy teddy bears to reach the shore. The shed is my only refuge from the ripping wind, but when I reach it, the door won't open. There's a padlock through its rusted hasp. When did that happen? I look back at the house and see my brother and daughter silhouetted in the window, the firelight shuddering behind them. My eyes fall on the ax beside the woodpile and I grab it—it's heavy and unbalanced. I grip it just below the head to shorten the arc of the strike I intend for the door. I don't want to miss and chop down into my thigh—can you see me lying a hundred yards from the sunless sea, blood gushing from a severed artery: a tragic story for the children I'd have failed.

The rusty hasp and new lock break off at my second blow, and I pull open the door, half-expecting a greeting from the frozen man. But his chair is empty. As are the dark corners and dirt floor—there's no place to hide. There's just the cooler of frozen milk beside the garden hose. After a moment, I sag into the lawn chair and let the ax drop. Did the frozen man just up and leave, like those hermits-for-hire my father told Austin about? What's my responsibility now?

My thoughts spin. What I need is an explanation—a story—one I can share someday with my brother—and Briggie, and even Greta, years and years from now. *Remember the trip down South*, I'll say, *to Chincoteague and Nag's Head? Remember the beach house, the ocean, the shed made of Bankers' wood?* I'll tell them about the man they never knew existed, and they'll be shocked and thrilled, but they'll understand why I'd been silent about him for so long. By then they'll have learned that accounting for the frozen men in our lives will always be a dicey matter.

The frozen man, I think, imagining that I'm reading from Austin's AAA guidebook. What if he were the last in a long line of pirate-kings, the last of the Bankers? His death at a ripe old age marked the end of their reign. Banker tradition dictated that his widow leave him for one last, symbolic day in a crypt made of blessed Bankers' wood. If I rise from this lawn chair and peer inland out the shed door, past the house, past my dead car in the driveway, I might catch a procession of headlights following a hearse toward a Nag's Head funeral home. Maybe Widow Smith rides in the first car behind the hearse. Maybe she tells the driver about her recent encounter with panda-worshippers.

Those headlights, wavering over the pocked beach road like a string of lantern-bearing ponies . . . there's a story I can live with.

ABOUT THE AUTHOR

Having raised two children and spent more than three decades as an educator in upstate New York, Gregory Wolos currently resides with his wife of forty-two years in a small town not far from Boston, Massachusetts. Gregory's daily regimen includes writing, running, and tending grandchildren. He holds a doctorate from the University at Albany.

Over one hundred of Gregory's short stories and reviews have been published in journals and anthologies like *Glimmer Train, Georgia Review, Michigan Quarterly Review, descant, Florida Review, The Pinch, Post Road, Baltimore Review, Los Angeles Review, PANK, Superstition Review, Tahoma Literary Review, Southern Humanities Review*, and many others.

Gregory's work has won awards sponsored by *Solstice, descant, Gulf Stream, New South*, the Rubery Book Awards, *Emrys Journal, Gambling the Aisle*, and the White Eagle Coffee Store Press.

Gregory has published three other story collections: *Women of Consequence* (Regal House Publishing, 2019), *Dear Everyone*, (Duck Lake Books, 2020), and *The Thing About Men*, (Cervena Barva Press, 2023). For full lists of Gregory's publications and commendations, visit www.gregorywolos.com.

More often than not Gregory's stories reflect Kafka's assertion that a literary work "should be an ice axe to break up the frozen sea inside us."